*The Diamonds* tells the universal story of how the inordinate desire for great wealth and success can lead to the corruption of life and of the human mind, and ultimately to ruin and downfall.

*The loss of the human essence and the emergence of an encompassing materialistic culture, is one of the topical issues raised in Dr. Conteh's novel.*

- Dr. Sheikh Umarr Kamerah,
Department of English, Humanities &
Foreign Language, Shaw University

*Of high level literary value and a cultural relevance of the highest order.*

- Professor David Rubadiri, Malawian
Ambassador to the United Nations

# The Diamonds

## J. Sorie Conteh

Lekon New Dimensions Publishing
New York

The Diamonds © 2001 by J. Sorie Conteh
All Rights Reserved
No part of this book may be reproduced in any form, except
for the inclusion of brief quotations in a review, without
permission in writing from the author and the publisher.

Library of Congress Control Number: 2001131271

ISBN 0-9704389-1-5

Published 2001
Lekon New Dimensions Publishing
P. O. Box 504
Yonkers, New York 10702-0504
USA

Printed in the United States by
Morris Publishing
3212 East Highway 30
Kearney, NE 68847
1-800 650 7888

# Acknowledgments

I am grateful to all those who have graciously supported me in writing *The Diamonds*—family, friends and colleagues.

A special thanks to Don MacLaren for his professional insights and judgment in guiding the manuscript through its development stages and always providing encouragement. Thanks to Bruce Chadwick, Ph.D., for being a very helpful editorial consultant.

To my wife, Fatmata, and children, Mariama and Isata, who had the patience and humor to let me work the extra hours it took to write this story.

# Chapter 1

Gibao sat under a kola nut tree dreaming the evening away. It was the time of night when the stillness and solitude of his concentration seemed eternal. The gentle wind caressed Gibao's moist body.

He had made several pilgrimages to this tree. Each journey left him with an unforgettable image. He would never forget those nights as long as he lived. How could he? Since his birth, he felt his life had received its sustenance from the solid roots of the kola nut tree. He came there to communicate with his departed ancestors, but only on occasions when he thought they would assist. Each time he visited the kola nut tree he felt at one with his ancestors and at peace with his past.

He remembered another time when he had come to this place. It was a few years ago at the time his mother told him to monitor the food that Manu, his first wife, ate. He was innocent and did not know what she meant, until his mother told him that his wife was expecting a child, which made his mother happy because she longed to have a grandson. Gibao was thrilled with the news. He knew that his mother was serious. It was his mother who had asked him repeatedly after he had been married when the first child would arrive. Gibao felt only confusion and embarrassment at such questions.

At this particular time, he had gone on a pilgrimage to sit under the kola nut tree. He never forgot that visit. His memory absorbed every detail of what happened. His feet were wet as he brushed against the dew-soaked grass on the pathway leading to the tree. The spirits of the land were restive and attentive.

## J. SORIE CONTEH

"*Ndebla, Maadaanee,*" he summoned his ancestors. He knew they were listening. Under the kola nut tree, he found the peace he wanted.

"*When I am happy, I come to you to express my appreciation. When I am in pain, I come to ask for your relief, for healing. I come when I am in good health, and I come when disaster strikes. I come when the crops are threatened, and when the river overflows its banks, and when there is too much sun and the rivers dry up and famine threatens,*" Gibao intoned. He was in the company of the spirits.

"*Manu's belly is getting bigger every day. That is why I am here. I am a son of the soil. I am a farmer. I also hunt. I dance. I wrestle. I tap palm wine. I drum for people to dance and be happy. I want a baby boy to help me farm, to hunt with, to wrestle with, to drum with and make people happy. I want Manu to give me a son. Ndebla. Maadaanee, that is why I came to plead with you.*"

Tonight Gibao came to solicit his ancestors' assistance. Gibao had collected two gourds filled with palm wine to compliment himself on his decisions for what he planned to do. He had come here in the late afternoon and wanted to remain here alone for several hours. He was celebrating his final decisions this night. He would not be the same man once he started his quest. This was a good night to change his life, he reassured himself. The moon's light shone with great brilliance, helping to focus his dreams more vividly.

The wind blew the kola nut leaves high above him. His thoughts ran deeper.

"*Gibao,*" a voice called to him suddenly.

Gibao turned his head to listen.

"*Gibao,*" the voice said again.

"Father!" Gibao said in a hushed voice.

"*Gibao, why do you call on your ancestors?*" His father's voice asked him.

Gibao began trembling. He recalled how his father, when he was alive, had warned him about the parental curse on recalci-

# THE DIAMONDS

trant children. He was aware that he was being watched by his father's spirit. He was aware that his father's spirit could hunt him down. Gibao hoped that his father, in death, would be a kinder and more merciful parent. He prayed that his father would accept his request to go seek a fortune. He wanted his father to understand what he was about to do and grant him safe passage. Gibao's concentration deepened.

"*What is it, Gibao?*" his father's voice asked.

"Father, I want to start by thanking you for your help. The harvest this year was very good. Mother is well. Your daughters-in-law are well. Your grandchildren are well. The community is doing fine. I have no problem to report, father," Gibao said.

"*Gibao, I know you want something,*" his father replied as the wind blew past Gibao.

"I am here because of something I am about to do. I cannot do it without informing you and asking for your blessing. Besides, I have stepped into your shoes. I take care of my three wives, my children, mother and grandmother. It is a big burden. I have been doing my best," Gibao said.

"*I have seen this to be true, my son,*" his father said.

Gibao rose slowly, dazed. He felt elated to be in the realm of the spirit world, the abode of his father and his many ancestors. His father was listening.

"Father, remember when you used to tell me that a man needs to be strong? You said that, if one were determined, he could fight a baboon, kill a boa constrictor, and climb the highest kola nut trees. I took your words seriously. I worked hard as a farmer, a fisherman, and a drummer. I have never allowed anyone to beat me in a fight. I am happy you taught me these things."

"*You ask now for my help?*" his father's voice came to Gibao.

"Father, I seek your approval before that of the ancestors, mother, or the elders. I am here, father, to seek my fortune in diamonds, like other men who have already gone and returned as rich as they could imagine. The landscape of our town has started changing. People have built houses with zinc roofs, have opened stores and bought Bedford lorries to drive everywhere. You cannot imagine how rich some men have become." Gibao paused to make sure his father heard his words clearly. "On Friday, I shall go to the shrine in the house and make a sacrifice to you and the ancestors. I shall kill a white cock and offer the white cock, cooked rice, rice flour and kola nuts to appease you and the ancestors so I can accomplish my mission and come back safely. This is my request, so I may be like the other men here."

"*I hear your request, my son. If you must do these things, I understand. You should be as great as other men,*" his father's voice said, as the kola nut leaves rustled above in the wind.

Gibao finished his request and sat down. He began to feel relieved. He sat still as if he were awakening from a deep hypnotic sleep. The anxiety he'd felt in approaching his father's spirit began to dissipate.

The tropical kola nut trees reached fifty feet into the sky above Gibao. The kola nuts, which reach maturity after five to seven years, are cultivated, harvested, processed and sold like any other farm produce. People who used to travel in caravans during the trans-Saharan trade took kola nuts with them. It was believed that when these nuts were ingested along with water, they enhanced people's endurance and enabled them to travel long distances without food or sleep. Through the centuries, kola nuts had acquired value because of their importance during ceremonies such as funerals and weddings. They were used to appease ancestors, seal bonds of friendship or welcome a visitor.

The kola nut tree under which Gibao sat had additional symbolic significance, which justified his presence there tonight. In fact, on the day he was born, his placenta was buried near that kola tree, which then became more than just a tree.

■ ■ ■

# THE DIAMONDS

"Gibao!" Gibao's mother, Mama Yatta, called out, thinking her son was somewhere on the farm or rice fields. "Gibao!" She called a second time but much louder. There was still no answer. Strange, she thought. "Manu," she called Gibao's first wife. "Where is your husband? I thought he was in the field."

"He was around earlier today, but for some time I have not heard his voice," Manu replied. Manu was of average height, slim and beautiful. Her face was round like a cat's, with prominent and voluptuous cheeks. She had a beautiful smile which produced deep dimples. She had large, firm, sensuous buttocks which she swung deliberately and provocatively as she walked. It was said that she captured Gibao because of her sinuously sensual walk. Manu was a friendly woman, but she was known to become aggressive when her interests were threatened.

"Where is my Nyake?" Mama Yatta wondered aloud to herself. "Nyake" or "father" was an added name of endearment which she gave to Gibao at birth to indicate respect or reverence. It was Mama Yatta's father's name. Nyake, her father, like Gibao, was the only surviving son in the family. Because of the significance of the name, no one could call Gibao "Nyake," except his mother.

Gibao had grown to be a tall and slender man with prominent features. Though slender, he had a muscular frame, which he carried well. He was by nature, like his father, very aggressive, and when he talked, he pronounced his words very clearly. This aggressive quality stood him in good stead in real life. His father had prepared him as a boy to be equipped to meet the challenges of life. Though he was kind by nature, he had antagonized a few of his elders and peers because he had affairs with their wives. This was one reason his late father had scolded him and warned him to mend friendships with those he hurt.

Mama Yatta turned and tried to find out Gibao's whereabouts from the second wife. "And what about you, Yebu?"

Yebu considered the question. *If he did not disclose his destination to you, what makes you think he would disclose it to his wives?* Yebu thought. Mutual distrust had developed over ten years between Yebu and her mother-in-law. This mistrust was unrelenting and grew stronger every day.

"I cannot harvest the rice and look after your son, too," Yebu said impatiently. She said nothing more and continued to tie the bag of rice she had harvested.

Yebu was the most aggressive of Gibao's three wives and the most jealous and disrespectful. She had a plain face though she always thought she was pretty. Being the tallest of the wives, she walked regally like a princess, sometimes bordering on arrogance. She had been the child of a rich father, and so felt freer and more confident than the other wives in making acerbic comments. She never hesitated to speak her mind whatever the consequences.

Harvest time was starting when the village people had dinner together, to drink in fellowship, to group and tell stories, sing songs and dance. Harvest time was a time of celebration and happiness. The harvest time was always a time of festivities, a time of merriment and jubilation. This was the time when people enjoyed the local brew, omole. It was a time when lovers made presents to each other and proposed marriages.

Everyone was hurriedly packing the remaining bundles to prepare for dinner and the festivities. Only lunch was eaten in the community farmhouse. Dinner was taken at home. People from all parts of the farm trudged in lines back to the farmhouse with bundles of vegetables, wood, or herbs. These ancient customs were a part of the day's harvest, the little rewards of their yearly efforts.

The homeward journey was full of activities. The women would pass by the stream to bathe and collect water, which they would heat when they got home, so that their husbands and children could wash. The routine of collecting extra water to carry home for their husbands to bathe was normal, except for those husbands who refused to wash in hot water. Gibao was one of those men, for he always associated bathing in hot water with old people. His wives were happy about this aspect

## THE DIAMONDS

of his behavior because it saved them the extra work of heating the water.

On arrival at the farmhouse, Mama Yatta continued to inquire about her son. "Teneh," she called. "Did you see Gibao?"

"He had come by earlier and left," Teneh, Gibao's third wife, answered, pausing in her cooking and cleanup duties long enough to answer her mother-in-law. Teneh had retired to the farmhouse earlier to prepare lunch since today was her turn.

Teneh was the favorite of Mama Yatta's daughter-in-laws. She was not only the youngest, but according to many people she was also the most well-mannered. Mama Yatta had come to like her very much. The other wives knew it, but never showed any animosity towards Teneh who, in turn, showed respect to them as rival mates. She was taller than Manu but shorter than Yebu. She was not as plump as Manu and not as slim as Yebu. She was somewhere in the middle between the two co-wives. Because showing respect to her elders was so important to her, she seldom displayed emotions even when she was hurt. She was a shy person who held her emotions inside and spoke very rarely, unless spoken to. Unlike Yebu who expressed herself whenever she felt like it with heavy, ponderous words, Teneh expressed herself by singing. She knew how to sing and sang often when she was alone. In fact, she preferred to sing, especially to express her happier feelings.

Mama Yatta was glad someone had finally seen Gibao. Mama Yatta had been a beautiful woman when she was young. Old age eroded her beauty and blurred her facial contours. She walked with a stoop and had to steady herself using a walking stick. Her height gave her an emaciated look. Her voice was coarse, but powerful. She was a caring mother with a very strong personality which became stronger after Gibao's father died. She raised her children by herself, courageously protecting their interests. She had turned her efforts to being fanatically supportive and protective of her grandchildren.

Harvest time made children seem extra happy as they reflected upon the joys of the adults. They would play hide and seek in moonlight. They ate with abundant abandon and recklessness. This was the time when mothers would wake up several times in the night to accompany their overfed children to the toilet.

Mama Yatta had continued searching and instinctively went to the kola nut tree where she spotted Gibao sitting, away from the merriment in the village. When she approached him, she saw the somber look on his face. She knew the tree's spiritual importance to her son.

Gibao was not aware he was sitting on the mortar, a log hollowed out and used by the women to prepare food. A mortar was to be used only for the pounding and preparation of food by the women. He thought he had sat down on a big log. He was confused. His mind was tormented. He felt overheated even though the wind from the thick over-grown kola nut forest was cool and comforting. Perspiration drenched his forehead and dripped down his face. He tried to brush it away. He heard footsteps. Then he turned around, still confused. He saw his mother, standing near him.

"Gibao!" Mama Yatta called in an anxious voice.

"Ummm," Gibao answered carelessly.

"Gibao, do you realize that you are sitting on a mortar?" she asked in a serious tone.

Gibao seemed unaware of this transgression. But it suddenly dawned on him that sitting on the mortar was a taboo that could leave him impotent.

"You are not to sit on mortars where food is prepared. You're not to sit on tables where food is served. Don't you remember what you were taught? Are you not well?" She continued her cross examination but did not get the desired effect when Gibao refused to answer. She sat down quietly near him.

Gibao continued to sit, not moving at all. He coughed slightly then spat on the ground, feeling uncomfortable in his mother's presence.

# THE DIAMONDS

"For the past few days," Mama Yatta said, "I have detected unusual behavior on your part. This is why I am worried." Mama Yatta was now resigned to the fact that her son would not change his seat even though she had alerted him to his open transgression of a taboo. "Are you well?" she asked. There was no answer, no movement, no coughing this time. "What is troubling you, my son?"

Silence hung in the air between mother and son. Gibao moved slightly to secure a more comfortable position. He had been sitting a long time and his backside felt the discomfort. Mama Yatta kept silent, waiting for a reply. It was now very dark, oppressively dark, the moon having set.

Thunk! Thunk! Thunk! The sudden sounds of kola nut pods broke the silence as they fell in the darkness. Mother and son were used to the familiar sounds. The people in the village could hear the sounds in the surrounding trees. The fall of the nuts did not stir him, but his mother's silent presence did. Gibao coughed again in a rather subdued manner. He prepared himself to talk to his mother.

"Gibao," his mother called out. "I am listening. I would like to join the others for dinner." She untied her wrapper and brought out a kola nut. She broke it in two and put half into her mouth.

There is something about mothers, Gibao thought. They have plenty of patience. Gibao knew, like anyone else in the village, that his late father never had his mother's patience. People used to say that Gibao's father had a viper's temper. But here was his mother, who would not eat dinner, sitting with him to find out what was wrong with her son. He felt guilty for putting his mother through the trouble.

Gibao meant the world to Mama Yatta. He was her only living son. She had had it rough during her pregnancy; indeed, she once thought she would not survive the pregnancy. Even after she gave birth to him, she thought Gibao would die, because he was a very sickly child. She had already lost two sons. Gibao was the third and she was determined he would survive, hence the name Gibao, meaning, "save this or let this be well." Gibao did survive to become what he was. He was now a grown man with three wives and six children. He was the most successful and accomplished farmer around his home village called Semabu. He was a hunter, fisherman, palm wine tapper, carver and a good dancer. The people admired him and were proud of him. None of his equals nor his elders could defeat him in a wrestling contest. It was said that he acquired his prowess when he was a boy of ten. His father could not stand the sight of his son being beaten by another, so he took Gibao to a doctor who injected baboon fat into his arm. The Mende people believed that this potion could provide their sons with the prowess and strength of a baboon. It worked wonders, for since then, he became so strong that his contemporaries feared him. The potion enhanced his physical prowess which was why every year he made the largest farm and had the most abundant harvest. The elders, both men and women, loved him dearly because he gave liberally to them.

These were the very reasons why his mother was extremely concerned about Gibao's behavior. Indeed, to her, Gibao was a pillar of strength. His survival gave meaning to her own existence. Both Gibao and Mama Yatta had developed a strong bond based upon trust and mutual respect. They confided in each other. Seeing her son sitting silently by himself and not responding to her pleas made Mama Yatta uneasy and afraid. She wondered what was bothering him so deeply that he could not immediately reply to her.

They both continued to sit in silence well into the night.

"Mama," Gibao finally said.

His mother turned toward him.

"I am sorry that I have made you so worried."

"Never mind," she said with pleasure. Mama Yatta moved slightly closer to her son.

Bmmm! Another kola nut fell in the darkness. A goat bleated in his pen when the nut fell.

## THE DIAMONDS

"I have not been able to tell you what I have in my mind. The reason is I know it will trouble you a lot. I have been behaving badly because I could not tell anyone about my plans until I let you know first. For some time now I have had thoughts about the possibility of going to try my luck elsewhere. This has been my problem. I have suffered in silence for so long. Now, I feel better to have admitted it. I want to prospect for the diamonds in Sewa. I want to prospect for diamonds like all the young men are doing. I mean like Pesima here in this village who has just returned with lots of money."

Mama Yatta sat silently, not believing what she was hearing. His news shocked her. Her heart began to beat wildly. She could not comprehend nor accept the logic of her son's ambition. She was convinced at that moment that either her son was going mad or that he was under some spell. She got up and tied her wrapper tightly, as if to say I am going to seize my son to knock some sense into his head.

"Gibao," she said standing. "Do you mean you want to leave me, your wives, my grandchildren and my own mother? You don't mean it, do you?"

"Mama," Gibao responded. "Please, listen to me."

His mother sat down again.

This time Gibao got up. "Pesima is my equal. You know that I can beat Pesima in almost anything that has to do with work. Now look at Pesima. He left here nine months ago and went to Sewa to prospect at the alluvial diamond mines. Look at what he has done on his return. He has built the only zinc roof houses in this village. He has opened shops, and, most of all, he has bought a Bedford lorry to drive himself around. Do you think I will ever get to that level by farming? Don't you see how Pesima's mother and wives walk so proudly now in this village? Many people don't even seem to recognize my presence here anymore since the return of Pesima. I want to go and double what Pesima has acquired. My ambition is to make you and my family happier than you are now. That is what has dominated my mind lately. I had to go into hibernation to plan what to do. If I get plenty of money, all of you can even join me in Sewa. But, I will have to go first. This is what most people do. Now, I need your consent and blessing before I leave." Gibao looked over at her. "This is what I request from you."

Mama Yatta felt confused. Life was safe and peaceful in Semabu, but on some level, she understood Gibao's need to do more with his life. She knew that Pesima's image now dominated her son, and that he wanted to do what Pesima had done, to compete and even to surpass his rival. What good fortunes came to Pesima was God's way of doing things. Would her son have the same good fortunes? She didn't know. So, let it be. That was destiny. People are endowed with different destinies. Whatever is destined for you will come to your doorstep. These were Mama Yatta's thoughts.

"Gibao," she spoke carefully. "You have wives, children, your mother. We are here. Do you not think that your destiny is here? You are a man, a strong man who is meant to be a leader in the village. You have responsibilities. I do not see that you should go. Your ancestors lived and died on this very soil. You cannot forget your destiny here. Sewa can destroy you."

"I respect my ancestors. I respect you, mother. I want to go only for a short time and make the money so I can come back wealthy like Pesima."

"You must ask advice for such a risky undertaking."

"Mother, we can go to a diviner to ask for advice. We can go to Ndawa, the famous diviner! But I want you to know my heart is set. I will make more money to help you and the others."

"We will see what Ndawa says," Mama Yatta said hesitantly. "If he shows a good future for you, then all I can say is may God go with you. I will stay and pray for you, for your safety. To leave your village, your land and your family is not a light decision. I must talk to the elders and we must see Ndawa. If you go, I still worry for you."

## THE DIAMONDS

Gibao felt his heart glow with delight. This was all he wanted. He would have been somewhat terrified to step away from his mother without her blessings, even as strong as he was.

Mama Yatta repeated her need to consult others first. She wanted to hear from the elders and to see from a diviner what the future might hold for Gibao in that strange land where so many had been tempted to go. Rumors about the diamond fields have proven them to be both a blessing and a curse.

By the time mother and son were home, everyone had gone to sleep. The village was quiet. Nature itself was at rest, as were the hearts of mother and son.

# Chapter 2

The following morning Mama Yatta started her rounds of consultations very early. She first called on Samai, the old man, whom everyone reverently called Maada, a farmer and confidant of Mama Yatta's late husband. On his deathbed, her husband had told everyone that he was leaving his wife and children in the care of Maada, who took this responsibility very seriously, and considered himself to be Mama Yatta's "husband," without actually being one. He was the embodiment and repository of tradition and traditional values in the village. A man of firm convictions, he could only occasionally be made to bend. He believed that the ancestors should be consulted on all important decisions.

Maada was awake early that morning when Mama Yatta came to him. He was sitting by the fire, wrapped in an old blanket in his hut, to warm himself and to prepare the cassava, a type of manioc. Maada poked at the fire to keep it going. Mama Yatta came and sat down, waiting for the old man to get settled before starting her topic. Maada moved his bony hands from place to place in search of his clay pipe which he found in addition to his snuff box, which held the powdered tobacco.

"What is amiss woman that you come so early this morning to see your husband about?" Maada asked. "You women. You always have something to talk about," he joked a little without smiling.

Mama Yatta sat on the only bench in Maada's hut. She gathered her wrapper in between her legs to ensure that her bare legs did not offend or arouse the old man.

Maada had grown quite fond of Mama Yatta. She reminded

# THE DIAMONDS

him of his own late mother who had so many things in common with Mama Yatta. Besides, they shared the same last name. He referred to her as Yeitoma, meaning "mother's namesake," for sentimental reasons.

So when she did not respond right away, he asked her again, "Yeitoma, what can I do for you this morning?" He assumed a more serious tone. He knew that Mama Yatta never came to see him unless she was very concerned about something. "Each time I see you first in the morning I consider the day will be a day of luck for me," Maada added. "Maybe someone will give me some tobacco to put into my pipe." He was fidgeting constantly with his pipe which was virtually empty. He put cinders in it. After some time, realizing the futility of his effort, he dropped the pipe near his left foot on the floor. He then took his snuff box and opened it. He poured out some snuff in his palm before putting it in his mouth. Instinctively, Mama Yatta stretched her right hand for some snuff. Maada gave her some. She put the snuff into the space between her lower lip and gums, forming a small bulge just above her chin.

"You always have good snuff," she commented.

"Grinding snuff is an art. It takes plenty of patience, you know," Maada commented. "But, you women of today do not have the time." Maada made snuff for himself, admittedly the best in the village.

Mama Yatta cleared her throat to talk. By this time, Maada had taken the cassava from the fire and was processing it. He was listening for Mama Yatta to deliver her speech while he worked. There was a calabash dish nearby made from a gourd, a very small one, which contained some ground hot pepper mixed in palm oil. They were the condiments with which to eat the roasted cassava.

"If you recall, last night you did not see me around," she began. Maada put the cassava aside to give Mama Yatta his full attention. "I was busy with Gibao. We were sitting under the kola nut trees. We were there until almost midnight."

Maada assumed a more serious posture. He attended to the fire to eliminate the smoke that was about to take over the hut.

"I have come to you this morning as a result of what happened. You see, for some time now, Gibao has been behaving like a sick man. I know him. He is my son. Even when an ant bites him, I know how he behaves. Yesterday he left us while we were harvesting. Yebu, that witch, could not tell me where he was. Teneh told me that he walked by without saying a word to her, that poor child. I finally found him under the kola nut tree sitting on a mortar."

There was a look of disbelief in Maada's face. He wondered why Gibao should have sat on a mortar. It must be due to some madness.

"He told me he wanted to talk to me about his desire to go elsewhere and try a new life. Because he was not able to approach me on this matter, he decided to behave like a mad man. I told him that before I gave my final consent, I would inform the elders to hear what they say. Maybe we will have to see a diviner to find out what the future will be for him," Mama Yatta said.

Maada's countenance changed. He felt sad and despondent, and even lost his appetite for breakfast. Was Gibao not already an accomplished person in his own right? Oh! Children of today, he said to himself, they are not content.

"Where did he say he wanted to go?" he finally asked.

"You know, where everybody is rushing to go, the place where Pesima came from, where they say you find money scattered all over the ground. This is the place where Gibao is itching with madness to go," she explained.

Maada looked up at the ceiling of his hut as if to seek guidance from above. If Gibao were to go, Maada knew he would surely not get his daily quota of palm wine, gifts of meat, fish, tobacco and many more things that Gibao brought him. Gibao was his protector. After the death of Gibao's father, Maada became Gibao's alter-father to guide him as he grew up. Maada

## THE DIAMONDS

knew that a male child was a blessing, an asset and a gift from God. Maada felt himself unlucky. He had eight children, all girls. They had married and vanished into their own lives with their husbands, and he was the only one left. He felt abandoned, even though a few of the daughters occasionally paid him a visit.

"If he has made up his mind to go," Maada said, "we can't prevent him. Children of today are different from us. He will learn his lesson. I think the best thing is to go and see Ndawa, the famous diviner. His words are final."

Yatta agreed and thanked Maada many times. She got up to go. She asked for more snuff after spitting the wad she had on the wall of the hut. Maada gave her some more after fumbling with his blanket.

"Yeitoma," Maada called after her. "Do you think it is Pesima that has put this idea into Gibao's head?"

"You are right," Yatta agreed. "He said that if he went to Sewa he would come back soon with double of all the possessions that Pesima has."

"What makes him so sure? Doesn't he know that it is God that gives?"

"Well, he said that he is more hardworking than Pesima. This is his reason," Yatta said.

"Children like to imitate." Maada scratched the back of his head. "Do we know whether Pesima stole everything he has? Do we know? Do we know whether he found his money in the right way? Chai," Maada said. He felt a sense of disgust.

Mama Yatta departed after hearing Maada's advice, but she still wondered whether Gibao's mind should be changed. Maada remained squatted on the floor near the fire. There was nothing more he could do for Yatta.

Mama Yatta decided to see three other elderly men. She informed all of them about her son's plans, as she had told Maada. Two of them agreed that it was good for a young man of Gibao's energy and industry to try his luck elsewhere. They endorsed his plans.

Kinawova, the third elder, disagreed and did so vehemently. As one of Maada's peers, his counsel was not to be taken lightly. He was known as the stubborn one. He shared the view that traditional values should be kept and protected. He believed that Gibao was motivated by greed, not ambition, and a particularly bad strain of greed of the type that possessed men's souls and eventually consumed them like wildfire. An old man with much experience, he recalled many such tragic cases of this greed.

To illustrate, Kinawova told a story to Mama Yatta. "When I was a young man, I had a colleague who decided to start hunting, not that he had the know-how of a hunter, but because a friend of his was making a handsome livelihood in the trade. Many people advised him to concentrate on his farm work for which he was well trained. He never heeded that advice. He bought a gun and went hunting. What happened? He was attacked and killed by a bush pig. I know of similar incidents, but I have given my warning with this story. The final decision is among Gibao, his mother and Maada."

Mama Yatta left the elders after thanking them and went over to the farm to talk to her mother. She wondered whether it was a judicious idea to inform the old lady about her grandson's decision to go elsewhere. The old lady might just get a heart attack and die after hearing the news.

Yatta found her at the farmhouse sleeping on a mat with two of her great-grandchildren. Her mother awoke as Yatta approached.

"So, you came to the farm house to help us today?" Mama Yatta playfully asked her elderly mother.

"Oh, I just did not feel like staying in the village today," the mother said.

Since Teneh was there to look after the children, Yatta asked her mother to accompany her to the stream to splash some water on her body before taking lunch. Her mother suspected that her daughter was about to tell her a secret.

# THE DIAMONDS                                    19

Mama Yatta began her story only to realize that Gibao had already discussed the matter with his grandmother because he presumed that Mama Yatta had already explained everything beforehand to his grandmother. Mama Yatta was relieved to know that her mother knew what was going on and would not have a heart attack over the whole idea.

At this point, Teneh hollered out to Gibao and to others in the fields to call them for lunch. "Joe's father-r-r!" Teneh called her husband. She always called Gibao "Joe's father." Joe was her first boy.

Gibao said they were coming. He had some rice he had harvested bundled in his left hand. He hurried to make sure that the bundle was a complete handful before departing for the farmhouse. Manu, the first wife, was also attending to her work on the rice. Yebu had other plans.

"We have been at this all morning. It is now time to eat and rest, so I am going. This work will not finish today or tomorrow," Yebu remarked and started off.

Gibao felt offended by Yebu's abrupt remark. His heartbeat quickened. He huffed at her arrogance and the independent spirit that she liked to show him.

Knowing how Gibao reacted to her abruptness, she attempted to explain what she'd meant. Gibao controlled his temper. He would not engage in a quarrel now. Yebu decided not to reply and walked away from him. There was no more grumbling or huffing noises from Gibao.

Yebu got to the farmhouse, but she still had to rest and wait. She could not eat before her mates. Her face was speckled with beads of sweat. She entered the farmhouse and immediately went to the big clay pot which was half full of water and emptied a full calabash into her throat. Her daughter came near her.

"I cannot take you now. I am tired," Yebu said. The child was full of happiness at the sight of her mother. She also wanted to suckle. "Child," Yebu continued, "there is no milk in my breast.

Since this morning, your mother has not even chewed a kola nut, let alone eaten. So, where is the milk coming from? You only want to suck me dry."

By now, Mama Yatta and her mother had returned to the farmhouse after their private talk about Gibao's secret plans.

"My daughter, thanks, thanks for the work in the field," Gibao's grandmother told Yebu.

Yebu did not answer. Her baby was now sucking her breast. She sat down on one of the big logs in the farmhouse. Manu and Gibao arrived at about the same time. Manu went straight to the clay pot to drink water. Her children gathered near her. Manu was perspiring heavily. She yanked the tail-end of her wrapper and wiped impatiently at the sweat on her face and neck.

Other people were entering the farmhouse where the commotion of dishing the food turned into silence as everyone concentrated on eating. Nobody bothered to spend extra energy on talk while they ate. Occasionally, the silence was punctuated by the shouts of one child over another.

Joe, Teneh's young son, was eating with all the women. He was fond of grabbing the fish or meat, which was on top of the rice. His actions embarrassed his mother who was responsible for disciplining the young boy.

"Put the fish down, you witch," Teneh would say. "When you are eating with your elders, you should wait for them to give you fish. You should not put your hand on top of the rice and grab the fish. That is how you learn bad manners," Teneh said in a threatening way as she showed her son the acceptable way to observe Mende customs at the table. It was a moral imperative that he should wait until his elders have satisfied their ravenous appetites before he could feed on whatever leftovers there were. It was one of the first lessons a Mende child was taught about eating with his elders.

By the time Gibao and his family came back to the village that evening, the news had spread like wildfire that he was preparing

# THE DIAMONDS

to go to Sewa. He was, therefore, not surprised when Pesima came to talk that evening about his memories of the diamond fields.

Gibao was sitting in a hammock in the veranda. His two friends, Gbegima and Mattia, lounged comfortably with him. They had finished the first gourd of palm wine, which Gibao provided, and were starting the second, which Mattia had prepared. Mattia was known all over for tapping the most potent palm wine. They used to joke that before you drink Mattia's palm wine, you must make sure that your belly is full of rice. If not, your head may spin off your body. The old people, who liked Mattia's palm wine very much, said that the quickest way of getting drunk was to take two cupfuls of his wine.

Gbegima and Mattia were considered ordinary jolly farmers in the village who were satisfied with tilling the soil. They were content with the status that God and the ancestors had given them and didn't have any interest in making the journey to Sewa to search for diamonds. Many believed that Gbegima and Mattia were afraid to take risks, rather than go search for great wealth in the diamond fields. After all, everyone had always warned about the dangers of mining diamonds in Sewa.

Pesima greeted them all and took a bench to make himself comfortable. As soon as he sat, Gibao called his eldest daughter, Jeneba, to bring an additional mug for Pesima.

Pesima was a typical village man who never pretended to know about the larger towns. He was neither as good-looking as Gibao, nor as aggressive, but he was cunning and smart. Like Gibao, he was deeply religious, believing that the ancestors should be consulted often in matters of health, harvest, good luck and physical security. Consequently, he offered many libations to the ancestors. If one neglected the ancestors, he knew that they would be swift in their revenge. His one vice was that he loved women, perhaps too much for his own good.

"Gibao," Pesima called. "I hear you are planning to go to Sewa. It is a good idea."

Gibao had tried to keep Pesima away from him since the latter's return from the diamond fields of Sewa. Gibao could not enjoy his rival's triumphant return. He maintained an independent posture. He knew the people of Semabu. The villagers were capable of calling him Pesima's beggar, meaning he would have to beg loans from the richest man in the village.

"Tell us about Sewa," Gibao asked.

"Sewa is a wonderful place," Pesima began. All of a sudden one of Gibao's children dashed into the veranda. The children were playing hide and seek outside and he came in at a time when Gibao and the others wanted silence.

"Get out, you untrained juvenile!" Gibao shouted at his son. The boy sped off in terrifying fear. Gibao, Gbegima and Mattia returned their attention to Pesima.

"Any hard worker should have no fear of going to Sewa. He will make money," Pesima started again. Gibao became intensely interested. "You need to get a job as a digger with one of the rich men who have a license from the government to prospect for diamonds. You and the group you work with get paid when he sells the diamonds. Your pay depends on the quantity and the quality of the diamonds your group finds."

Gibao poured some more palm wine into his mug. Pesima continued, "Many rich people look for young men who have energy and stamina. The boss divides his men into groups. In each group, there is a leader. The boss always has some spy in the group. This is so because, in the diamond business, there is no trust. You sift the dirt with water. When you find something, you give it to the group's leader." Pesima made it known the diamond area was a no-man's-land of distrust, where employers searched for worker thieves like dogs smelling out their prey.

Outside the veranda, Gibao could hear the whole village singing and shouting. Everyone was in a festive mood. Those in the village had banded together in their own select groups to forget their work fatigue—the old people, the women and the children, and the men.

# THE DIAMONDS

Gibao looked up at the bright moon, which, once again, was shining on the village.

A few times Manu made the attempt to pass by Gibao and company, as if trekking to the toilet. It was done just to ensure that Gibao would see her hard looks and come to the realization that he ought to be in bed by now since tonight was her turn to be warmed by her husband. As she passed, Manu cursed silently, in frustration. Pesima was deep in his lectures about Sewa and nothing diverted Gibao's attention.

Gibao went to bed late that night. He went to Manu, but she had already gone to bed, as they say, "to warm the bed for her husband." Her eyes searched the darkness for Gibao. Manu could not sleep as long as Gibao was not with her. She turned her plump frame impatiently several times in the bed in anticipation of Gibao. She knew what the wine did to Gibao. She cursed the others several times for letting her husband get drunk. If he had had too much palm wine and was feeling fine, the moment he got in bed he would fall asleep, snoring, oblivious of her. She worried she would not have any of Gibao's warm attention tonight.

As it was, Gibao had no energy and no thoughts about sharing sex with Manu that night. He had enjoyed gaining new information about Sewa from Pesima. In respect to his mother and Maada, he had to journey far away with them to Kpetewoma to visit the diviner, Ndawa. He had to be rested for the long journey. He got into bed and wasted no time in getting himself engrossed in snoring.

Manu was disgusted, dissatisfied and felt neglected once again. She knew she would not be held closely tonight nor tomorrow night because she had heard Gibao would be away with his mother and Maada to see Ndawa. By the time they returned, Manu's turn would be over. It was a miserable thought. Her body itched with hot desire but was cooling down from the intrusive feelings of disgust and resentment.

Gibao was unaware of the discomfort he was causing. He

was too busy snoring the palm wine out of his brain. Manu felt that Gibao's behavior was deliberate. This was not the first time that he had become too drunk and forgotten her. She worried that she had lost her youthful looks after three children. She recalled that, when she was the first woman Gibao had, she certainly had plenty of Gibao's attention. She was young and had many men competing for her. But now, he could dare to abandon her, to play such tricks with her when her night came. She was certain that, if it had been Teneh's turn, Gibao would not pretend to be drunk. If he feigned to be drunk now, Manu thought, it was because of her age, her deteriorating beauty. After all, her first child was now fifteen years old. What does a man want to do with her after fifteen years? Still, Gibao would get angry if Manu teased or laughed with other men. Men, she felt, were bloody selfish. Here Gibao had neglected her again, and, yet he would still be jealous of her if he thought she was interested in another man. Manu sighed knowing she was not to be satisfied this night. It was hard to sleep the night away next to the unsavory, insulting snores of Gibao. She kept her lips tightly closed and rolled away from Gibao.

# Chapter 3

The distance to Kpetewama was uncomfortably long, but it was even longer for Gibao since he had to travel with two older people. The route was well-traveled by other people either going to or coming from Kpetewama to see Ndawa. People said Kpetewama could not exist without Ndawa.

Kpetewama had received notoriety because its inhabitants were known to be lazy. The big swamp next to the village was underutilized because the inhabitants always made excuses not to tend to it or develop it for farming. People said the Kpetewama villagers, instead, devoted their lives to brewing and drinking omole. Kpetewama, all the surrounding neighbors agreed, had degenerated into a Bacchanalian existence. If one was awakened in the dead of night by sounds of drumming, one knew the noise would be from nowhere else but Kpetewama. Not only were the people lazy, they were notorious beggars. Their women would travel long distances to beg salt or onions from their neighbors.

Despite Kpetewama's reputation, people came from all over the country to see Ndawa. He never moved from the village. It is the sick who have to look for a doctor, as people would say about Ndawa's influence.

Ndawa was a short, stocky man. He was a very confident diviner, who had acquired fame beyond the frontiers of his environs. He was known to talk a lot and slept very little. He claimed that, because of his profession, he knew all the prominent people in the country. Ndawa would look into his mirror and determine one's future. His predictions and prescriptions were sacred.

People came to see him to find out if they would become rich. Women came to find out how fertile they were. Some men came to see if they would win an impending election. Students came to see Ndawa about passing their examinations. Chiefs, who were unsure about their positions, came to Ndawa to find out about the future. This was the man Gibao, his mother and Maada set out to see.

The sun was shining beautifully that morning when they left. The birds were already warming their feathers. Reptiles were warming up on the roadside. The insects were in the air. Nature itself was awake.

Nonetheless, Gibao woke feeling somewhat apprehensive. He worried that Ndawa might not predict his dreams of wealth. Pesima, it was true, had consulted Ndawa before he left for Sewa, only to return with a fortune. Also it was this same Ndawa who said that Gibao's first wife, Manu, would bring forth a baby girl as her first child, and it had happened. Gibao tried to remain optimistic.

When they got to the first village, they spent some time greeting old friends. It was a long time since Maada passed through, so all his friends and admirers were glad to receive him, to drink the morning palm wine with him and Yatta, to eat kola nuts with him, to share his potent snuff and some tobacco.

"Let us go now," Yatta finally intervened. "It will be good to be near our destination when the sun is overhead," she said. Yatta knew that her son was eager to reach Ndawa.

The forest through which they now passed was always cool so they did not feel the heat of the sun. Overhead, they saw monkeys swinging from tree to tree. Some made faces at them and screeched in high pitched voices, reminding Maada of his more youthful days, when he would easily pick off a few of the creatures with his gun. He had then a gun that never missed. This morning, he could have cleanly shot and killed many of these creatures. He would have returned with plenty of meat.

# THE DIAMONDS 27

But, he was a young man no more. Age had caught up with him. The monkeys seemed to sense this and were mocking him.

Some distance to Ndawa's village, they heard singing and drumming. The evening air was calm and soft as the sun set in a crimson sky. The closer they approached the village the more the sound of music resonated in their ears. The people of Kpetewama were in their usual merry mood.

Gibao, Maada and Yatta prepared to cross the last river to the village. Maada and Gibao pulled their trousers above knee length to facilitate the crossing. They stayed ahead of Yatta, who as many womenfolk did, lingered behind in the river to wash up before crossing. The river washing was almost a ritual for women. Men were supposed to proceed and not to turn and look at what was happening behind them.

The last batch of people they met were a group of people who had come to see Ndawa. They were now returning home. It was dark, but they had to go on. Maada inquired about Ndawa. He was told that Ndawa was there, but they were not sure Ndawa would see them that night because there were many people who had come. Some had been waiting as long as a whole day and more were still coming. Maada was not bothered. It was important for the people that in the end they accomplished their goal.

Ever since he was a young man, Maada had known and heard about Ndawa. He had met him several times. But one thing was certain, Ndawa had never changed. He had lived in that same hut for as long as Maada could recall. Ndawa was doing good business in the land. What did Ndawa do with his money? The story had been circulating for sometime that Ndawa had to pay for his art. He gave all his earnings to a water spirit. He would remain famous as long as he was paying the spirit. The moment he defaulted, his fame would vanish in the air. No wonder then his family was always in need.

But, why should a man seek fame if it does not better his condition? Gibao wondered to himself.

They were now in the village. No one questioned them. It was an open secret—any strangers in the village were there to see Ndawa. There were about fifteen people already waiting their turn.

Maada arranged to send Ndawa a message, but the messenger rebutted Maada's request saying that Ndawa was busy and saw people only according to their sequence upon arrival. But Maada instructed the messenger to tell Ndawa that his friend Maada had come to see him. The errand man left reluctantly to give the message because he thought he already knew the answer.

Meanwhile, Gibao was busy with a young man of his own age who lived in Kpetewama. Gibao told him what they had come for. The young man assured Gibao that Ndawa was a wonderful man in his trade. But the man was rather surprised that a young and good-looking man like Gibao was thinking about leaving his people to go to Sewa. People told horrible tales about incidents in Sewa. The young man said that he got several invitations to go to Sewa, but he had declined every one. He said he was happy in his village and had no intention of going to Sewa.

Gibao was shocked at what he was hearing. How could a young man be so unambitious? He thought to himself.

"Are you going with your wives?" he asked Gibao.

"No," Gibao said.

The young man laughed at Gibao. Gibao did not like people laughing when he spoke. What was wrong with this man? Is he trying to torment my life? Gibao wondered.

The young man had a warning for Gibao. "Tell me the truth, my friend. Both of us are young. How do you hope to survive in Sewa without women? How? Women, they say, go there to make money. Moreover, I understand woman damage or payment to an offended husband, is very expensive. It is not like here. So, think twice."

"But, I will send for my wives when I am established," Gibao defended.

## THE DIAMONDS                                    29

"My dear friend, they say that the place is very cold, so how would you manage to put up with the cold while your wives are away?"

Gibao coughed, but gave no answer.

Meanwhile, Ndawa said he would see Maada even though it was not his turn. Maada was called in to see Ndawa. Other people, who had been waiting all day, did not know that Ndawa and Maada were good old friends. Ndawa also knew that, if Maada was around, he was sure to get good snuff and some tobacco.

Maada, Yatta and Gibao were now seated with Ndawa.

"Ndawa," Maada said. "You never move. You are always in this village. You are like a rock by the river."

Ndawa did not answer. He was busy trying to assemble his divination tools. The walls of the room were full of feathers, skins, skulls, shells and hanging cloth and all sorts of talismans. The ceiling and the entrance of the hut held a wild assortment of divination charms. Ndawa himself, after years at his art, was an extraordinary embodiment of a talisman.

"Ndawa, you will not now remember Gibao. Many years ago he came here to find out whether one of his wives was going to have a baby boy or girl. That was a long time ago," Maada explained.

By this time, Ndawa had brought over his mirror with a red piece of cloth and four cowrie shells. Ndawa sat down on a leopard skin on the floor. He crossed his bony legs, put the mirror down, and spread the red piece of cloth over it. He placed the cowrie shell in the middle of the cloth. He rubbed his hands vigorously and wiped his face. Then he took one cowrie and gave it to Maada, gesturing towards him to take it with his right hand.

"Say all you want to say to that cowrie shell. Say what you have come for, do not leave anything unsaid," Ndawa instructed Maada.

Yatta watched Ndawa, who was concentrating on the red cloth while Maada spoke his requests.

30        J. SORIE CONTEH

Gibao scanned the hut. He marveled at the many amulets hanging on the walls. His mind was active, wondering what was to be his fate. Soon, the truth will be known, he thought.

Maada had spoken and given the cowrie shell back to Ndawa along with the consultation fee. It was not much, only two shillings. That money had to be paid even if it was Ndawa's father himself who came to ask for his services. Ndawa put the money on top of the mirror. He rubbed his hands again and placed them on top of the cowrie shell and the money which were lying on the mirror. He took off the red cloth after he had uttered several statements at the face of the mirror. Ndawa reached over for a small bottle that held water. He sprayed water on the face of the mirror and the water flowed off the edges while some drops stayed, making miniature puddles. It took some time before he picked up the mirror from the floor, gazing at it. The mirror now held answers for Ndawa, and he uttered words incomprehensible to his clients. Soon, he was in a trance as the muttering continued and his eyes closed.

Gibao and his mother knew this ritual was to be expected. It was part of the art. His revelations from the mirror would be nothing but the sacred truth. Because Ndawa was reputed to be the embodiment of divination, he was the symbol of prophesy in the whole country. The most hardened skeptic never doubted him.

Ndawa had communicated with the spirits. His clients now had to be told the message. They were expectant and attentive. The moment of truth had arrived at last. Gibao would know whether his ambition would be realized.

Ndawa cleared his throat a few times, to speak clearly of his revelations. "Maada," Ndawa called instantly. Gibao felt like jumping from his seat. "It has been a long time since I ate your snuff, please let me have some."

Gibao felt his stomach begin to churn. Ndawa at any moment would divulge his future, but Gibao was sensing the need to move his bowels from worrying so much.

# THE DIAMONDS

Ndawa carefully placed some of Maada's snuff inside his lip, and finally spoke "The way is clear" he said.

Gibao saw diamonds floating past his eyes.

"There is no doubt that he will get money. He will make money," Ndawa predicted solemnly. "That is destined. It is written. It is so clear. But, let me repeat. He should come back home when he gets money. Let him have a contented mind. This is the message I have for you."

Mama Yatta was as happy as her son and reached over to touch his hand briefly. They had come to Kpetewama and were hearing such good news.

For a second time, Ndawa cleared his throat and this was a signal. He wanted to talk. Gibao had to stop thinking about where he would be spending his money and become attentive. Each word Ndawa uttered was taken seriously. They could not afford to disregard a single word that came from his mouth.

"Now, there are sacrifices Gibao will have to make before he leaves for Sewa," Ndawa told them. One thing people did not like about Ndawa's prophesies were his sacrifices. His consultation fees were minimal, but he recommended elaborate sacrifices which people dreaded. The story was told of a sick man who had seen Ndawa. He paid a consultation fee of two shillings. The man was seriously ill, and had come to find out whether he was bewitched. Ndawa had told him he would recover from his illness if he sacrificed one hundred white pennies. He had to throw these into the river. But, that was not all. He had to sacrifice a white ram. The man was penniless. In the end, the man had died.

Ndawa instructed his clients that night that on their return to Semabu, and before Gibao's departure for Sewa, they should prepare a sacrifice of twenty-one dishes of cooked rice. But that was not all. They also had to sacrifice one hundred red kola nuts and a similar number of white ones. Finally, they were to sacrifice seven white cocks. The twenty-one dishes of rice were to be eaten entirely by children not more than ten years old. There was to be a communal bowl where all the children were to wash their hands after eating the food.

In the end, they were to throw the communal water at all road points in the village of Semabu. The kola nuts were to be given to elderly people. The chickens were to be taken some distance from Semabu and left to wander until they came back to Semabu. Ndawa assured them that, if they were able and willing to carry out all the sacrifices he had prescribed, Gibao would surely get money in Sewa, more money then he had ever before seen in his lifetime. "I have spoken," Ndawa said.

Maada, Yatta and Gibao arrived the following day in Semabu as the night darkness descended on the quiet village. There were no welcome noises, as they had heard when they arrived in Kpetewama. The quietness of the young night was now merging imperceptibly into the vastness of the kola nut plantation through which they were passing to make their entrance into Semabu. They had at last returned from their mission. They were all tired, but happy that they returned with good news. Gibao felt confident and relaxed. Ndawa had spoken. He had made his predictions. The way to Sewa was clear, or so it seemed when Ndawa had gazed into the mirror.

# Chapter 4

The diamonds of Sewa were rumored to be abundant. One only had to dig them up to become wealthy. The easy, quick wealth had devastating social consequences. Villages became depopulated as people rushed off to Sewa to dig for diamonds. As a result, Sewa became over-populated, but had none of the social resources to accommodate the surplus population. It was a boom town, in the old gold-rush tradition. It was said that if children deserted their homes one would only have to journey to Sewa to find them. If a wife was missing, she could be found in Sewa. The whole nation converged on Sewa like hungry vultures on a carcass. Gibao was one of these vultures. He had developed a vulture's appetite for money and wealth.

Gibao left Semabu in the early morning darkness while the other villagers were asleep. He had to leave early enough to make the train connection at Moyamba. He would join the Pendembu Express train from Freetown that would take him to Segbwema. From Segbwema, he would travel by lorry, the last leg of the trip.

When Gibao left Semabu that morning, he felt spiritually clean. This feeling sustained him morally and psychologically. He felt a sense of inner satisfaction, of moral wholesomeness. He felt happy and free. It was a new type of freedom that he had never known before, one motivated by a challenge and a purpose. He was on his way to match Pesima and bring back more than Pesima.

Gibao started out with a torch in one hand and a small luggage case in the other. Yatta saw him off by the roadside.

She took her son's right hand and looked at his palm. Then she spat on it four times, saying, "Rub it in your face." Gibao obeyed. "May God go with you. Take care of yourself," she said with a heavy heart. Her voice trembled. It was hard for her to smile as she said goodbye to her only son embarking on what she considered a dangerous journey.

The others who had come to say goodbye were almost half asleep. All of Gibao's young children, except for Jeneba, were asleep. His three wives were present. They stood transfixed. Manu, the first of his three wives, uttered goodbye. His grandmother did not come because they said she would not be able to control her tears if she saw her grandson giving her his back.

Gibao carried with him only twenty pounds sterling, part of the proceeds of his harvest. Although the money was enough to live on comfortably in Semabu, it would not be enough in Sewa where costs of living were higher because of the abundance of diamond money.

Gibao moved ahead into the darkness with his torch. He knew the road to Moyamba. He pointed the torch straight ahead, just to make sure he would not be surprised by any of nature's creatures. All his life in Semabu there had not been an incident whereby anyone had been attacked. He traveled by torchlight now towards a strange, mysterious place called Sewa.

Sunrise caught up with Gibao after several hours of walking. He started seeing the trees, shrubs and insects. He turned off the torch and listened to the pleasant sounds of birds and crickets beginning to awaken in the morning light. The monkeys began chattering above.

Gibao's heartbeat quickened along with his steps. His scalp tingled as he imagined his destiny ahead.

Gibao stopped to wash his feet, mouth and face in a nearby stream. He broke a shrub which he used as a toothbrush. He had to prepare himself to dress like the inhabitants of Moyamba. He opened his suitcase and changed his khaki shorts for a pair of white trousers, tying them with a black belt. He then

## THE DIAMONDS 35

put on his black crepe sole shoes and white socks. He took his powder, the latest in *Bintu el Sudan,* rubbing some on his face and on his neck. The powder blotched parts of his skin while giving him a conspicuous look, as if he had just graduated from a secret society dubbed with a white clay. He stuffed two handkerchiefs in his clothes, one in the back of his trousers and the other in the second pocket just enough so there were no protrusions. Then he stuck a comb in one of his pockets which did protrude. He put on a red shirt. He had rehearsed these changes many times in his mind. He dressed himself this way in a bold attempt to look like an educated person from Moyamba, rather than like someone from a remote village.

Gibao looked at himself in a pocket mirror and smiled. He looked like a caricature, some overdressed doll, like one of the scarecrows he used on the farm. But, he believed he dressed now to fit in with the townspeople.

When he arrived in Moyamba, Gibao did not notice that people were looking at him. He felt great.

He had arrived well in time for the train. As he went to the railway station, he passed by the famous Harford Secondary School for Girls, a boarding school which Jeneba, his eldest daughter, attended. Gibao and Manu were proud of Jeneba. She was the joy and emotional pillar of their very existence. Funny how things happen, Gibao thought to himself. Two illiterate people with an educated and brilliant child. How God works wonders! A child from Semabu who knew the white man's Bible and other books. A child, as the teachers told him, who should be allowed to do everything to further his or her education.

The teachers at the school, as the story goes, were American missionaries. Anne Smith, one of the white teachers, told Gibao not to take Jeneba prematurely out of school to give her to a man in marriage. The teacher knew many good students who had suffered this fate.

Mrs. Smith talked Mende fluently, having been in Moyamba

for over twenty years. She admired Gibao for his unpretentious simplicity. Unlike other parents who came in cars or Bedford lorries, Gibao had occasionally visited his daughter at school, wearing tattered clothes and no shoes. His daughter did not feel in the least embarrassed by Gibao's tattered clothing. When Anne Smith met with Gibao, she told him that Jeneba could be a doctor or a lawyer. Gibao was very impressed by what Anne Smith had said. Jeneba was now approaching fifteen years of age. If Jeneba had had other village parents, they would have made money out of the innocent girl by giving her to an elderly man in marriage. Gibao told Mrs. Smith that he saw Jeneba as a gift to the family. This was God's way of doing things. "God works in mysterious ways to perform His wonders," the white woman told Gibao. He had left the compound then feeling buoyant and reassured. Jeneba was happy, too, after the meeting. She had accepted the fact that her father, though an illiterate man, was an honest and a caring parent.

Jeneba became famous in her own right. When the Paramount Chief's clerk was ill and the Chief needed a letter written to the District Commissioner, it was Jeneba who had written the letter. And, the District Commissioner had replied. The news spread all over about the young girl who had written to the District Commissioner. That year when the women's secret society was in session, one of the wives of the Chief composed a song about Jeneba, which became the leading song of the society that year.

Gibao brought his revery to an end when he realized he had been waiting a long time for the train. The wait for a train was painful because the trains were never on time. Gibao then realized that he would arrive in Segbwema at night without any accommodation. He reached into his back pocket for his handkerchief to dust his face. He had rechecked to be sure he had his money and ticket. He had been warned to be alert for professional thieves at the train station who preyed on potential victims who looked vulnerable.

## THE DIAMONDS                              37

Finally, the Pendembu Express arrived. There was an instant rush as people boarded the train from every available opening, including the windows. The boarding problem was complicated by many of those already aboard who were trying to prevent those from outside entering, a tacit demonstration of human greed, meanness, and selfishness. Some would close the doors while others would close the windows. The boarding turned into chaos and pandemonium.

Gibao was lucky. He had plenty of brute force. His initial problem was to identify his third class coach. The first class coaches were for the white colonialists, the second class for the well-to-do African bourgeoisie and the third class for the poor population.

When the train came to a halt, Gibao tried to enter the coach directly in front of him, which happened to be first class.

"Get out of here, you fool! Don't you see it is first class? Don't you see how it looks inside? You don't have common sense!" the white man shouted at Gibao. All the white people, made up mostly of African residents, shouted a chorus of insults at him. Gibao moved away from the coach.

He then tried to enter the next coach.

"This na second class oh, mister," said a subdued voice. It was an African who turned to a nearby guard instantly.

"Show me your ticket. Let me see," the guard snapped at Gibao. He looked at Gibao's ticket for just a moment. "Go to the third class. You don't belong here."

Gibao was not first-class nor second-class material.

He had walked all these weary miles to enter into this chaos. He went to where he saw the majority of people boarding.

A man looking through the open window agreed to take Gibao's luggage, thus facilitating his entry. Gibao barely managed to get a place to stand, and his luggage was pushed compactly between his feet. He stood tight and straight in the aisle. This would be his place on the train. Meanwhile, the young man had managed to sit next to Gibao. The train began moving. Air started blowing through the open windows, allowing everyone to enjoy the fresh air while diluting the foul smell of human sweat.

"Ah! My broder, tenki, ah bin for lef if noto for you," ("Thanks, my brother. Were it not for you, I would have been left behind") Gibao said, expressing his gratitude.

"For some, it is a pleasure to see their fellows in trouble," the young man commented. "Sometimes some people think they own the train."

"Where are you going?" Gibao asked his helper.

"I am going on a trip," the young man answered, evasively.

"Where are you going to come off?" Gibao persisted.

"I will come off in Segbwema," the young man answered.

"I am going there myself," Gibao said excitedly. "Tomorrow, if I get direct transport, I continue to Sewa."

Gibao was happy to know that this good Samaritan was going in the same direction. He, too, was one of those going to Sewa. Gibao would need his fellowship. The man told Gibao his name was Amadu.

When the train arrived in Kangahun, many people disembarked, thus allowing Gibao to have a convenient seat by Amadu and they engaged in further conversation. Unlike Gibao, Amadu had brothers he was going to meet. The brothers had been in Sewa for some time and had established themselves. But Gibao was going to Sewa blind, someone who was desperately searching for a new kind of happiness.

The train arrived at Bo in the dusk. There was a layover before departing the station. The train was called an express, but trains stopped at almost every station, so they seemed more like locals. The people said the trains usually arrived late so the train engineers, guards and porters could claim overtime.

The immediate concern of Amadu and Gibao was finding accommodation in Segbwema. They were going to arrive there in the dead of night. Amadu told Gibao that, when they arrived at Segbwema, they would look for lorries waiting for passengers

## THE DIAMONDS                                        39

for the next morning. They would have to sleep at the lorry
park, if they did not have anywhere else to sleep. There were
always passengers at the lorry park waiting to travel to Sewa.

■ ■ ■

Back in Semabu, the people of the village woke up and found
themselves grieving over Gibao's departure. It was as if people
were mourning the death of the head of a family. It was the
sort of feeling people could not explain; they just felt it. They
stood in little groups for comfort and support. The chicken in
their coops and the goats in their pens felt the difference.
Towards midday, nobody bothered to go and let them out.
Everybody was engaged in talking about Gibao's departure. It
was indeed an undeclared mourning. No one wept, but their
hearts were heavy. Many would have wept, but the Mende
people say it is not nice to cry for the departure of a living
man. They cry only for the dead. This was the restraining
factor, an imperative for all of the somber ones.

Arriving in Segbwema, Amadu and Gibao made their way
to the lorry park to wait for the first lorry ready to leave in the
morning. The lorry park was full. There were traders going to
sell all sorts of produce and commodities in Sewa at exorbitant
prices. There were single women going on business trips to
entice men in their seductive trades. They had heard how
lucrative Sewa was for their trades of the flesh. There were students going to meet relatives and parents to take money for
school fees.

Amadu and Gibao tried to make themselves as comfortable
as possible with the others. They had each bought two large
bottles of *Allsops Lager Beer*. The beer helped to enrich their
conversations. Amadu had heard more about Sewa than Gibao
and had much to tell Gibao. Everything he said about the
place was positive. He spoke about some friends and relatives
who had gone to Sewa and returned to their homes. Those

friends and relatives could now boast of several houses; some had even bought Bedford lorries. Remarkable accomplishments. Gibao became more excited as he listened.

Amadu was also making the trip with a view to going back home to set up a business. He wanted to own a lorry and drive it himself and to build a house with a shop in it. These were his sacred ambitions. Amadu claimed he had worked for the P.W.D. (Public Works Department) for ten years and had risen to the rank of Road Foreman, but that he had to leave because his workers had all deserted for Sewa. Amadu had also left his family behind with the hope that he would send for them later. His father and mother were both alive and had induced him to go to Sewa and make money. They were impressed by what they saw when Amadu's contemporaries went to Sewa and came back wealthy.

Amadu and Gibao felt unanimous in their conception that diamonds were special. They felt there was something supernatural in finding diamonds. The spirts of the diamonds would give some men more luck or what the people called *babuyay*.

Gibao was the exception. He never really believed in luck. He believed in hard work and that only hard work could earn diamonds. But Gibao had never actually been to the diamond fields. He envisioned that the way to succeed was by working feverishly to ferret out the diamonds from the earth that held them. He would be like Hercules seeking to unearth these diamonds. His entire being was dedicated to this. He was ready.

Amadu and Gibao enjoyed their *Allsops Lager beers*, boasting about what they wanted to do. The beers gave them added comfort while they waited the slow, tormenting hours in the park, and fueled their dreams with excited anticipation.

The townspeople in Semabu went to sleep that night without comfort, thinking about Gibao. Gibao's absence had touched every aspect of the town's social and physical life. When people met to dance, his absence was felt. For who could drum better than Gibao? None. Who could dance or sing Wunde songs

## THE DIAMONDS

better than Gibao? None. Those who were most affected were Gibao's mother, grandmother and Maada. Maada's life was changed dramatically without Gibao. He had lost his quota of goodies that had come from Gibao, so Maada could only wait for the return of his good provider. He was destined to become more miserable and lean. Despite the obvious gaps in provisions and the absence of Gibao's life sustaining gifts, Maada continued to pray for Gibao. The feelings of grief continued for the other villagers as well.

# Chapter 5

When Gibao and Amadu left for Sewa that morning, the harmattan, the dry, forbidding wind that blows from the Sahara and the northwestern coast of Africa, had not completely stopped. It was sunny, but oppressively cold. The discomfort to the passengers was compounded by the fact that the vehicle they were traveling in was not completely covered. The tarpaulin on one side of the lorry truck had been stolen and the big opening let in plenty of the harmattan air.

The people crouched together to protect themselves from the harmattan which blew mercilessly against their skins.

As the lorry rumbled along, one of the passengers gossiped that a few days before when he was in Sewa the harmattan was so severe that many people were dying of pneumonia.

There was also the total lack of certainty about the length of the trip. Amadu and Gibao did not know the delays the lorries faced. The only reason why Amadu, Gibao and many other people decided to travel in this lorry was because the driver left earlier than the rest of the lorry drivers. The problem was that each lorry had to cross three rivers on three ferries, which were small and criminally slow because they were manually operated. Each ferry transported one Bedford lorry and one car at a time. There could be about twenty vehicles or more on each side of the river waiting to cross during peak times. People were forced to spend days waiting for their turn to be ferried. If one had to cross two or more such ferries, it was not uncommon that a trip of one hundred and thirty miles could take a week to complete.

# THE DIAMONDS

To make up for the ferry delays, the lorry drivers often drove very fast and tried to overtake other lorries to get to the next ferry first. The possibility of one lorry jumping ahead of another was a serious affair. A driver's pride was involved. The lorry in front would refuse to give way to those behind him. The lorry behind would start hooting the horn and would continue the noise until one of two things happened: a fight ensued or an accident took place. This latter danger was ever present, especially in the dry season when the roads were full of dust stirred up by the fierce winds and the drivers could not see very far in front of them.

Amadu and Gibao were traveling on a lorry named "Na God De Gi." The Bedford lorry just behind them had written on it "The Evil That Men Do." So, the lorries sped on, the one chasing the other. Some of the passengers on "Na God De Gi" felt that, though they wanted to get to Sewa, the driver should not speed recklessly in a bid to get there too fast. An argument between the driver and the passengers ensued. The lorry driver finally gave way to "The Evil That Men Do," which sped past the "Na God De Gi," spewing a cloud of dust as it did. Gibao and the other passengers were left covering their faces from the swirls of choking dust.

Then, the driver in Gibao's lorry abruptly stopped to talk to the driver in another lorry returning from the ferry, to find out how busy it was at the ferry. The people in "Na God De Gi" were informed that on this side of the ferry there were about twenty vehicles waiting. Unfortunately, the delay was not the only matter. There was also a rumor that the ferry workers might strike for more pay and better working conditions. These were worrying revelations. The lorries departed from their brief meeting, leaving Gibao in despondence about the delays.

Three miles before the ferry, they came upon "The Evil That Men Do," which had become involved in a serious accident with an on-coming Bedford lorry, "Man Pass Man." Seven people lost their lives on the spot and several more still lay seriously wounded.

Gibao and the others mumbled that it was God's will that saved them from the accident. One of the passengers suggested that maybe it was because they had as one of their passengers an Alhaji, a Muslim cleric, who was constantly praying.

This was the first such accident that Gibao had seen. He became frightened seeing how the lure of Sewa affected those who rushed dangerously to get there. He started wondering about the wisdom of his trip.

The passengers on "Na God De Gi" spent a day and a half at the first ferry. They took their meals at a nearby cookshop called "Mami Yenoh's Cookery," which served rice, yams, cassava and fufu. The eatery was famous and was the only one where passengers could buy food at this ferry. It catered to all people, including Christians, Muslims, villagers and foreigners.

The trip to the last river took four days of speeding lorries and long waits at the ferries. Gibao had suggested that Amadu and he stay together, once they arrived, until such time that Gibao himself could find himself some dwelling. Amadu opposed the idea believing that Gibao would be too much of a burden for his brothers. He explained that even a fly can sometimes be too much a weight or an annoyance on a person's back. Thus, it was at Njama, a fast growing town in Sewa, that Amadu and Gibao said their farewells after a week's trip by lorry and wished each other success.

The only traveling companion Gibao now had was his luggage bag. He had nowhere to go immediately, but he was thankful he had reached this far safely. He reflected on the accident he had seen on the way. He could have been one of the victims, a dreadful thought. He had been lucky. His immediate need now was to find a place to sleep for the nights ahead.

Gibao's movements as he walked the streets of the town that morning were cautious. No one spoke to him and he spoke to no one. People went about their business hurriedly. The sun

# THE DIAMONDS                                    45

shone brightly, which seemed to be a good omen, and he watched his shadow repeatedly. A house in the distance seemed to attract his attention. Why of all the houses he had passed should this one catch his attention? He thought about this. He remembered what the old man in his village had told him. He would be guided by his ancestors during his adventures. He then walked up to the house with some confidence.

The owner of the compound and its accompanying shop introduced himself as Mr. Kemoh, and he was curious to find out why someone like Gibao who had a family, would come looking for a room without any of his wives accompanying him. The shopkeeper held the suspicion, like most people in the diamond area, that people who traveled alone were trouble-makers. Mr. Kemoh was, furthermore, a man with several wives and grown-up daughters in his house. He was apprehensive about boarding an unaccompanied male who might be attracted to one of the women.

Mr. Kemoh was a short, elderly man. He loved his stomach, as people said about those who loved food. He also loved women and made sure he had plenty of wives. A curious thing was that all his wives were taller than he was. He was very talk-ative and would gesture with both hands, flailing them in the air when he talked. He was especially assertive in his commu-nity, and was considered to be an elder statesman. He was also jealous and very suspicious of young men, whom, he felt, were not afraid of courting the wives of senior citizens like himself. The competition from the younger men bothered him much. Mr. Kemoh always walked fast, which left people always won-dering where he was going. Despite his jealousies, however, he was kind in his own way.

Mr. Kemoh spared no time in telling Gibao about some of the hazards of Sewa. According to him, it was strangers like Gibao that gave Sewa its bad reputation. This was an interesting comment considering that Kemoh himself was not a native of Sewa. He had initially come here like Gibao. He had become prosperous and had gone on to buy a shop and a Bedford truck to operate as a lorry. He spoke the language very well, and felt that his hard work had entitled him now to be a native of the place. There were many like Mr. Kemoh who had permanent residency status and had stayed for such a long time that they were no longer strangers in Sewa. Such men could be very hostile to people who were coming into Sewa for the first time.

Was this what human nature was all about? Gibao thought to himself. Mr. Kemoh finally allowed Gibao to stay at his compound, but Gibao had to wait before he could go to work. Gibao found himself lonely and bored as he sat on the veranda day after day. Here he was, being quizzed about his residence permit by a man who had also come here as a stranger. What a world!

Gibao used the time to review his thoughts and Ndawa's predictions. He thought about the sacrifices he had made. Ndawa had said all would be well if the sacrifices were done as he had ordered. He thought about the kindness of Amadu, his traveling companion. Maybe, if he had not met Amadu at the right time, his journey would have turned out differently, as he had seen at the lorry accident.

■ ■ ■

Since Gibao's departure, his mother and grandmother had hardly ventured out. They stayed in the hut, talked about Gibao fondly and prayed for his safety and prosperity.

Mama Yatta prepared the family for a special ceremony at his father's grave in order to ask the father's spirit to continue the blessings and guidance for Gibao. The women pounded rice flour mixed with sugar and formed the mixture into three small balls topped with one kola nut each. The ritual request also involved pouring palm wine on the grave site on Gibao's behalf. That day all of Gibao's children and wives went to the grave site to witness the ceremony. It was Maada who officiated.

## THE DIAMONDS                                         47

Maada himself had grown leaner since Gibao's departure, without the regular supply of good things that Gibao used to give him. However, Maada continued as the surrogate father and guide to Gibao's family. He would visit Yatta and they would discuss Gibao and the prospects ahead and Yatta would drop in to see Maada occasionally to get some snuff.

Kinawova, the elder who had advised against Gibao leaving, still remained implacably opposed to him even in his absence. He viewed Gibao's departure differently from the others. He believed Gibao's quest was due to greed, envy, and dissatisfaction. Was Yatta not aware of the horrors of this diamond place, horrors that were reported every day? Why should she condone her son's departure to Sewa? Kinawova would ask the others. Kinawova felt a sense of disgust. He said that the youth of those days were condemned. They were doomed to a dismal future. Woe upon them. The earlier days were better. They were better in the sense that their parents had control over their children. But, these days, see how free the children are? He recalled the sense of revulsion over the immoral behavior of Gibao's sisters, Njabu and Miatta. It was terrible. Kinawova thought about all these things, not with pleasure, but with sadness and an acute sense of moral repulsion. He was now an old man, with a frame dangerously thin and delicate, but he was still strong in mind. In the end, he said he wished Gibao would learn a lesson in Sewa which would serve as an example for others, a lesson he thought that would help resurrect the moral strength of his society.

Yatta had acquired an addiction for smoking tobacco in her clay pipe. The pipe itself was very short, after it had suffered several mishaps. No one ever asked Yatta why she never acquired a new pipe despite her son's prosperity on the farm. Mama Yatta tended to misplace the pipe. When she could not find the pipe, she would engage the assistance of many people around her, including her grandchildren and in-laws.

"Ndoma Nya, did you by any means happen to see my

pipe?" Yatta addressed Teneh, who happened to pass by while Yatta was searching for the pipe in the main sitting room.

"I have not seen it," Teneh replied and walked away. Yatta continued her search by herself, beginning to look frantic. She took a moment to reflect on the likely places to look for the missing pipe. She stood still in the middle of the room and thought she should ask Yebu.

This particular day Yebu was not prepared to be part of a search team for her mother-in-law's pipe. Yebu was busy with her mate preparing food for the workers. As usual, the task was backbreaking and an element of urgency went along with the preparations.

But Yebu had on occasions secured Yatta's pipe when it was mislaid. Yatta was not aware that when she referred to Teneh as "Ndoma Nya" (a name of endearment) that Yebu heard her. Yebu was fuming from that moment on as she continued to cook.

"Yebu, did you by any chance see my pipe?" Yatta asked when she came into the kitchen.

Yebu and her mate, Manu, sweated in the kitchen from the roasting heat of the fire. She ignored Mama Yatta's question.

"Yebu, did you hear what I said? I have been looking for my pipe for a long time now. Have you seen it?" Yatta asked again.

Yebu stood up and secured her wrapper around her waist. Manu thought she was ready to pounce on Mama Yatta and watched with apprehension.

"Go and ask your Ndoma Nya to help you. From the beginning of the day, I have not had time to take care of myself. I have been busy cooking. Do you think I have time to look for your pipe? Mama Yatta, I know you came here to provoke me. You have no sympathy for me and my mates. Let me tell you, you are pushing me too far. If only you can leave me alone I shall be happy," Yebu said firmly.

"What have I said that makes you talk to me so rudely?" Yatta asked.

# THE DIAMONDS                                    49

"I have never been Ndoma Nya to you. We are not the loved ones," Yebu said, looking over at the silent Manu. "Yes, you can ask about your pipe, but not when we are killing ourselves to cook for you and everyone else. Your pipe is not important right now. I am fed up with all your little provocations. Honestly, if I have to get out of this marriage and go eat grass, I am prepared, but today I shall speak my mind to you because I am fed up and frustrated."

Mama Yatta stood silent with her mouth half open.

"Yebu, don't say anything more," Manu interceded. "You know that in the end people will misunderstand and misinterpret what you have said. In this relationship, we, the unloved wives, are never right. So, please do not say anything again," Manu pleaded with Yebu, who now busily dished up the food.

"I hope you don't dish food for me. I shall not eat food cooked by you anymore. I shall wait for Gibao when he comes. I do not trust you anymore," Yatta told Yebu.

"Your Ndoma Nya will cook for you. You have no problem," Yebu replied.

"I told you not to talk again, didn't I?" Manu asked Yebu.

At this point, Yatta walked away quietly.

Gibao knew nothing about the growing frictions back at home between his mother and his wives.

■ ■ ■

Once in Sewa, Gibao had to start from scratch. He needed to find work, which is how he met Kemoh's elder brother, Alhaji. Alhaji was, at this time, in need of more workers, so when he went on a business trip, he had asked Kemoh to recruit potential workers for him. This was how Gibao found a place to live, got a permit and was accepted for work.

Alhaji Jimoh was a tall, elegant, slender man of sixty-two years, though he could pass for fifty. As people say, men with plenty of money do not get old. He was very religious and prayed five times a day according to the teaching of Islam. He always carried his prayer beads with him. He was soft spoken. His head was neatly shaven. He had developed the habit of rubbing his head with his left hand so much that people observed that maybe Alhaji's left hand should be grafted onto his shining head. He loved money and worked hard to get it. He made lots of money and displayed his wealth by building a big house, and owning a Mercedes Benz car and several Bedford lorries. He had seven wives and many children, but his one weakness was that he was fanatically jealous of his wives. People called him Alhaji. He was a very popular diamond prospector.

Alhaji's presence was felt everywhere in Sewa. He had many workers who were mining diamonds. He employed, fed and housed them. Houses were needed by the new arrivals until they could afford their own. He also knew the workers needed housing for their safety and their sleep which would allow them to work better in the diamond fields. He was responsible for getting permits for all of them, a difficult task in those days. Without a resident permit, one was constantly harassed by the police and often sent to prison.

The problem remained that Gibao still had to wait for Alhaji to return before going to work. Gibao accepted sitting on the veranda and waiting. He philosophically accepted that life was moving him in a favorable direction. He considered how he had made his first contact in Njama by coincidence. Here he was at Kemoh's house. Kemoh was the first person he had spoken to upon his arrival in Njama. This house was the first house he had really entered and into which he had been accepted. Gibao could not understand the wonders of his God. They had always baffled him and would continue to baffle him. Didn't Ndawa tell him that his trip would be safe? He could have been one of those seven people killed in that other lorry. The imponderables of nature, the facts of life and death were hard to understand. He thought over many more things

## THE DIAMONDS

while waiting day after day for Alhaji. Kemoh had made sure Gibao understood that Alhaji would be his boss, and about what would be required for living at Alhaji's compound. After a lot of reflecting about his new life with Alhaji, Gibao thanked God that he would have a leader like that to help him, and he waited some more.

"Young man," Kemoh called. Gibao was jolted into consciousness. "Are you a hard worker?"

"It is not good to praise oneself," Gibao replied humbly.

Kemoh accepted the reply. He went on to emphasize that diamond-digging was not only physically exhausting, but dangerous as well. However, Kemoh said, there was plenty of money in it, if one worked hard.

This was the sort of talk that Gibao liked, the fact of physical prowess, brute muscle power as an index for success in the mines. Gibao took his time at this juncture to tell Kemoh about his past achievements in Semabu. He said many more things while Kemoh listened. Kemoh had heard many such utterances before from young adventurers. They said such things when they were desperate for a job. The moment you provide them with a job, a place to sleep and a permit, they turned their backs on you. Then they are always ill and so on. However, Gibao told him that, if Alhaji employed him, he was sure some day Alhaji would sing his praise to Kemoh.

Kemoh's house had ceased to be exciting compared to what it used to be when he was actively engaged in diamond digging. He had dispersed his workmen a couple of years ago and had decided to open a shop and to operate two Bedford Lorries for a transport business. Gibao wondered why a man of Kemoh's financial standing should leave the diamond business. Kemoh had his private reasons.

Diamond money, people said, never lasted. The people said there were mystiques attached to the diamonds. If the diamonds did not like you, you could be ruined in the process. The diamonds first tempt you, lure you and then all of a sudden they can ruin you. Kemoh believed this and had washed the diamonds from his hands.

One morning while Kemoh still slept, Gibao's boredom, which developed during the long wait for Alhaji to return home, suddenly disappeared. From the veranda, Gibao watched the people in the early hours. The workers trudged along with their usual mining implements with them. This morning he noticed that some faces were contorted. Other workers showed expressions of dismay and agony, yet, they moved on. Gibao decided to take a walk and to find out what it was that had changed the people today.

As Gibao moved to the south of town, he noticed that the crowd there was thicker and more solemn. He quickened his pace. At one point, he made an attempt at asking a passerby what was happening, but the man ignored him. The snub may have been unconscious, but nevertheless Gibao felt ostracized and humiliated. He felt that he did not belong. He did not feel important. He went along, anyhow, determined to see where this solemn procession was heading.

Gibao arrived at the place and he stood in the midst of the crowd. People were jostling and pushing at each other. There was a horrible smell. The more people moved to the center of the crowd, the more they cupped their hands over their noses or held their hands over their mouths. Everybody was rushing to see the four dead bodies lying in front of Pa Kinawa's house. They lay outside in a row, a very pitiful sight. The four young men were not over thirty years old. They now had bloated eyes, protruding tongues, inflated stomachs and smashed heads. Two had their stomachs punctured, which had to be tied to prevent their entrails from spilling out in the open. All four men had been buried alive in a pit when they were prospecting for diamonds.

Here and there men stood with handkerchiefs to wipe away tears from their eyes. The sound of women wailing echoed in the chilled atmosphere. Some women fell to the ground and

## THE DIAMONDS

rolled around in abject grief. Some tore their hair and shouted to God. Two of the dead were never identified because no one knew their home villages. Everybody knew the other two were from Sewa because someone knew their names. Someone in the crowd had gone for the mother of one of the young dead.

There was a lady who was chasing her eight year old son who wriggled his way into the crowd in order to have a view of the dead bodies. She grabbed him and showered blows on him. "You! I have given birth to you for nothing! You will not benefit me in the future." She was beating him further. Children are not supposed to show such interest in corpses. They are supposed to be afraid. She mistook the boy's inquisitiveness as a bad sign. Later someone intervened on behalf of the boy. But by then he was weak, the mother had sapped his energy.

Gibao stood there like many others who had come to the land of diamonds. All of a sudden his mind went back to the ferry incident. The incidents of death were increasing, but they did not seem to keep people from coming to these diamond fields. Men went about their mining business that very hour. The pit that had terminated the lives of four would continue to be mined later today.

People said that the spirits of the river where the mining was taking place had taken their yearly pay. It was the spirits of the river, people said, that had complained they were neglected by the community. This was the reason some had to die. Before the prospecting, the Sewa people of Njama religiously appeased the spirits at an annual ceremony. They had stopped this ceremony since the start of the diamond digging. None of the strangers who came to dig at Njama cared about appeasing the spirits, so the spirits of the river chose whose lives would be terminated.

Gibao had left the scene in a daze. He went by the river where the spirits and the miners were. He did not go to tell the spirits he had come and that he himself would be digging so they should protect him. He said nothing to the spirits. He just went there to reflect. He was depressed as he looked down at the muddy river. It was in the river that the miners processed their mud, silt and dirt until they discovered the glittering gems. Gibao saw all around him people prospecting, washing their clothes or urinating. The river was a place of human activity and energy.

Gibao returned to Kemoh's house about lunch time. The others already there were various friends or business associates who came to lunch with Kemoh, just as others had come earlier to share breakfast with him. The conversations would be about Njama. They would talk in detail about the pit incident. These things happened every day. Their talk would go on about other related matters in common and beyond. Toward the end, the most important aspect of their conversation would be about who had made the best diamond find of the day or the week.

Gibao returned full of sadness. Kemoh could sense his heavy heart. He knew that Gibao had been to the scene. People like Kemoh never bothered to go to such scenes any more. They had been through the scenes of death several times already and had dealt with such matters by treating the whole affairs with callous indifference.

That night in bed, Gibao felt no wide-eyed excitement about the diamonds. He found it difficult to sleep, wondering what his future was going to be like. He thought about the four corpses, the ferry incident, and all that he had heard Kemoh and the others say. Then, the thought of his family came to his mind, his mother and grandmother. He thought particularly about his son. The boy was a jewel. Would he see his family again? Then, Jeneba came to mind. He thought about what the missionary lady had told him about her. Many other strong men in this state of mind would have shed tears. But, Gibao was different. He just lay there in a state of uncertainty, wondering, ruminating.

# Chapter 6

Alhaji was still at large. Gibao was without work, and his funds were dwindling dangerously low, making him extremely anxious. He wondered if he should go somewhere else and try his luck. He had only five pounds sterling left in his pocket. He realized the idea was an exercise in self-deception to say the least. What guarantee was there that he could get a job soon after leaving Kemoh's place? He would still have the problem of having to meet someone, explain his problems and establish confidence.

Gibao finally told Kemoh about the problems that were developing, and that he was becoming extremely worried that Alhaji had not yet returned from his business trip. He explained that he had left his family behind and that they would not be happy to hear he had been spending all his time waiting for someone who never arrived. Kemoh consoled him by promising that, if he needed pocket money, he would lend him some periodically until his brother came back. Gibao could repay the money when he started work. This was very kind of Kemoh, but Gibao continued to worry.

Feeling lonely, Gibao took comfort in cigarettes and beer, *Guinness Stout* where possible. Sometimes he would walk to the north end of the town to buy the locally tapped raffia wine called *Baaneh*. A cup or two of this wine warmed his spirits considerably and took the edge off his fears and loneliness.

Yet another issue surfaced that started tormenting him. Since his arrival, he had noticed something about the food. Earlier, the food the women dished for him had been enough to fill him, but there had been a progressive paucity of his rations, possibly because Kemoh did not want to extend too much food or credit to him. How long was he going to be subjected to this state of affairs? But he felt strongly that it was not his place to complain to his host.

Gibao, therefore, developed the habit of going to Ya Digba's Cookery. There he would eat extra side dishes, trying to ensure that no member of the Kemoh household saw him. It would bring him shame if they did. They would criticize him by saying, "What kind of guest is this who is not satisfied with our food and has to eat in the street?" Gibao would hide while eating, in order not to be surprised by any of his host's children or wives.

Ya Digba's Cookery had acquired a good notoriety in Njama. Rumors had it that Ya Digba, the owner, put exotic ingredients in her sauce, which attracted customers at the expense of other restaurants in Njama. Ya Digba was a plain middle-aged woman who was devoted to her profession. She joked with her customers and as a result acquired a large clientele, making her the envy of the other restaurant owners. She was fat and shapeless. She even made jokes about her fatness and her unattractiveness to men, but her size only matched her generous love for the people who, in turn, loved her. She was fondly referred to as "a woman of the people."

The most unscrupulous cook of tainted food, that meat that included monkey, dog, and cat flesh, was the man the people referred to as "Alhaji-I-want-more." He was a well-known dealer in roasted meat, a tall, well-built man, with conspicuous scars running perpendicularly on both sides of his jaw. Of all the people engaged in the business of roasting and selling meat, he was the most famous in Sewa. His meat, they said, was so delicious that children and adults of all faiths would buy from him and ask for a second or even third serving. His customers always told him, "Alhaji, I want some more." At first, the people did not know he sold tainted meat, along with the accepted goat, sheep, and cow meat. Eventually suspicions mounted about his meats, and he was arrested. He confessed

## THE DIAMONDS

his guilt, but said that he had only wanted to give his customers variety. By the time the trial ended, Alhaji had escaped from custody, and he was never seen again. From that day, many people in Sewa refrained from eating roasted meat. Some, on hearing the news, vomited while others had more severe stomach problems. It was a theatrical sight seeing only his customers in the streets retching and clutching their stomachs, and there were many.

Gibao had solved his ration-for-food problem, but he was confronted with another problem. It was difficult for him as a married man to have been sleeping alone all these days. What added further insult were the cold winds of the harmattan that were still in the air. He entertained the thought of seducing one of Kemoh's wives, but then he remembered his friend's saying that the women of Sewa needed plenty of money. They wanted to be paid well for having sex with a man. The idea of seducing a wife would mean continuing to spend money on her, but his money had dwindled to only five pounds sterling. He was repelled by the idea of negotiating with women for sex. After debating with himself over a course of several weeks, he finally rejected these things and renewed his determination to suffer in silence.

One morning Gibao noticed a number of posters placed at strategic places throughout the town. One poster was at Ya Digba's Cookery. There were others at the north side of town for people who walked through that end of town to drink raffia wine in the small restaurants.

The poster showed the picture of a man standing and gesturing dramatically, with his right hand clenched in a fist stretched towards a microphone. Gibao had never seen such a picture. He did not know what the microphone was. Many people stopped to look at the posters, but they were more fascinated by the man in the picture than whatever the poster said. Most of them, including Gibao, could not read or write, so they had no idea about the meaning of the poster, but the sensational picture was causing all sorts of attention. Eventually, the news spread that speakers were coming to Njama that day to talk about issues relating to the mining of diamonds. The townspeople collected automatically into little groups trying to analyze the likely effect of the talk.

Gibao got caught up in the anticipatory excitement without fully understanding what was going on. He stood by the poster and waited for something to happen, but nothing happened within the hour, so Gibao finally headed back to Kemoh's. He refused to ask people what was going to happen for fear of being rebuffed again. People seemed to welcome those with information into their circles with open eyes, but Gibao had no information to give.

Later in the day, Kemoh encouraged him to attend the meeting which was to take place at the center of town. Kemoh told him that the speakers were young men who were well-educated and had traveled outside the country. Gibao's curiosity was aroused once again, and he was ready to hear the speakers.

By 4:20 P.M., two Bedford lorries with loud-speakers attached to their roofs arrived and parked in the center of town. A man's voice boomed through the loud-speaker, inviting people to come at 5 o'clock to listen to the speakers. "If you want to know how the white man took our diamonds from us," he said, "then come this evening." He repeated his message and continued with other ideas. He warned that, unless steps were taken to stop this trend, no diamonds would be left in Sewa and each person would be forced to go back to where he came from. The speaker pleaded for people to come. These announcements coming out of the loud-speaker generated such a furor that in less than half an hour the center of town was crowded with people.

The crowd, thick and animated, was assuredly upset by this message and worried that there would not be enough diamonds left for them. At 5 o'clock, the people awaited the speakers. People's tempers flared sporadically. Some were becoming

## THE DIAMONDS 59

impatient and began cursing the organizers. Some hissed in disgust at the empty lorries. Others angrily pushed and shoved.

"People who know book (those literate) should respect time," one man shouted after he had looked at his watch. Just after that observation, there was a continuous blaring of vehicle horns. A convoy of Land Rovers drove slowly through the crowd. People clapped their hands and made way for the speakers. People startled jostling each other again, but without anger this time, as they tried to secure better places to view and hear the speakers.

"Don't push me!" one man warned another. The man had been trying to displace him. He, in turn, was determined and continued to hold his position. He had come earlier and had laid claim to his place, defending his right to it. He was not going to be displaced by anyone. A verbal quarrel ensued.

Another quarrel erupted from the other end of the crowd. One man stepped on another's corn-addled foot. He jumped with pain and then stooped to see how much damage the other had inflicted on him. Blood was oozing out. The pain became so unbearable that he had to leave. He went reluctantly, cursing the other man's mother in his mind. He would try to come back after attending to his sore foot. His eagerness to return made him walk faster, increasing his pain at every step.

The crowd was alert, held together by anticipation. Unfortunately, technical problems developed with the microphone. Here and there individuals, who had to go on to do other work, became antagonistic towards the organizers. Some heckled and suggested that they should do away with the microphones.

"The microphone is artificial mouth," one man said so clearly and loudly that the entire audience heard him. There was laughter.

Gibao had secured a place at the periphery, but from which he could see as well as hear clearly. It had been a long time since he had seen such a crowd. The last time he had seen a crowd of this size was when he was initiated into the Wunde secret society. That was a long time ago. He recalled vividly that there had been no Bedford lorries or Land Rovers, nor microphones or loud-speakers, and that the initiation meeting had been better organized, that things had gone as planned. Gibao realized that times had changed. No longer would a council of elders administer the laws—it took microphones, lorries and lawyers.

One man looked at his watch and realized that he and his workers were losing time. They should have been at their site in the swamp to wash the gravel they had dug during the day. If only these people would talk! In the end, the man left in disgust. He had to go.

The man departed cursing the organizers. He hissed several times over his shoulder. He grumbled much on the way and observed that these speakers could not expect progress if things were never done on time. People always came late, he thought, as if coming early made things malfunction. He remembered years of complaints, demands for independence, but what good would independence be if everyone would always be late? His top priority was to sieve the gravel that bore the diamonds, so he could earn his wages. He needed to start as soon as possible.

A man clambered onto the roof of one of the Bedford lorries to try to calm the crowd.

"Let them talk! Let them talk!" people started shouting throughout the crowd. It went on like this for a while. The noise was incessant. The crowd was keenly eager for something to start, but too many people could not stop the impulse to complain.

The man on top of the lorry appealed again for silence. People murmured to themselves as they continued standing, but began to settle down.

"You see," the speaker said. "If you can lend us your ears, then we will start. The fault was mechanical. It was not ours. Please bear with us. I know that some of you want to go to your gravel. You want to go and wash them, but, wait, please!"

# THE DIAMONDS                    61

he implored. People were still talking in little groups. They were fed up. "Allow me to introduce the first speaker to you." There was instantaneous silence. "How many of you have heard the name Ngombu?"

Mr. Ngombu was a very dramatic speaker, just as his name, which meant fire, suggested. He was well-known for his political speeches. He was well-educated and well-traveled. He had studied in the American University in Beirut, Lebanon, then had gone to England to continue his studies. Some said he went to the States and, later, to France and on to Nigeria. He wore a dark brown gown with a hat to match. There were talismans, sewn on all sides of the cloth and even on the hat. These precautions were necessary, people said, because there were many enemies capable of shooting their adversaries with witch guns. To survive the battle, one had to be well protected. Whenever Ngombu wanted to appear in public, he would dress accordingly. Ngombu was a lawyer by profession. His cheeks were round, and he had piercing bloodshot eyes. He had eaten so many kola nuts that his teeth had become permanently brown.

Ngombu mounted the Bedford lorry with a microphone in hand, and a thunderous applause erupted from the people around. It was not easy to get the crowd under control. Ngombu appealed to them several times. Finally there was silence. Ngombu then asked that prayers be said briefly first by Muslims, then Christians. When the prayers were finished, he said, "For those of us who do not belong to Mohammed or Jesus, may our ancestors guide us safely." The people showed their approval for what he said with clapping and hearty laughter.

"I want to talk to you this evening, so that you will listen and understand me," Ngombu started. "Most of you are here to prospect for diamonds. But most of you do not know what we went through before you were allowed to mine. It was a big fight for us in this country. I refer to our struggle with the

WHITE MAN'S GOVERNMENT to release land to us for mining. Prior to this, it was a crime to be seen in this part of the country with shovel or sieve. So, if you needed to dig a pit toilet, they must have expected you to use your teeth or fingers!" He waited while the crowd laughed loudly. "Do you know the reason?"

"NO! NO! NO!" the audience thundered.

"The colonial government with a colonial administration created a colonial mining company which led to a MONOPOLY —an exclusive right—to mine all diamonds that were found, not only in Sewa, but in the whole of this, *our* country. A contract was signed by which OUR LAND was leased for ninety-nine years to the colonial company. Yes, a contract for ninety-nine years. Now, how many of us are going to live for ninety-nine years?" he asked, his eyes roving through the crowd from side to side. His lips curled mockingly. People were now fervently absorbed, their eyes barely blinking. "The white, colonial company had such a monopoly, a big monopoly. Do you know that we here in this part of the country were never consulted? This was what so-called democracy meant then and now."

There was laughter and applause.

"You see, fathers and mothers, brothers and sisters ... you see, children ... this was how we were deprived of our wealth." Ngombu waited a moment and there was silence. "The White Man was here in 1929. He was here in Sewa and he has been here ever since."

Somebody in the crowd wanted to know how the White Man had managed to get to Sewa at that time when even today the roads are virtually impassable.

The speaker laughed heartily at the question. People joined him in the laughter. He coughed a little. "I like that question. Let the young man who asked the question please raise his hand," Ngombu requested. The man complied. "Let us all give him a hand," he ordered. Everyone clapped. "He is a clever man."

"My brother," Ngombu went on. "When it comes to seizing our land and wealth, the White Man can pass through the eye

## THE DIAMONDS                                    63

of a needle. If that was the necessary way, yes, he could. And
he will not complain of mosquitoes, or malaria. No. He can
do anything to deprive you and me. So, they had no problem
coming here. They came. But, can you believe that at that time
our people already knew the diamonds and had them in their
houses?" Ngombu asked, his voice rising.

A chorus of outrage swept through the crowd.

"Well, if you don't believe me, ask the elders. In those days,
when it rained, people could pick diamonds on the road, by the
streams. Our people admired these gems and put them into
bottles and kept them. They used them for spiritual purposes.
Then the White Man came and saw these gems, and told our
people that, unless they got rid of the gems, an epidemic
would descend on them. The word went round and people
collected all of them. The White Men took the diamonds away
without paying for them. Why else do you think the White
Man is so rich today?" Ngombu thundered.

"Because they stole our diamonds, by cunning!" a voice
boomed within the crowd in response to the question.

"Yes! Yes!" said another voice.

"These people who did this were said to be geologists,"
Ngombu said. "Do you know who is a geologist?"

Everybody said "No!" in a loud chorus.

"Well, I will tell you. Geologist are people who prospect for
diamonds, so we are all geologists."

There was laughter.

"According to the White Man's law, the diamonds of this
country belonged to them. Yes, they belonged to *them*, not us!"
Ngombu shouted. "We found this law difficult to accept. They
got permission to prospect, mine and distribute all diamonds
in this country. We, the people of this land, said this law was
unacceptable to us. We, also, wanted to mine. They said,
"No." You know what happened? We organized ourselves and
at night we would go to the mine in what they now considered
their land! They complained that we were encroaching on

their land! They said we were thieves! Well, tell me. Have you ever heard of someone stealing from his own land? Now, can you steal that which belongs to you? In Africa, we do not entertain such laws. Maybe they allow for something like that in English law. But this is Africa!"

There was applause. Many people shouted that he was speaking the truth.

"So, they brought in troops to protect their interests. They brought in African troops. Yes, that is what they did. But, as it happened then, the troops were not able to cope with us. We were well organized. And, now!" Ngombu exclaimed. He stopped talking and held an arm in the air. His eyes roamed from one side to the other across the crowd. This was an electrifying moment. Everyone held their breath in anticipation of Ngombu's next statement.

"I have come to appeal to you ... so that we can become organized once more! If we are organized, we can get the government to ask the company to give us rich, gem-bearing land. You all know that in unity there is power! There is strength! They used to call us 'illegal miners.' When we were organized before, we succeeded in getting the government to persuade the company to allocate land to us to mine." Ngombu stood silent for a moment and then let out a booming laugh.

"Hah! That was another of the White Man's tricks. The government instituted the Alluvial Diamond Scheme!" Ngombu spoke more about this scheme. He was sweating and constantly wiping his face with a white handkerchief. He kept readjusting the large sleeves of his gown. He explained that the White Man's mining company realized that there was constant encroachment on the company's land by illicit mining. Consequently, the White Man's government and the White Man's mining company made a law that part of the alluvial mining land should be made available to only licensed miners.

"This is the point at which we are today. The changes came through our efforts! All of you are here because of what we did!

## THE DIAMONDS 65

But! All of you know that the land allocated to us for mining is less fertile with diamonds. It was a big trick. Now, we have decided to ask for a better deal! We want more and better land, land that bears diamonds! We are going to put our case to the government, but, if an impasse follows, then let our organization be ready for more action! We will be organized! This is why we came to talk to you, to help you to be informed and ready for action!" Ngombu leaned forward with a raised fist.

People again shouted with loud applause, and lavished praise on Ngombu. They felt ready to die for the changes that Ngombu wanted.

"Another point we want to drive home to the government is that they should stop calling Sierra Leoneans strangers simply because we are in Sewa. They should stop harassing us. One cannot be a stranger in one's own land. Now, it appears to me fascinating that I am a stranger in England, in Lebanon, in France and, now, in my own country," Ngombu added in a mocking tone.

There was laughter around him.

"Who are the strangers in this country?" he shouted.

But the answers to this question were confused. All sorts of foreigners were fished out indiscriminately.

Ngombu laughed and clapped his hands in recognition of their intelligent answers. He had ended his speech. The second speaker took the microphone. He was smallish, but he was known to have great power in his voice. He fidgeted constantly with his round glasses. He was well-known, so he needed no introduction.

"I greet you all, comrades," he began.

The people used to call him Money because he always had something to say about money.

"Money! Money!" different people shouted in approval.

"Money is sweet," Money answered back. "Without money, your home will be disorganized. Without money, you will always say 'yes, sir' to people. Without money, you always owe thanks to people, and are never thanked yourself. Without money, your wife will desert you." After muttering a few more such aphorisms, Money paused. This was another reason why he was called Money; he could admonish people with these sayings about money almost endlessly.

"All of you know that we have been labeled radicals, rabble-rousers. They even call us communists. The only reason is that we demand our share in the riches of this land. They say that we go through the country causing trouble wherever we speak. But is it troublesome to remind the people of what is rightfully theirs? Only to those who would keep it from them. What I find most insulting is that they call us communists. Why give credit to communists at our expense? The meaning is this. They are accusing all of us here, those who speak and those who hear, of being weak in the head—that we are passive creatures, that we do not know what is good for us, and so can only ape the communists who travel to this country and tell us what is good for us. You see? That sort of thing," Money said in a very serious tone. He went on to tell them that such tactics were designed by the colonialists to distract the people from the essential issues. When he finally stopped, there was much wild cheering.

The whole town was lively and buoyant after the meeting.

Gibao was happy, but he realized he was in the midst of volatile political and social changes in Sewa and the whole country. He had never heard such speeches in Semabu. He wondered how this political and economic turbulence might some day affect his village.

If things went as envisioned by the speakers, then the future was promising. That night, Gibao felt lucky and, for the first time, at home. People he had never met before talked to him. They thought he was from Sewa. On his way to Kemoh's house, he stopped by Ya Digba's to eat a plate of rice. He went back home very tired after all the talk and exuberance. When he went to bed that night, he had no time to reflect on the

## THE DIAMONDS

day's activities. He went to sleep feeling his sacred mission to improve himself was blessed again. Gibao thought himself protected by God and the ancestors, once again. All he needed now was at get to the diamonds.

# Chapter 7

All miners looked forward to the day when they would be paid according to their hard work. Payday, unfortunately for some, was a day of agony. Some had debts equal to their pay. They either owed their masters, neighbors, friends or Ya Digba. Many had to repay credit from Mr. Cole's bar. When rumors circulated that a particular diamond prospector was to pay his workers, creditors would assemble by the workers' houses ready to demand their money.

Whatever the situation, payday was the reason they were all here. All the diamonds they had accumulated would turn into money. Workers would be able to enjoy themselves, if only for a day or two. Their families and relatives would also share in the merriment. Njama, itself, would be a place of pleasure. The men and women in business could sell their wares for cash, and the town would be buoyant. This happened often, and the debt collectors got their share.

Alhaji had finally come back and held a meeting where he paid his workers. Those groups of workers who had made big diamonds finds, and the ones with better quality diamonds, got more money. There were those who made few finds and got less money. This was nature's balance of equity, so no one complained.

This time Alie's group came in on top of the list. There were only four in their group, like the other group led by Buya. The rumor spread that each of Alie's party had over 2,000 pounds sterling. They were lucky to have picked up one of the most beautiful gems, which was of the best quality. It was pure and

# THE DIAMONDS                                    69

clean. Alie, as leader of the group, received 3,000 pounds sterling.

Because Alie was older and showed a sense of responsibility, sensitivity, and maturity, Alhaji had made him the group leader. In turn, Alie never disappointed his boss or behaved in a way that would tarnish the flattering image that Alhaji had of him.

It was said that, before the White Man came, there was no word in the dictionary for inflation. Money was money. It had plenty of value. It harnessed many men's dreams. And people were happier back then.

On this night, all of Alhaji's workers got paid. They rarely got paid at the same time. When everyone was as lucky as they were on this night, the merriment in the compound was even greater than it was on other paydays. People set their gramophones in motion, and there was music all around.

Having a gramophone meant that people would come to you. Everyone wanted a gramophone. The lack of a gramophone in the compound would produce discomfort for husbands, because their wives would complain about not having music. In a shop without a gramophone, the silence was guaranteed to drive customers away. The gramophone was a symbol of affluence. Owners took pride in it as a social symbol. People played their gramophones that night and danced with reckless abandon. Children were conspicuously awake at such times, their bedtimes overlooked by adults too joyous to remember petty rules.

Gibao was the only one who went without pay, because he had not worked for any money. This was as it should be and he blamed no one. His own turn would come, he thought to himself, as he sat on a long bench alongside five other people.

Prior to Gibao's arrival, the workers had devised a system whereby they catered for the happiness of everybody in the work force. Whenever two or three groups were paid by Alhaji, each worker paid a contribution to a common fund. Part of the fund was given to the rest of the workers who had gone unpaid.

On this day, the common fund was not necessary. Everybody was paid and happy. There was a unanimous decision to contribute to Gibao, as a way to welcome him and admit him into the diamond prospecting community. In the end, Gibao got 320 pounds sterling.

This was the largest amount he had held at any one time in all his life. Yes, for Gibao, the land of diamonds was indeed the place to be. He remembered that at one time Pesima had told him how easy it was to come by money in Sewa. He started seeing why there was such a rush into the place. He remembered that at the height of his harvest and during a good year at that, he sold his rice for 50 pounds sterling, the biggest sale ever. That was big money then. It has caused much jubilation in Semabu. That was the time he bought many dresses for his first wife Manu and also had married Yebu, all from the proceeds of that harvest. Now, this Yebu had become a thorn in his flesh and a bone in his throat. Now, he realized that he could have a much better wife, if he so desired, with his 320 pounds sterling.

Gibao sat with others in front of their living quarters. The sounds of recorded music blared forth confusedly as gramophones played from all angles of the compound. Some people, especially the married ones, played gramophones loudly from inside their rooms. Some of the workers would spend a long time in their rooms counting their money. In the end, they would come out feeling happy. They would join the rest of the people in the compound, and the merriment would continue.

As they sat, they saw Ndoinjeh, a worker in Alie's group, rush in. You could tell from his glassy eyes he was feeling especially fine. He had disappeared for a time to celebrate receiving his pay. A remark was made that maybe he had been entertained by one of the women in town. He arrived carrying two pints of Guinness Stout in his hands. They were both open and half full. As he walked, he drank randomly from each bottle.

A man selling roast meat followed him in the compound.

# THE DIAMONDS

71

The man was of average height and had conspicuous marks running perpendicularly on both sides of his jaws. It appeared the marks were created for a specific purpose. The man carried a big bowl full of roast meat with powdered pepper and some salt, and a sharp, long knife and several pieces of paper. The lapels of his shirt had become brown, assuming the very color of the roast meat he was selling.

"My friends!" Ndoinjeh called aloud, attempting to drown out the music in the background. No one paid much attention to him. Some treated him simply as a drunk and waved at him, laughing. People were too busy enjoying themselves. This was not the time to listen to a drunken rambler. "My people, listen! I have a message for you all," Ndoinjeh insisted. Even mad people could insist on their right to be heard while they expressed their madness.

There was silence finally.

"We have a guest among us. He is going to be a permanent guest," Ndoinjeh began. "He is a lucky man. He came at the right time. I want us all to entertain him tonight."

There was silence in front of the quarter where Gibao and others were seated. Then someone told Ndoinjeh that he was late and that contributions had been made to enable Gibao to have some pocket money. Ndoinjeh immediately vowed that he would double all that they had given Gibao. No one took him seriously when he made the boast. The people watched as Ndoinjeh ceremoniously in his drunken way handed over one half full pint of Guinness Stout to Gibao.

"This is the time to celebrate! All of this roast meat is for us. Let us have our pleasures, people!" Ndoinjeh announced to the delight of all present. He ordered the man with the conspicuous marks on his jaw to cut up the meat into edible pieces, enough for everyone around and anyone else who might wander in.

People descended on the bowl and the meat, fresh from the fire. They liked to eat meat when their heads were spinning with alcohol. People began to quarrel in the process. One man told his companion not to rush since there was plenty to go around. Tonight, even the children were at liberty to feed thanks to Ndoinjeh's hospitality. They ate as if they had never eaten before. One man took out his handkerchief to clean his running nose after indulging greedily at the bowl. Some had teary eyes from the pepper on the meat.

"It is enough, you. Adu!" one woman told her son. "If you wake me up at night to accompany you to the toilet, I won't go," she warned. Everyone who heard her laughed, and saw Adu stuff his face with more meat; nevertheless, he nodded to his mother and smiled.

The man who was selling the meat stood watching, his face showing delight. When they had finished, the meat-man told Ndoinjeh that he had five pounds sterling worth of meat in the bowl. Ndoinjeh gave him ten pounds sterling and told him to keep one pound for himself.

Gibao was impressed.

Some people wished they had ice cubes in their mouths. Their mouths were on fire, as they say, because of the hot pepper. People gradually started moving away from the meat scene to other parts of the compound in search of more fun.

"Gibao!" Ndoinjeh called. "We are all brothers here. We are the children of Alhaji. He is our father. In Sewa, the man who brings you to money is your father. Is this not so people?" he asked, looking around. "You don't know Sewa, Gibao. You have just come. So, be our guest."

People decided to sit down and listen to Ndoinjeh talk, even though he was behaving like a drunk. But they were all drunk or nearly drunk themselves.

"Do you all know why I brought this man here? This man who sells roast meat? You know why?" Ndoinjeh repeated his question. "I came to Njama a long time ago. And I only buy roast meat from him. This is why I have brought him— to introduce him to my brother. My brother, my brother who is sitting here, Gibao Semabu," Ndoinjeh said. He stood, tipsy

## THE DIAMONDS

from drinking so much Guinness Stout. Then, all of a sudden
he started singing:

"We will drink tonight;
We will drink tonight;
We will drink alcohol tonight,
There is a place somewhere
Where palm wine is
Dripping into a gourd."

People joined the singing with wild enthusiasm.

"Listen. Listen, people! I am sending for two cartons of
Guinness Stout for our guest," Ndoinjeh announced. There
was thunderous applause. He put his hand into his pocket and
took out some money. There were ready volunteers to go to
buy the Stout. One man managed to clutch hold of the money,
and he sped off fast with it.

"Gibao," Ndoinjeh called. People had now become more
attentive to him than ever before. Whatever nonsense he wanted
to utter, there was a ready audience. "I want you to look carefully at this man who sells roasted meat." He was referring to
the Maraka man. "Look at him closely. Forget about the marks
on his jaw. We all have these marks. There are many more
here like him. So, look at his face," he pleaded. "The reason is
that, if you come to Sewa and you don't have someone to tell
you these things, believe me you end up eating dog meat, cat
meat and vulture meat, disguised as chicken. Ndoinjeh's eyes
widened as he looked at his guest.

The others who were listening knew that Ndoinjeh was speaking the truth. Some of the other workers would have wanted
Gibao to find out these things for himself. It was all part of the
initiation to Sewa. Gibao's eyes were wide with disbelief. Dog,
cat or vulture meat was unimaginable. The thought of eating
such meat was revolting. If he ever ate them, he was sure he
would vomit and know right away that he had been tricked.

All of a sudden one of the men was heard laughing very loudly. What was so funny about eating dog meat that someone should laugh? It was criminal to feed someone the meat of a dog or cat or vulture. Why should the man laugh? Someone felt offended. What Ndoinjeh had said was serious and not a laughing matter. But, the laughing man turned out to have been a victim, so that the topic rekindled his memories.

"Do you know why Komaaneh is laughing?" Ndoinjeh asked Gibao. "Well, he takes the whole issue lightheartedly. He has eaten cat meat here in Njama. That was how he was initiated into this Sewa. But he has the right attitude. He laughs at his foolishness and does not make the same mistake again."

A cold wind started blowing. It was refreshing, but it brought with it the foul, sharp smell of fresh urine.

"Brother," the laughing man finally called. "We have seen many things here. If a diviner had ever said to me I would one day eat cat, I would have said he was a liar. As my demia, my friend, had said, we have eaten all these things in Sewa. Not everybody who is in Sewa is a diamond digger. People are here for many reasons. That is why you should not say that you wish you could be like this man or that woman. You don't know how they get their money. This place was never like that until we, the strangers, started coming. Believe me. I am happy. There is not one diamond in my home village and I will pray that God will not give us diamonds. Let there be a place for diamonds, and places for all else."

Some people in the audience agreed with him, while others disagreed.

"But, what is wrong with eating dog or cat?" another man, named Vandi, got up and asked.

"Sit down! Sit down!" people shouted at him. But he refused.

"No," Vandi said. "You make too much noise over little things. Let me tell you. The White Man says that you can eat anything, once it is well cooked. In others parts of the world, people eat dogs, just like we eat sheep or goats or cows in this

# THE DIAMONDS    75

country. So, you people don't know about these things," he said authoritatively.

There was some silence. Some people were busy analyzing what Vandi had just said. It made some sense. To others, it was naked sophistry. Why should they eat dogs and cats just because other people in the world ate them? People murmured among themselves. The idea was not acceptable to them.

"Tell me," the sophist got up again. "Who ever fell ill because he ate roasted dog or cat meat? Tell me that person!" Vandi challenged. "God sent them for us to eat."

One woman left the place. She could not stand Vandi any more. She considered him a dangerous man, for preaching the eating of dogs and cats. He was poisoning the minds of innocent people.

But everyone forgot about Vandi and his message when the two cartons of Guinness Stout were brought in.

"ODOFO! ODOFO!" The people were shouting Ndoinjeh's nickname.

"Na God De Gi" Ndoinjeh answered back. Ndoinjeh believed very religiously that one should enjoy what one had. God would provide the next time. So, he enjoyed himself lavishly and shared equally lavishly. When everyone had a bottle, he started singing again. This time everybody got up to dance. He sang his own name and that of Gibao. People followed his lead. The compound was full of joy again.

There was even one lady who was crying because she was so happy. She had been drinking all sorts of different drinks. She went and sat by the gate, feet stretched out on the floor. She was holding on to a glass of rum someone had poured for her. She joined in singing the song of Ndoinjeh that the others were singing. In the end, she would cry. Those who knew her said that was her own way of enjoying herself. The fact of the matter was that some years ago she had come to the mines with a boyfriend. The boyfriend made lots of money and eventually opened a shop. Later, he abandoned her and went away.

She never saw him again. People said there were many stories about her and the man. She had defied her parents and come to Sewa. She had, at one time, enjoyed some prosperity. People realized that her drunken crying was a reaction to what had happened in her life. She wept and sang, and thus enjoyed herself in her own way.

The merriment continued late into the night. It was thus that Gibao was initiated into customary celebrating in Sewa when people have been paid well. He heartily enjoyed the excitement and celebration, thanks in particular to his full pocket and full stomach.

Meanwhile, Ndoinjeh had left the group unceremoniously to visit a friend who lived away from the compound. His absence caused no comment, everyone was too busy drinking Guinness Stout. Also, it was not unusual, and no one bothered to inquire about him. He had had his pay and could celebrate anywhere he chose. He could end up sleeping in his own bed or at his friend's place as sometimes in the past, no matter.

Ndoinjeh had gone over to see Momoh, his good friend. Momoh had bought a new Bedford lorry which had the inscription "MONEY PALAVER" written on its side, so people had started calling Momoh "Money Palaver."

When Ndoinjeh arrived at Momoh's place, there was as much merriment here as at the compound he had just left. But the people here recognized that Ndoinjeh was too drunk and advised him to go to bed.

"No! No!" Ndoinjeh protested. He said he was far from his limit. He boasted that he could still drink a bottle of brandy that night. He even put up 200 pounds sterling as a stake.

Someone else, partially drunk himself, got up and accepted Ndoinjeh's challenge.

Momoh protested, and Ndoinjeh became furious at Momoh's objections. Instead of listening, Ndoinjeh ran to Mr. Cole's bar, where he bought the brandy.

When Ndoinjeh returned, Momoh tried to take the brandy

## THE DIAMONDS                    77

away from him, but Ndoinjeh's devilish desire to hold on to
the brandy was stronger than Momoh's reason. Momoh continued to protest. Ndoinjeh bragged that this was not the first
time he had accepted such a challenge. He said that he had
acquired a charm that sobered him when he drank, while at the
same time it would make his opponent become very drunk.
The charm would influence his challenger by a sort of spiritual
remote control. When he said that, even the challenger became
afraid. Those around him agreed with Ndoinjeh, saying that
they themselves had seen it happen many a time. Hearing
these comments, Ndoinjeh's challenger asked him whether he
had been initiated into a secret society. That question did it.
Ndoinjeh was insulted. Anyone who valued his reputation
would have been initiated and accepted into a secret society.
It was like asking a Christian had he never been baptized.
Ndoinjeh stood by his challenge. He tilted back his head and
drank off the whole bottle of brandy in front of everyone. He
had demonstrated his powers, and he walked home with his
head held high.

But in the morning, Ndoinjeh was found dead by the gate
in the compound. This was the price of winning the bet.
Compounding the tragedy, no one could locate a penny of his
money. Prior to that evening, Momoh said, Ndoinjeh had
confided in him that this was going to be his last week in the
diamond mines. Ndoinjeh had decided to go home and settle
with his family and parents, and Momoh had promised his
friend he would allow his lorry to take him home in grand
style.

When Gibao heard the story in the morning and saw
Ndoinjeh's corpse, he could not help crying. He had known
Ndoinjeh to be a pleasure-loving man, whose abundant joy
bordered on carelessness and who liked to show off. He lived
the good life in Sewa and loved to make others happy, his
philosophy being that today we will have fun and tomorrow
will take care of itself.

# 78 J. SORIE CONTEH

Gibao wept at the sickening sensation that he had lost a new friend. He thought about how this young man had killed himself by becoming too drunk and dying in his vomit. But even as Gibao and a few others mourned, hundreds of other miners went on to look for more diamonds.

Alie, Momoh and another friend washed and dressed Ndoinjeh's corpse. It was ready to be conveyed to his home town. As previously planned, Momoh's lorry would take Ndoinjeh home.

Women were weeping all over the compound. The lorry had come from Momoh's place with the door wide open. People gathered around the corpse for a last glimpse of Ndoinjeh.

Alie was to say something before the body was taken in the lorry on its final journey. People stood tense and somber around him. He had worked with Ndoinjeh for almost four years. Alie's mouth trembled, and his eyes were red from the tears that he held back.

"People," Alie mustered up his courage to speak without faltering. "How do you say goodbye to a friend, a co-worker, to someone with whom you have had so many things in common for so long? How?" he asked in a soft voice.

People were weeping quiet tears. There was absolute silence. The women had been told to stop wailing, to wait for Alie to finish his eulogy.

"I find it difficult to believe," Alie tried speaking again. "I find it difficult to speak. I find it difficult to accept. Yesterday we were all here, happy and celebrating. Some of us were happy simply because Ndoinjeh was happy. The roast meat he bought, the drinks he bought, the songs he sang all made us happy, and we danced with him in his happiness. Who knew, but Ngewo our God alone, that was our last chance to see him, to be with him, to make merry together? Now, where is he? He came to Sewa well and healthy. He is about to leave with nothing. It is sad because he does not feel the departure as we do. When someone is dead, he has no feelings. It is you and me, his

# THE DIAMONDS 79

friends, his family and parents who feel all the pain. That is
death. Yes, his loved ones." Alie's voice faltered, trembling
with more emotion. Tears were flowing freely from his eyes.
"People, I only hope Ndoinjeh's death will teach us a lesson in
self-restraint. May he go in peace," he concluded.

Ndoinjeh's corpse was loaded into the lorry. His mining
group sent a shovel to accompany his body. The men said it
was the custom, and that his parents could use it in digging his
grave. Then the vehicle left, and the women began wailing
again.

Gibao eased his grief by being with the other mourners that
morning. Everyone eased his own pain by reminiscing about
others who had died in the area. Gibao had now been initiated
more closely into the ways and the logic of Sewa. He began to
understand how Sewa held a glamorous, yet a deadly attraction
for people. Death, Gibao realized, was a more sudden and
frequent visitor to Sewa than to his home village. Or, at least,
death visited in a different guise.

The mourners, except for Gibao, knew well the story of Pa
Bai. They remembered how he had plenty of money as a result
of a big gem find by his miners. Pa Bai told others he had sold
the gems for a handsome amount. People still argued to this
day about how much Pa Bai had collected. Some would put
it at 80,000 pounds sterling, while others thought 100,000
pounds sterling was the actual amount. The actual amount
was beside the point. The fact was that the amount was the
largest Pa Bai had ever had, the largest anyone among them
had ever earned.

The Lebanese man who had bought the gems was a good
friend of Pa Bai. People suggested to Pa Bai that he could
deposit the money at the Sewa Bank, but Pa Bai had thought
differently about the bank. He said he knew that money
deposited at the Sewa Bank finally found its way to the big
bank in Freetown but often by devious means. A few times, he
said, the people transporting the money had been attacked and

the money stolen. There was no sense in putting money in a bank, when it would not be safe.

"The bank," Pa Bai said, "could simply say that they can't see the money because it has been stolen by thieves."

Pa Bai decided that he was going to take the money to Freetown himself for safekeeping. In preparation for this journey, he bought a new Mercedes Benz. This was the car everyone looked forward to owning. It was common in Sewa. The black market dealers who wanted to buy diamonds directly from the miners were known to use the Mercedes cars as bait. They would not hesitate to give such cars as gift to diamond diggers who sold illicit diamonds to them.

Pa Bai's Mercedes was not a gift. He bought it and paid for it. Many myths surrounded Pa Bai's Mercedes. Many people were of the opinion that it was the fastest of all cars and that, if one accelerated up to 120 m.p.h., the car would take off like an airplane. When Pa Bai bought the car, he consulted the Greek man who sold it to him, and this man confirmed the story that the car had such power that to ride in it was like flying in an airplane.

Pa Bai had left his family in a festive mood, as the purchase of a new vehicle was always celebrated. At the end of the party, the owner would pour libation on the car to ensure its safety. The car, the Greek had told him, was the best made by the White Man, so Pa Bai was pleased.

The day Pa Bai was driving to the Freetown Bank, he left very early in the morning. His car was loaded with money. His family continued the celebration in his absence, while Pa Bai went on his way. The greater part of the road was messy and rugged. It was impossible for him to accelerate even to forty miles an hour. He drove his new Mercedes as cautiously as he could.

The roads from Sewa to Freetown or to any part of the country were nearly impossible to speed on, especially during the rainy season. There were a few stretches that were good, and Pa Bai was longing to come across one such stretch.

# THE DIAMONDS 81

About an hour from Sewa he thought he had his chance. He had just passed a town where the Public Works Department had finished work on a fifteen-mile stretch connecting two towns. But the road had two sharp curves, about which he had never been warned.

One of the curves included a bridge and a big sign was placed a mile ahead of the curve which read "DRIVE SLOWLY. DANGEROUS CURVE, NARROW BRIDGE AHEAD." The fact of the matter was that Pa Bai was unable to read. It was said later that he had accelerated on that road up to 100 m.p.h. Unable to negotiate the curve at that speed, he crashed his beautiful Mercedes car into the bridge, and he was crushed to pulp. He died a miserable death on the bridge. The speedometer froze at the highest speed anyone in town had ever known a car to be driven. People were aghast at such a hideous, unnecessary death.

Now, people were just as upset over Ndoinjeh's untimely death.

Gibao's grief for Ndoinjeh stayed with him for several days. He had lost a new friend in a matter of hours. There was no turning back to Semabu, even though death seemed close around him. He had been spared, he reasoned, in order to do other things. He felt he was still destined to be here in this strange, new part of the country. There were mystical powers that grew with the diamond and diamond spirits, especially as more and more people died searching for their diamonds. Gibao grew determined that he would succeed like Pesima had done. Gibao was still on a sacred mission, similar to that of the White Man's story about the Holy Grail, the quest to find the chalice used by Christ at the Last Supper. The diamonds inspired Gibao's spiritual quest to improve his life, his mission, to one day set himself apart from those lesser men whose dreams held lesser ambitions.

# Chapter 8

Gibao had to undergo a great deal of training before he understood proper mining techniques. However, he was taught something more than just mining. The leader of his group, Buya, was, for the most part, always with him. Buya was a short, plump man with a protruding belly, which he jokingly referred to as a symbol of affluence and good living. He was a soft-spoken man whom many regarded as very affable. He had displayed responsibility and sensitivity, qualities which had earned him the attention of Alhaji, who in turn had elevated him to the leadership of the group. Another reason for his prestige was that Buya was older than his co-workers. Buya sometimes took his age too seriously, even to the point of annoying his co-workers.

Buya had a friend, Tamba, who lived about two miles away from Njama in a place called Tokpombu. Tamba was a young, energetic man who was reputed to have the best raffia wine in and around Tokpombu. The raffia wine was known to be more potent than palm wine because it had more alcohol content. Its taste was usually sour, but it could also taste sweet depending upon the length of its fermentation.

Tamba and Buya had become friends in the diamond fields. Whenever Buya was less busy, especially in the evenings, he would take a walk to Tokpombu and have a drink. He would meet many other people originally from Njama who had decided to settle in Tokpombu.

Every morning Tamba would set aside a sizable gourd of raffia wine for Buya. He would only sell Buya's gourd of wine

# THE DIAMONDS

when it was past the time for Buya to visit. Some of the customers referred to the gourd as "Buya's gourd." Some would come to Tamba's shop with the express purpose of buying Buya's gourd in the event he did not show up. Others would ask Buya in Njama whether he was going to Tamba's that evening. If not, the person would go to purchase the wine in his gourd.

One day a man of good reputation was said to have taken a false message to Tamba, saying that Buya had gone on a trip and would be away for a week. He had then bought Buya's gourd. He was drinking his last cup when Buya arrived. The man jumped up and asked Buya if his trip did not materialize. It was an embarrassing occasion, they said. Everybody enjoyed Tamba's wine and wanted it, having known its pleasures real or imagined. These were some of the things that Gibao had to learn.

Buya arranged to take Gibao on the trip to Tokpombu. Gibao would provide Buya company on the trip, which usually Buya would take alone or, occasionally, with another friend. Buya had decided that he would use the opportunity to teach him about mining.

The journey made Gibao homesick. The two of them walked along a narrow path, similar to those in his home village of Semabu. Gibao saw people emerging from various directions coming from their farms, with logs or bundles of wood on their heads, the children carrying chicken coops on their backs as they trudged towards Tokpombu. Young men were carrying home gourds of raffia wine, with their machetes secured under their arms and their faithful dogs following behind. Somehow, their faces seemed familiar to Gibao, but he didn't exactly know why.

Buya and Gibao had to cross two streams before they got to Tokpombu. They would announce their arrival at the streams ahead of time with loud shouts, "Men are coming! Men are coming!" This announcement gave any women, who might be bathing in the stream, an opportunity to submerge their bodies in the water until the men disappeared. This was a common practice, and it was necessary in a small village. Men made their announcements because there was always the possibility that one's own relatives, whether grandmother, mother, sisters or daughters, might be bathing in the stream. The men felt a moral obligation to make the announcements.

The trip this evening to Tokpombu was Gibao's first journey outside Njama since his arrival there. Buya led the way, as he always did. His habit was to hasten his pace and walk past anyone he came across who was heading in the same direction. On one occasion, once there was enough distance between the two of them and the other group, Buya cleared his throat and took his snuff tin from his pocket. He always carried his snuff in a small flat tin. He opened the tin and inhaled some snuff. He stood there for a moment to allow the snuff to take effect, then turned towards the bush and sneezed loudly. He repeated the procedure. Gibao watched him clean his nose and noticed how he seemed to feel easy and light. Buya never ate the snuff, but used it only for inhaling.

"When you get as old as me, you will understand why I like to inhale," Buya told Gibao. "Tamba is a good friend of mine. Since I came here, I do not drink raffia wine anywhere but in Tokpombu. Tamba is a Sewa person, a very nice man. The people are nice. I give him money when I take my pay. I do this all the time. Sometimes he will not take money from me. I drink his wine free, sometimes. Do you know that some people are even jealous of me for this?" Buya asked without expecting an answer. Gibao listened intently. "As I was saying, the Sewa people are kind. They said that some time ago, a long time ago, a set of warriors from the north came and attacked them. The attackers were riding horses. Then there was another warrior, Nyagua. He also gave the Sewa people a hard time. Now here we are, invading their part of the land again. Is this not an invasion? Imagine the number of newcomers in Sewa

# THE DIAMONDS                                    85

country and the havoc they have caused." Buya continued his ruminations on the matter for a long time as they walked. He wanted to teach Gibao about the local people. Buya thought every diamond worker needed some instruction, not only in the methods of mining but their meaning in relation to Sewa land.

"Do you drink much raffia wine?" Buya asked Gibao.

"No, not much. We have palm wine, but we get raffia wine only occasionally. I tap palm wine myself. I think tapping for raffia wine is too laborious. You have to climb the tree with a machete and a small hammer. The top of the tree has to be cleared by cutting the fronds around the area where one has to put the gourd that will collect the dripping juices. When the clearing process is completed, you drill into the tree until enough space is available to secure the gourd. The gourd is connected to the hole by a small hose that passes the liquid to the gourd. After that, you have to wait ten to twelve hours for the gourd to fill. The gourd is usually collected in the evening, depending on its size," he told Buya. "Of course, you may know about this process already."

"Well, I tell you in Sewa we drink lots of raffia wine. I even prefer it to Guinness Stout or other beer," Buya responded.

Gibao coughed as if he was trying to clear his throat. He told Buya to go ahead while he relieved himself by the roadside. As Gibao adjusted his shorts, he noticed two women approaching from behind with bundles of wood on their heads. Gibao moved a little further into the woods. He looked over and saw Buya also relieving himself.

"This thing is contagious," Buya called over. "The moment one man does it, you feel like doing it yourself!"

The village of Tokpombu was much smaller than the town of Njama. There were only two houses with roofs of corrugated iron. The rest of the houses were thatched with palm tree fronds. Unlike Njama, there was no main street or road. The houses were built in a random manner, but no one complained about the layout. The location of anyone's hut had never been an issue. However, men and animals lived side by side just as they did in Njama.

Tamba's place was a small hut that was always well-stocked with an assortment of the merchandise that he traded, such as beer, tobacco, cigarettes, stout, clothes, kerosene, matches, sieves, shovels, corrugated iron sheets, nails, hammers and general mining equipment. At the entrance of the store, he had hung a talisman wrapped in a sheepskin, while another talisman hung from the ceiling. They were prominently displayed and were meant to ward off evil spirits and other malevolent forces, such as witches.

Buya relaxed at Tamba's place and started talking softly into Gibao's ear. "I want to tell you something very important. It is a secret. We workers have two ways of getting money."

Gibao leaned closer to Buya in eager anticipation.

"When we wash the gravel," Buya confided, "and the boss is not around, we usually keep one or a couple of the gems and give the remainder to him. Later, we sell what we have and share the money. We have our customer friends, who buy from us. But it is a big secret. If the boss finds out, it is big trouble. That is why we are like brothers. Of course, the other way we make money is when Alhaji pays us. I am telling you this because for us to succeed in this business, all of us must keep the secret. Any betrayal would mean disaster. People here in Sewa do not take kindly to having their diamonds stolen. There are several cases where people have lost their lives because of this. We need you to be fully with us, because ours is a kind of secret society and whoever discloses its secrets may regret it later."

"How is it possible to steal when Alhaji is around?" Gibao asked.

"He is not always present when we are washing the gravel to sort out the diamonds," Buya went on. "There are times when he is away on business. We do not have to wait for him. What Alhaji and others do is to employ one of the diggers as a secret agent. In the diamond business, you trust no one. The bosses

## THE DIAMONDS                    87

have had some of their relatives stealing diamonds from them
or conniving with us. You see, everybody wants money. Money
means independence. In fact, Alhaji has more faith in some of
us than he has in his relatives." Buya lowered his voice and
added, "As I said before, any betrayal, even a small one, could
be fatal."

Gibao was thinking how to answer. He moved a little closer
to Buya. "Thank you for what you have just told me. As for
keeping secrets, all I have to say is that I am a Wunde man.
The Wunde is a very secret society, just like the Poro initiation
society. I know the consequences of any infraction of the rules
of secret societies. I have come a long way to look for money. I
can assure you I will do anything to ensure that I get that
money. I do not want to return home penniless and become
an object of ridicule," Gibao ended in a whisper.

Buya and Gibao shared another sip of the raffia wine, as a
silent pledge to each other to keep their secrets. Gibao relaxed
again as Buya told him that success was the only real and last-
ing mark of hard work. Gibao had heard that kind of remark
several times. But he had concluded that diamond digging
could not be any more difficult than farming. He felt certain
about that.

"When you get money," Buya advised his younger worker,
"you should bring one of your wives over here. You can even
rent a room in town."

Gibao said he had thought of taking such action as soon as
he made his fortune.

"Women in Sewa love money and plenty of it, and other
men's wives can be trouble, too," Buya warned. "Alhaji is very
jealous of his wives, especially the younger ones, so one should
stay away from them. I know that some of the workers in the
compound are in love with Alhaji's wives. But it is a big risk,"
Buya told Gibao.

Buya poured some more wine into Gibao's gourd as they
relaxed.

"When I first arrived I was in love with a woman in Njama," Buya began, the start of a new story. "She was nice at the beginning, but later she changed. She used to cook two pounds of meat, then add fish and chicken to it, which meant she was not using all of the money. That was getting to be too much. The fact of the matter is that she was using my money to feed another man. You see, women in Sewa do not love only one man. It is very difficult to come across such a woman here. For example, I could not meet all the demands of Yeli, my former girlfriend. What's more, when women come to Sewa, they change and become greedy. Yeli was the first woman I had who smoked. She loved rum, too. How can such a woman keep money?" Buya asked.

Buya enjoyed the opportunity to reminisce about women with Gibao. "Yeli was always traveling, going to see a relative. Sometimes, she would take the money I gave her for food and wouldn't show up again until days later. If I asked her where she had been, she always gave me a good explanation. Her mouth was sharp, her tongue sweet like honey. I loved her very much, but she was making too many holes in my pocket," Buya concluded with a tinge of regret.

Gibao was grateful for Buya's talk. Many others who had made the trip here were not lucky enough to have a tutor like Buya. Some of the newcomers had made serious blunders in their first encounters with the diamonds. Gibao felt himself being taken around like a dignitary, by comparison.

When Buya and Gibao arrived back at Njama that evening, they were told that Ndoinjeh's father had come to see Alhaji. He had come in the lorry that had taken away Ndoinjeh's body, to find out whether Alhaji owed his son any money by way of salary. The father was told that his son had been paid the fat sum of 2,000 pounds sterling in cash on the day of his death. Prior to this, Ndoinjeh had received other handsome payments from Alhaji. Ndoinjeh had never had financial problems since he started working with Alhaji three years ago. His group had

# THE DIAMONDS

always been lucky. Alhaji swore by his religion that Ndoinjeh must have been worth over 10,000 pounds sterling considering his pay for the last three years. Alie and Buya confirmed Alhaji's estimate of Ndoinjeh's wealth.

Alhaji had no idea how Ndoinjeh had saved his money. Ndoinjeh had never given him money to keep, like the other diggers. Alhaji had one of his wives, N'tuma, who kept his accounts, bring out the book that contained his workers' deposits. N'tuma was somewhat literate since she had been educated up to middle school,, where she stopped when her parents married her to Alhaji. It was shown that Ndoinjeh's name had never appeared in the book of deposits.

There was speculation about Ndoinjeh and a lady called Nyahalo. This lady had a strange history. She was a fat woman who walked only when it was absolutely necessary. Nyahalo, people said, had been deserted by men, including two husbands who had had to run away. She was never able to trace their locations or find out what had happened to them. This woman, for reasons that baffled many people, was able to captivate young prosperous men. Her bulk made her a physical monstrosity, but her face was pretty. People said that there was no excuse for young men having any business with her.

Buya had warned Ndoinjeh to avoid Nyahalo. Ndoinjeh had flatly refused the advise of Buya and his co-workers. He had told them that young girls had too many problems, but Nyahalo, he said, was always stationary and, therefore, available. In the end, Buya said that Alie had told Ndoinjeh to remember what the elders used to say about the cockroach. When it should perish, the cockroach would enter a palm oil bottle, whose slippery sides it could not climb. But Ndoinjeh would respond that what was poison for one could be meat for another. Nyahalo was both meat and poison to many. She was an enigma, an incomprehensible phenomenon, one of nature's freaks drawn here to the diamonds—just as Ndoinjeh himself and other men had been drawn to them. People said some men were attracted to her by her conversation, but that they had all ended up in financial obscurity. Her source of income was no mystery, but no one had firm proof of this.

Nyahalo, they said, had charmed Ndoinjeh, like those before him, into her chambers. Such young men would forget about their parents and concentrate their love and their attention only on her. Once a man accepted her bait, only Ngewo the God could save him from moral and financial ruin. This was the woman many suspected Ndoinjeh to have been in love with, a suspicion his co-workers shared. There was no evidence to bring Nyahalo to justice, so Ndoinjeh's father could not pursue the matter.

Ndoinjeh's father was therefore unable to recover a penny of his son's three years of labor in the diamond mines. Alhaji gave him 200 pounds sterling as his own contribution to Ndoinjeh's funeral. Alhaji confessed to Ndoinjeh's father that Ndoinjeh was one of his most energetic workers and that his death was a big loss for his business.

Before falling asleep that night, Gibao tried to comprehend the complexities of this world. Before he knew it, he heard cocks crowing in the early morning. Their noises were mixed with the cry of the Muezzin at the mosque summoning people to prayers. This was the beginning of another day. All of Njama was slowly awakening.

# Chapter 9

Gibao was a son of the soil, as the people say. He had acquired a facility with the hoe, machete, axe and shovel when he was very young. Gibao was eagerly looking forward to his first day of work. Alhaji had acquired some new lots where they were to start prospecting for diamonds. Gibao saw this as a golden opportunity to see the process of prospecting from beginning to end. Gibao dreamed about his first day of working with the diamonds.

He recalled vividly another event in his life that caused him such anxiety, but it had not been an event he was looking forward to. It was a long time ago, when he suspected that he and other boys were going to be circumcised. The news was kept secret from the boys, but his grandmother, by a slip of the tongue, had indicated to him the imminence of the event. When he saw men building a big grove some distance away from the town, he was convinced that his grandmother knew something. For days, he was worried about what he thought was going to happen. He had lost his appetite. On the appointed day, very early in the morning, he and the other boys were awakened to make the trip to the grove. He then recalled his grandmother telling him that the whole exercise was designed to prepare them for manhood through the process of circumcision.

Gibao had proven himself as a man on that day. The challenge ahead of him now was to be one of the best diamond workers for Alhaji. Would he be up to the task? The first process in diamond prospecting entailed clearing the bush.

The second process, to which everybody looked forward, was digging and washing away the dirt, leaving the gravel. Buya had told Gibao that it was possible that they could pick up diamonds whenever they washed the gravel, but that it was also possible that they would not pick up a single piece for days, weeks or even months. An element of luck was necessary, Buya had said. Some people came to Sewa, worked a week or two, made lots of money and then went back home rich. Some, he said, had spent as long as five years prospecting without ever becoming so lucky. Gibao could not bring himself to believe this gloomy aspect of the story Buya told him. And as much as he trusted Buya's wisdom, he treated these anecdotes as simple cautionary tales that could not apply to the ambitious and blessed. And he had already been blessed. He could not foresee that such delays could happen to him. He knew, for example, that Pesima had spent less than a year at the diamond fields before becoming rich.

Gibao and Buya had stored so much gravel that it resembled a small mountain. Gibao wanted to know from Buya if Alhaji would be present at the time they would be washing the gravel. He prayed that they would make significant finds, so that he could make money quickly. Gibao wondered, What are the prospects that Ngewo our God will answer my prayers quickly?

While waiting for their turn to wash the gravel, Gibao decided to visit the other group that was about to wash theirs. This was the group headed by Alie. Gibao not only wanted to see how the gravel was washed, but more than anything else he wanted to actually see a piece of diamond. He had never seen one before. He had no idea what a rough diamond looked like. When he accompanied Alie's group that morning, he was surprised to find Alhaji already there waiting for the workers. Gibao remembered Buya's lessons about how the boss cannot trust anyone when it comes to his diamonds.

The workers wasted no time in starting the long search. Each knew his assignment. They started loading the sieve with

# THE DIAMONDS

gravel and washing it. The washing process took most of the day, and Alhaji remained with them throughout. When they finished, they were all exhausted, but happy with the results. They had collected several pieces, including one piece which they called "number two."

Alhaji made Gibao take a look at the pieces and explained how to distinguish between them. To Gibao, the pieces could pass for pieces of any glass or bottle. He was delighted to have finally seen these magnetic gems that had lured him to Sewa. These gems in the palm of his hand had attracted people from other countries to this obscure place in the world.

Gibao was surprised to find that the diamond did not look as impressive as he had imagined. However, he understood that this was due to the fact that they were not polished. What was it about these gems that made them so valuable? He thought he should send a letter to his family, especially his mother, to say that he had started work and had, in fact, seen diamonds. After thinking about it, he concluded that it would be difficult to send a letter home from Njama. It was a long way, and communications were extremely inadequate. Ah! Gibao thought again. Maybe after I have washed my own gravel and found a diamond I could send the letter home. With the money, I could get someone to write it and another person to deliver it.

That evening, Gibao, Buya and Mulai, a co-worker, headed to Ya Digba's for drinks and some food. On the way, they stopped by Momoh's shop. Momoh had returned from Ndoinjeh's funeral but had not yet been to the compound to see the others. Momoh told them how he had been unable to control his tears when he saw Ndoinjeh's mother weeping on the day of the burial. The other workers who were sent by Alhaji to accompany his body said the same thing, that they also had wept the entire time. All of Ndoinjeh's sisters and brothers had been wailing, pulling their hair and beating their breasts. The whole town had been ablaze with mourning, like fire sweeping through summer hay. Buya stood silent as Momoh spoke. It was simply another sad event to add to the others that he had witnessed in Sewa.

"You know the most pitiful part of it all?" Buya asked as they walked along towards Ya Digba's. "The parents did not get a penny out of him," Buya answered his own question.

"How can one come to Sewa for three years and not save a penny?" Mulai asked.

Ya Digba's was full of customers seated outside, drinking and talking. The people would talk about the biggest gem found, smugglers intercepted, a missing child, and other things.

"Ya Digba, please help us with some food," Buya called out to her.

"You! Buya!" Ya Digba called back without lifting her head. She recognized his voice, but went on preparing the food. "Where have you been hiding yourself all this time? Do you know someone came and reported you to me?" She joked. "We shall talk about it. Please behave yourself and do not give the lady heart trouble." She then looked up and saw Buya and his company. "Hey, young man, long time no see here." She was referring to Gibao. "It is Buya who has been keeping you. He is a bad man. You watch out," Ya Digba teased, smiling. Without needing to ask, she dished rice for each of them. "What do you want to drink?" she asked them. Her little daughter was busy helping her prepare food for the other customers.

People liked the way Ya Digba recognized her customers and teased them. Her customers were special to her, not just faceless participants in a commercial transaction. She had the human touch. Her friendliness, as much as the enjoyment of the food, made people flock to her stall.

"Ya Digba, when are you going to cook fufu?" one of the customers called out.

"Ummm, you like fufu, as if you have no teeth. No wonder you always look dull," a customer replied.

"Leave him alone," Ya Digba joined in. "People have the right to eat what they want. Come here next Friday. Since my

## THE DIAMONDS                              95

sister went away, I have not been able to prepare fufu. You know that cooking fufu requires lots more work than cooking rice," Ya Digba explained, smiling broadly.

"Which of you Alhaji workers killed Ndoinjeh?" somebody hollered, trying to tease Buya. Buya did not bother to answer the man.

Ndoinjeh's death was known all over town. Even before the mourning had formally ended, people had started joking about it, Sewa fashion. Gibao could not appreciate that type of joke. He was not ready to accept the ease with which people forgot others when they were dead. If a death occurred in Semabu, he thought, the village would be in mourning for a long time. But in Njama, people could forget the dead in a matter of days. The people in Ndoinjeh's compound went to work the very day his body was conveyed to Taninihun, his home town. These were aspects of the diamond mentality that Gibao did not like. If he died in Njama, he knew by now how people would treat his death. Was it that people lost their feelings once they were in contact with money? Was it that they had no more regard for life? Gibao asked himself these questions, while taking a critical glance at the man who had asked the insensitive question about Ndoinjeh. But the man was only busy trying to get the most out of his plate of rice and licking his fingers to make sure he got all of the delicious sauce. He looked no different from anyone else, no different from Gibao himself.

When the time came for Buya to leave with his company, he teased Ya Digba by promising he would see her sometime to discuss any gossip made to her about him. Ya Digba teased back that his return had better be soon, or she would forget.

As the three of them walked to the compound, Gibao asked Buya the name of the man who had asked the question about Ndoinjeh. The man was called Kalilu.

"You don't know, Njama people don't care. Death does not mean anything to people any more. People die everyday. It is because you have just come that you are surprised by the way people talk. Wait until diamond money starts to come into your hands. Then, you will think differently," Buya remarked, nodding his head sagely.

Gibao refused to accept Buya's remark. Life to Gibao then was important. The opposite of life, the finality of death, should be treated with soberness, deep concern and regret. Death should not be a topic for a joke. Men, he thought, were degenerating to the level of animals. But then he realized this comparison was not accurate because even animals could express concern for the loss of their kind.

The following morning, Buya, Gibao and the co-workers went to wash the gravel which they had stored for the past week. Gibao was not surprised to find Alhaji already at the site. Alhaji was extremely pleased with the enthusiasm and determination with which Gibao was working. It took Alhaji some time to believe that Gibao had not before had any knowledge of diamond mining. Gibao swore by his mother that this was his first time of coming to Sewa and seeing the process in operation. Alhaji stayed with the men for the rest of the morning. Whenever he had to stay longer at the site, he would conduct his Muslim prayers there, and one of his wives would bring a snack for him some hours later. Alhaji had been warned not to stay long without food because he had ulcer problems. He heeded this medical advice as religiously as he conducted his prayers. By the close of the day when they left, the workers had found several gems but none of much value. When they returned for the evening shift, Gibao was given the opportunity to do the washing. Alhaji was not present in the evening, so Gibao was praying repeatedly that they would make a significant find. They were lucky and picked up a few big pieces, but Buya decided to give them to Alhaji.

Gibao could not understand Buya's action. Why give the diamonds to Alhaji when he was not around? Gibao wondered. Why did Buya tell me that they stole often in order to make

## THE DIAMONDS
97

extra money? If you cannot steal when the master is away, when was it a good time to steal? Certainly not in his presence!

Gibao was a novice. Buya and the others knew what they were doing after three years at this work. The other workers had told Gibao repeatedly that it was necessary to be shrewd and calculating. One must not act rashly because mistakes could be fatal. But like all newcomers, Gibao wanted money to come his way very quickly.

Gibao was glad that he was now a confirmed member of the group. Also he had succeeded in showing Alhaji how industrious he was. All his co-workers were impressed with his performance, although they thought privately that such vigor would not last long.

The find that they gave to Alhaji did not measure up to the prospector's requirements for undertaking a trip across the border. Gibao was speculating all the time about how much his own share would be when the gems were finally sold. But Alhaji was in no rush to dispose of the gems, as he was busy negotiating about some new plots of land to be mined. There was speculation that the newest land the government was releasing was particularly rich in gems. The rush to get even a square foot of this land was ferociously rough, and the cost of the plots rose accordingly.

This was not a problem for Alhaji. People like Alhaji never really had problems when they had to relate to government officials. It was a common saying that "money no ba lie" (money never misleads). People who had money could do virtually anything and get away with it, if they knew the right channels. But, if one had money and was tightfisted, then one's business stayed like a fallen fruit and even began to rot.

Soon after this first find, Buya took Gibao to Tokpombu again. He impressed on Gibao how lucky he was. There were good prospects ahead in the newly acquired lots. They would all make lots of money. Buya asserted that he had had a premonition to that effect.

Gibao wished this could be true. He asked Buya at what time they would be able to steal diamonds. Buya would not say. He only told Gibao to take it easy. The strategy was that one had to create a high degree of trust between master and workers. Alhaji was certain that his workers stole the gems anyway, and the workers knew that he knew. Buya assured Gibao that he would see how they would go about it when the time came. Gibao was relieved to have the information, so he tried to be patient and wait for his next lessons on stealing diamonds.

# Chapter 10

Gibao was happy on his first pay day, one Friday, to receive 400 pounds sterling. The pay served to boost his hope for the best in the newly-acquired plots that Alhaji had bought.

Alhaji had given his workers a holiday. They spent much of the day in the compound drinking, eating and talking. Many of the workers took the opportunity to lecture Gibao about life in the mines. They narrated one story after another. The diamond business was full of cheating, where each player tried to outwit the other. It was savagely brutal.

Gibao was told about a servant who was falsely suspected by his master of stealing diamonds. The master alleged that his servant had swallowed the gems. He commanded the servant to answer, but the servant denied the accusation. However, the master was not convinced, and so he butchered the servant, searching through his bowels for the gems. There were no gems to be found. The master was tried for murder, found guilty and hanged.

Gibao listened in stunned disbelief. How could such a thing happen? He tried not to get too upset as he listened.

The second story was about four workers who had conspired to defraud their master. They had succeeded and made away with diamonds worth thousands of pounds. The leader of the group escaped with all the gems. The rest pursued him for three days and finally caught him in a jungle, while he was still running. They found out that he had swallowed the gems by sandwiching them in a banana. The three overpowered him and disemboweled him. They retrieved all the gems and left his body in the jungle to rot.

The stories were told in a light tone, but it was hard for Gibao to see or enjoy the humor the others enjoyed.

Another story was about a Lebanese dealer who was caught smuggling. He had a big, fierce-looking Alsatian dog which looked more like a wolf. The man had come to the border in his Mercedes Benz with the dog sitting in the back seat. He had many diamonds he was trying to take out of the area. It was said that he had hidden pieces of these gems in meat and given them to his dog to swallow. How he was going to get these pieces from the dog was his own problem. One of his servants at home had seen him giving the "diamond meat" to the dog and tipped the police. On his way to Freetown, he was naturally stopped at the border. The dealer said he appeared exceptionally nice to the police that day.

"Officer, how de morning oh?" the dealer greeted the officer.

"How are you, boss?" came the officer's reply.

The dealer was said to have panicked when he saw it was O.C. Samba who greeted him. O.C. Samba had acquired notoriety at the post. He was said to be the only officer who could not be bribed. He was efficient and strict. The dealer had deliberately chosen that day for his trip because he was told Samba would not be on duty. There were many that day who had traveled to smuggle diamonds. It was told that these would-be smugglers were afflicted as if by hot pepper that day.

"Officer, it is a long time since I saw you," the dealer remarked.

O.C. Samba was busy inspecting other travelers. He uttered no word. No one was going to rush him. He took his time. The police post was full of travelers and smugglers. When O.C. Samba got to the Lebanese dealer, he searched him thoroughly, and then asked him to accompany him to the car. O.C. Samba saw the dog in the car and made the remark that it looked like the type that ate diamonds. One could see the dealer's color assuming various shades of pink. His stomach turned, and his hands started trembling.

## THE DIAMONDS

"Boss," O.C. Samba called. "Sorry, but you cannot pass with this dog. I suspect it."

"Officer, to God, to my mother who bore me, there's nothing like that in this dog's belly."

"Boss, we are familiar with these things. Don't worry. We will find out," O.C. Samba said firmly.

"Officer, but the dog only knows his master; the dog is a dangerous dog," the dealer said in a trembling voice, hoping that the tremors would be understood as expressing his fear for the officer's safety.

"I trained at Hendon Metropolitan Police College in England and I know my job. I will take care of that dog when I am ready, so you leave him and go to Freetown," O.C. Samba said in an authoritative voice.

The dealer never saw his diamonds or his dog again. And he never returned to the border.

That very day, another interesting but sad incident happened at the police post. Another important and very rich diamond dealer was also smuggling gems to sell across the border. He knew from experience that the police had devised all possible means of searching prospective smugglers. This man, with one of his wives, devised an ingenious plan. They decided to hide pieces of gems in the woman's sanitary napkin, pretending that she was having her monthly period. The wife dressed gorgeously in flowing gowns with wrapper and head ties to match. Her man was tall, elegant and robust. They succeeded with their plan until they got to the border. The man went through the search without any incident, and then he had to wait for his wife to be searched by the female police. But it was a painful wait.

"Ah, our world is coming to an end," his wife said to the female police. "See. Big woman like me, children are searching me all over. They are not even afraid. I could be your mother," the wife told the girl searching, while two others looked on.

"Mama, it is not our fault. It is the law," the girl replied, continuing her search.

And then, another female officer brought out a new sanitary pad and said that the lady had to change the one she was wearing. "It is the law," the lady was told again. The police woman said there was no negotiating.

The husband and wife ended up losing all the gems, but they managed to get away before the police actually found anything. O.C. Samba had done such a good job of catching smugglers and he was promoted to the rank of Sub-Inspector and given special responsibilities for Njama, Post No. 1.

However, the smugglers still tried to devise new ways of smuggling. They would even put gems in the inner tires of vehicles, but the police caught up with them almost as quickly as they could devise new tricks.

Gibao heard many such stories. But no matter what, he was ready and willing to cooperate with Buya and the others to steal diamonds from Alhaji. He was determined to pursue his mission in Njama because he believed in the predictions of Ndawa.

■ ■ ■

Soon after the holiday, Alhaji was driving his Mercedes car in Njama when he decided to stop by and talk to his Lebanese friend and customer. This Lebanese man was known as a devout Muslim, he was not the same one whose dog had been confiscated. Alhaji found him in his shop sitting in his armchair with his prayer beads in his hand.

"Salaam, Alhaji," the Lebanese friend said and stood up immediately.

"Salaam," Alhaji replied. They shook hands, and Alhaji noticed the smell of coffee in the shop. The fan was pointed in Alhaji's direction, so the gentle breeze brought the coffee's aroma to him in all its freshness.

The wife of the Lebanese also greeted Alhaji, and all the children came to salute him. Alhaji was known to all the family members. They could even recognize his shadow. It was Alhaji

# THE DIAMONDS 103

who had made the Lebanese man rich and prosperous in Sewa.

"Alhaji, some coffee or tea?" the Lebanese asked his friend.

"No, thank you. I was just passing by, I am expecting some workers to bring some finds the day after tomorrow. You know I obtained some plots in the new area that has just been released," Alhaji said.

"Alham dulilai, God is great, Alhaji. I understand that place is rich in diamonds," the man said excitedly.

"Oh, yes, there was a great rush, and many people could not get even a single square foot of land."

The man was a chain smoker. His thumbs and index fingers were stained with nicotine, but, whenever Alhaji was around, he felt inhibited about his smoking.

"I meant to tell you about the new man I have got," Alhaji started, boasting. "I have put him in Buya's group. I think he is a better worker than anyone else there. Even Buya says that about him. I am very happy to have him." Alhaji was talking about Gibao, and had said the same to his brother, Kemoh, and thanked him for recruiting Gibao.

By the time Alhaji left his friend's place, it was raining lightly. He decided to go home, where he found several visitors waiting for him. His house was always like that, one guest after another from many places in and outside the country. Among his guests was a distinguished visitor from Njama named Alhaji Kabba. He was one of the rich men in Njama and had come to congratulate Alhaji Jimoh for having succeeded in getting several plots at the new sites, whereas he Alhaji Kabba had got nothing. One complaint people had about Alhaji Kabba was that he was tightfisted, despite his wealth, but sometimes he paid for his tightfisted ways.

"Alhaji, I know you are going to make money this season. Walai, I know that," he told Alhaji Jimoh.

"Were you late in applying? What happened that you have no sites?" Alhaji Jimoh asked.

"No, believe me. They said they did not see my papers and the closing date for the application had passed," Alhaji Kabba told his friend. The fact of the matter was that those who processed the application forms knew Alhaji Kabba to be a miser, so none of them had felt obliged to waste time on his papers. His papers would be "missing" until he made up his mind to open his pockets to help the processors.

Alhaji's wives put together some food for the guests. Alhaji told his guests that his acquisition of the plots coincided with the presence among his workers of a young energetic man who had recently been recruited, again referring to Gibao.

"This is God's work," Alhaji Kabba said.

"N'tuma!" Alhaji Jimoh called his wife. She came hurriedly and meekly. She was trying to tie her wrapper securely around her waist. "Go and bring the book," he instructed. These were the accounting books where his workers' money was credited. Gibao was doing well financially, and Alhaji Jimoh was proud to advertise his success.

Both Alhajis could not speak English, the language in which the accounts were noted, so N'tuma explained meekly how much Gibao had in his account.

The rest of the evening Alhaji and his friends sat and talked about diamonds, events of the day, and other matters of interest in Njama. They observed that there were signs to show that the rains were going to be heavy that year.

Gibao, meanwhile, wanted to send some money to his mother and family. The amount he was going to send was small. Buya knew a driver of a Bedford lorry who would have to pass through Semabu at some point. Buya talked to the driver, who was called Nyandeboo (beautiful neck), and the driver agreed to help Gibao. The man's name had nothing to do with his looks. Nyandeboo was really an ugly, short man, whose neck could not be distinguished from the rest of his body, and this gave him the appearance of an oversized toad. How he acquired his name remained a mystery. He consented

# THE DIAMONDS

to take the money, along with a letter indicating how much each person should get. The money was to be shared among Gibao's relatives and close friends including his grandmother, his mother, the three wives, Maada and Kinawova. Nyandeboo's Bedford lorry had an inscription on it that read "MONEY NEVER LIE." The inscription became his nickname.

All of Alhaji's workers were looking forward to prospecting in the newest plots of land. They were happy their master was not tightfisted like Alhaji Kabba. Alhaji Jimoh believed in the saying, "You should throw money to catch money." He had always been able to catch plenty of money by throwing some in the right direction. Many of the workers could not sleep well the night before prospecting in the new plots, thinking about what they might find the next day and how it would enrich them.

Alhaji and his workers left for the site earlier than ever before. This particular day, they had their meals at the site. No one would risk leaving gravel without inspecting it, so they decided to wash the gravel the same day, even if they had to spend twenty-four hours at the new site. They finished their work at the pit at about 11 o'clock at night, together with Alhaji. It was one of the happiest days in their lives at Njama. They made lots of quality finds. This was sensational news that could not be kept quiet, and it spread overnight all over town.

Gibao was puzzled as to whether Buya had secured a few good pieces for themselves to sell as they had planned. How did Buya manage to elude Alhaji? Gibao was not aware of Alhaji's being away for even more than five minutes all through the operation. He admitted to himself that he was new to the game and might have missed an important trick. After all, if it had been meant to fool Alhaji, it would certainly have fooled him also.

The diamonds Gibao and the others had found would send Alhaji across the border for sure. The following day, Alhaji's compound was invaded by visiting dealers seeking to buy the diamonds. The following evening, Alhaji disappeared from Njama.

The black market contacts for diamonds included characters from Greece, America and England, who represented only a small part of the international influx of white people into Sewa. Mr. Kazantas from Greece was a major player. His name was too hard to pronounce, so he was popularly known as Mr. Baker because he was the only white man who went into the profession of baking bread, as a cover for his diamond activities. Mr. Bradford was an Englishman, whose cover profession was school teaching, and he was married to a missionary. He was usually called "Mr. Bedford," after the name of the Bedford lorry truck, then the most popular means of transportation. Mr. Puttman's cover profession was that of motor mechanic. He was good at this, however, and he repaired all the vehicles for everyone in and around Njama. All these people had to have their cover professions, because their diamond dealing activities were illegal under the laws of the country.

The Lebanese dealers were shopkeepers by their official profession and they competed with the other dealers to win the attention of the local diamond dealers and transporters. Some of these, like Alhaji and his brother, Kemoh, preferred the Lebanese shopkeepers because they were all Muslims, and the Lebanese shopkeepers exploited this commonality of religion for getting customers. As for the other dealers, they knew that the workers liked inducements in the form of radios, gramophones, goods from Europe, bicycles, boots and, for someone like Gibao, a promise from the missionary lady that she would assist in helping his son or daughter to study abroad. The only other inducements the Lebanese merchants gave to the diamond workers were brandy and rum.

Buya was very knowledgeable and would tell Gibao in detail about these three important contacts and also about the Lebanese shopkeepers. Gibao learned from Buya that the Lebanese knew that these workers stole diamonds from people like Alhaji

# THE DIAMONDS

and Kemoh, and that, as a result, the Lebanese merchants would try to blackmail them in subtle but effective ways. They had to be subtle because, if their threats became too strong, the workers would not go back to them a second time.

Buya walked Gibao past all three of these contacts, so he would know who they were and how to approach them some day.

Mr. Baker, the Greek, was tall and handsome with dark hair. He talked a lot and had acquired the ability to speak the main languages in Njama: Krio, Temne, Kono and Mende. He had no problem communicating with people in all the groups. He was very friendly, but his bread was good and this earned him additional popularity in Njama. People ate bread at any time of the day, and he worked hard to make sure the bread was always available and affordable. He had tried the fishing profession before, but he was lured to Sewa, when he learned he could make quick money there. He was not married and enjoyed a lively, happy and sociable single life.

Mr. Bradford was of medium height, on the plump side, but physically agile. He was soft spoken. He mostly went about dressed in a white short-sleeved shirt and khaki shorts. He was drawn into the diamond business by his missionary wife, who had acquired an extensive knowledge of Sewa when she had carried on missionary activities there.

Mrs. Grace Bradford was pretty, slim, tall and graceful. She had developed the habit of carrying the Bible wherever she went. She always wore long dresses, and she was well known in Sewa because of her missionary activities. Her knowledge of the diamond business was extraordinary and, consequently, she was an asset to her husband in his smuggling activities. Few people outside the trade suspected that she and her husband were involved in smuggling, since women were never involved in the smuggling of diamonds. As a missionary wife with her bible, Mrs. Bradford was in a good position for smuggling diamonds to Antwerp, and her smuggling trips always went

108          J. SORIE CONTEH

smoothly. Like Kazantas and Puttman, she and her husband
became rich and lived very comfortably.

Mr. Puttman was a very efficient automobile mechanic, and
he became well-known throughout Sewa because transportation was very important to business in Sewa; Bedford trucks
were used all the time. Mr. Puttman was shrewd and industrious. He was also secretive about his diamond interest,
though many local diamond workers knew about this his
underground business. Like the rest of the foreigners who
trafficked in diamonds, he made occasional trips to Antwerp
to sell his diamonds.

Buya warned Gibao that the foreigners would try to exploit
the diamond workers, so Gibao would have to learn how to
exploit the foreigners in turn. One way to do this, Buya explained to Gibao, was not to have just one foreign dealer as a
customer, but however to give the impression to the dealer that
he was his only customer. It was all a corrupt game, but in the
socially and economically explosive diamond era, the practice
of stealing diamonds for one's quick wealth was not morally
frowned upon. What Buya, Gibao and the other workers could
steal was sold to foreigners such as the Bradfords, Puttmans,
Bakers and the Lebanese. The business of exploitation was
color blind and went beyond religious or ethical beliefs. Buya
reminded Gibao that, although they were illiterate and did not
know the white man's book, they could still become wealthier
than any white man, as long as they knew the art of reverse
exploitation.

Buya, Gibao and their companions went to see the Lebanese
man who was also Alhaji's friend. The moment the Lebanese
man saw them, he knew they were bringing gems to him. He
was very warm towards them and took them to his lavishly
furnished living room. The workers sat down on a long settee.
They had the serious look of those who had something
important to sell. The Lebanese man hovered around them in
a flutter of movement, trying to be cordial and helpful.

# THE DIAMONDS

"Wetin una de drink, what would you drink?" the Lebanese man asked them.

No one answered. This was part of the game of negotiation.

"Beer, stout, whiskey or brandy?" the Lebanese man asked again.

The workers look at each other, as if trying to make a collective choice.

"The place is cold," Mulai said, almost inaudibly.

"Me, a go takam stout. Brandy, it burns my throat and chest," Buya added.

Gibao opted out, so the Lebanese brought two bottles of brandy and six pints of stout and put them all on the center table. The workers' faces were glowing now with pleasure, while the Lebanese man's wife was taking care of the shop in the back.

"Any good for me?" the Lebanese asked.

"Yes, boss," Buya answered. "Good number two and other nice ones, boss."

Buya took out a white handkerchief. He looked happily at the pieces. They were good. Buya and the Lebanese embarked on hard negotiations. The discussion was protracted and difficult. The Lebanese was insisting on bargaining for the lot but the group on the other hand wanted a piece by piece sale. They ended the meeting by selling at 300 pounds sterling, which everyone thought was a reasonable price.

That night, when his companions went to sleep, Gibao sat alone in the veranda of their house. The rain was pouring hard on the zinc roof. He was taking stock of his newly acquired fortune. Should I be content with what I have and return home like Pesima? But his answer came quickly. No. He rejected such a thought. His mind told him that he had an even more prosperous future ahead of him. He had demonstrated his ability for hard work and, in a short time, he had made more money than he would have thought possible. He decided he would wait until a time when he could return home in splendor, when he would dwarf Pesima in all respects. There was no compromise on this for Gibao, now that he had begun to realize his greatest expectations.

# Chapter 11

Gibao's self-confidence grew as he started to make more money. A new identity, perhaps dormant before, began to take shape. He convinced himself that he belonged to Njama and was a definite part of its community. He fraternized and moved around with an air of importance and familiarity.

He was, however, confronted with one problem: Buya. He appreciated the fact that Buya had been nice to him, and had actually initiated him into Njama society. Buya was much older than Gibao and treated him like a younger brother. He was grateful to Buya for this, but he realized that he was becoming unhappy in Buya's company. Gibao felt tense, never free with Buya. Part of the problem was that Gibao felt he always had to censor what he said in Buya's presence particularly about his long-range goals for operating his own business.

There were other workers who were Gibao's peers. There was Mulai, but Mulai belonged to another class. The one that appealed to him most was Brima. Brima and Gibao had many things in common. They were younger than their co-workers. They enjoyed what they called "the fast life," centered around women and alcohol. They loved to dress up, like other successful young men. They were disposed to a flamboyant style of life in Njama.

But Gibao still needed Buya's help in learning to deal with the foreign buyers. One Friday evening, after a meal, Buya, Gibao and two others left Alhaji's compound but told no one where they were going. This was not unusual. On Friday nights, most people would go about their business privately, with euphoric abandon to engage in Njama's pleasures or to enter the hidden world of bartering in gems.

Buya had the gems in his custody. He would press his hand repeatedly against his pocket to be sure they were safe because he knew what the consequences would be if he lost them or tried to play tricks on his friends.

"First, we shall go to Mr. Bradford, then to Mr. Puttman and finally to Mr. Baker," Buya explained to the other three. "I am almost certain it will be Mr. Baker who will buy them. The others, as usual, think we are fools. They do not know how difficult and dangerous this our job is."

"I agree with you," Gibao said. "I personally feel that of all our customers among the foreign people, Mr. Baker is the best. He is considerate and kind. For instance, when we casually drop by, he offers drinks, gives us brandy or whiskey, and sometimes he assists, when one is broke, unlike the others and especially Mr. Bedford, who is very stingy with everything, but still wants us to do good business with him.

Alie laughed rather sarcastically though he supported Gibao's observations. "You see why I like Gibao. He is very realistic in his assessment of issues. Even though he frequently suspects that both Mr. Baker and that single girl Fudia have something going on between them, he is the first to admit that Mr. Baker is our best customer. That is why I like Gibao because whether one likes it or not the main reason we are all here, including Mr. Baker and the others, is to make money and go back home."

Alie added, "Well, the way I see it, Mr. Baker is trying to please Gibao so Gibao can leave Fudia for him and him only."

Alie knew about Gibao's attraction to the girl Fudia and was teasing him about it. Gibao had recently met Fudia formally and had begun to use her "female services." Now that Gibao had money, he could enjoy more female company, and more than company.

Alie was disappointed because Gibao showed no interest in talking about Fudia. What Alie didn't know was that for the

# THE DIAMONDS

moment, Gibao's mind was rigidly focused on how much the gems would fetch and how difficult the negotiations would be, thoughts about money, not about Fudia, were Gibao's only concern. For him, women were not important when it was time to negotiate for money .

As they approached, they saw Mr. Baker lying in his hammock on the porch. His Aladdin light glowed brilliantly as if he were signaling to potential customers that he was still around and awake on this Friday evening. Dozens of moths and other insects swarmed around the light, keeping his company as unwanted guests. But they didn't bother him; he seemed used to them.

Mr. Baker recognized the four men who were approaching. He held up his pipe in a friendly wave. He had had a feeling that he would get some visitors that evening.

"Come in, my friends. Sit down. It is funny. I was thinking of you people today," Mr. Baker said as he stood to greet them. "News is all around town that many people found diamonds today, including your boss. So, I was happy for all of you. I made sure I kept some fresh bread in case you dropped by and, to tell you the truth, I was sure you would. I know that miners work hard and need to eat, so I always make sure fresh bread is available for you. It is not easy these days to come across good and reliable friends like you. You should know how much I cherish your friendship."

Buya and his friends listened attentively and warily.

"We also appreciate your friendship, Mr. Baker," Buya said, acting as the spokesperson. "You have been very helpful to all of us. You are not only a customer, but a friend. You assist us when we are broke. People like Mr. Bedford and Puttman and the Lebanese only help people like Alhaji and his brother, those already rich. As for Mr. Bedford, all he gives us to drink if at all is *Guinness Stout,* and Mr. Puttman gives only beer whether the place is cold or hot. The Lebanese give us only soft drinks because they say that they are Muslims, even though we know that some of them drink whiskey, brandy and beer in their houses."

Mr. Baker casually waved at the insects which had invaded his porch, as he listened. "Well, as the place is cold, let us have some hot drinks," He said with a smile. He went into his house and came out with glasses, then went back and came out with a bottle of whiskey and a bottle of rum.

"I also have beer and *Guinness Stout*, if anyone is interested," Mr. Baker said.

Buya and his friends laughed away the suggestion. "At this time of night, whiskey is the best drink because the place is cold," Alie responded to Mr. Baker's kindness. "When you take it, you feel it in the chest and stomach. It makes you feel warm and you start to sweat." Alie took a glass of whiskey without ice. He drank it in one gulp and put his right hand on his chest, as if to illustrate his point.

"Are you coming from your compound, or from Mr. Saad, or from Mr. Bradford or Puttman?" Baker asked them.

"No, Mr. Baker, whenever we have something good, we come to you. We only go to those people when we have gems that are not good. I think they know that too. Always, they tell us that we only go to them to dispose of the gems that you don't want," Buya cleverly replied.

The night was early as the five of them started their negotiations on Mr. Baker's porch. There was an intense stream of human traffic in Njama that Friday evening, as always when the heavy rains ended, so that bars and social clubs were alive with music and dancing. Many voices could also be heard.

"Buya, since you are the one who buys bread for the whole group, let us go into my room so that I can show you the fresh bread I kept for your people," Mr. Baker said. The two of them got up. Mr. Baker began escorting Buya into his house and into his bedroom. "As I said, I had this feeling that you would be coming, so I kept the bread I baked today for you. I hope you will enjoy it for your breakfast tomorrow morning."

# THE DIAMONDS

Buya had not started drinking his brandy. He always waited until the bargaining was completed before he took a sip. This was a principle he observed very religiously, and he earned the respect of his friends for keeping to this practice. His rationale was to keep a clear head so he could negotiate the top dollar and debate any resistance his buyers might conjecture as to why the buying price should be lower.

Buya handed the gems over to Mr. Baker who gazed at them in admiration. The pieces sparkled with brilliance. Mr. Baker silently trembled with excitement at the thought of having these quality gems.

"No bargains, just pay one thousand eight hundred pounds," Buya told Mr. Baker, who was still looking at the gems in his hands.

Baker frowned. "No bartering?" he asked quietly.

Buya shook his head, "No."

"Alright," Mr. Baker said. He knew that to haggle too much on the price could mean the loss of these diamonds. "No bargaining between us. We are friends. That is why you came to me. I will give you one thousand six hundred pounds," Mr. Baker added cageyly. "You see, as you know when I go to Antwerp, I have to buy a ticket, then pass through the police posts, where I have to grease the palms of the numerous police people. You understand what I mean."

"Okay," Buya said relenting to the small bargaining. "But put fifty pounds on top of that for me. You too know what I mean. I need the additional fifty pounds , and that will be just between the two of us. Let me go out and get them to agree to what you have offered." That way, I get my fee of fifty pounds for convincing them that you will only be able to pay us one thousand six hundred pounds, and you get your small bargain."

Mr. Baker nodded his head in agreement.

When Buya met his friends, they looked at him and waited for his message. They had agreed earlier that they would not accept anything less than one thousand five hundred pounds from Mr. Baker and nothing less than one thousand seven hundred pounds from the other buyers, so they were happy with the news that Mr. Baker had offered one thousand six hundred pounds. The deal was concluded that night to everyone's satisfaction.

■ ■ ■

In time, Buya noticed that Gibao had grown restless in new ways by spending more of his free time with Mulai and Brima and seemed interested in joining another digging company. Gibao simply wanted to get away from Buya's controlling grasp. When Gibao became closer to Brima and Mulai, Buya was not surprised. He held nothing against Gibao. His main interest had always been to find and retain a good, permanent worker. He was satisfied that he had helped Gibao to adapt to his new surroundings and to cope with life In Njama. Buya ignored Gibao's more youthful desires and activities. He wished him, Mulai and Brima good luck in their newfound friendship.

Buya had also befriended Mulai when he had first arrived in Njama. The men complained that Buya tried to play the role of elder brother to the others. Buya wanted his juniors to honor his age, though he did not say it in any explicit manner. But he made the implications too clear to be ignored. Buya would take on each newcomer as his little brother, leading him on occasional walks to Tokpombu for a drink. The young employees ultimately fought to be free to associate with others of their own age, outlook, and temperament. It was not a surprise that Gibao defected from Buya's big brother controls as the others had done before him.

Alie and the other older group leaders simply did not care. They socialized with men of their own age and left the younger ones to themselves. They would generally intervene only if they saw the younger ones doing something wrong that would affect the morale of the group as a whole. The offer of sage

# THE DIAMONDS

advice was given, usually by Brima, only if it was deemed urgently necessary.

Gibao had at one point met Brima's sister, Bintu, who had followed her brother a year ago to live in Njama. She was a single girl who had found life in Njama too interesting to leave. She opened her own business in rice and palm oil after Brima gave her some money to get started. Gibao had at one point toyed with the idea of pursuing Bintu, but she had made it obvious that she did not want him. Bintu was friendly, not only to Gibao, but to all of Brima's co-workers, but she had never had amorous feelings for any of Brima's friends.

Gibao soon realized it would be better to dismiss the idea of pursuing Bintu. He knew from experience that just because a girl acts friendly to a man, he should not assume that she wants to accept him as a lover. He had on a few occasions made this mistake with different girls and had been embarrassed. Gibao now allowed plenty of time to get to know them first before he would make overtures to girls.

He recalled one particularly unnerving experience from his boyhood days. He and others had been initiated into the secret all-male Poro society. News spread after graduation that he was the best dancer. Before his graduation, he had been attracted to Nyahawa, a girl who had been nice and friendly to him. He summoned up courage to approach Nyahawa. He felt that, since he had graduated from the society and was recognized as a famous dancer, Nyahawa would not reject him. As was the custom, he had sent an intermediary, but he was rejected by Nyahawa, to his great surprise and disappointment. He had miscalculated his worth compared to what Nyahawa thought of him. That was a long time ago, but he still remembered how humiliated he'd felt at the time.

Gibao accepted the idea that it was not prudent to fall in love with or marry a close friend's sister or relative. He forced the prospect of such affairs out of his mind. However, he thought he could use Bintu as an intermediary for accomplishing another project that he had been thinking about for some time. He wanted Bintu to give a message to N'tuma, Alhaji's young wife who kept her husband's financial accounts. Gibao wanted to find out if N'tuma would be willing to establish a romantic relationship with him. The idea of infidelity was not of any concern to Gibao because it was known that wives took lovers.

Gibao realized that it would be easy for Bintu to act as the intermediary. Her own brother, Brima, was in love with one of Alhaji's junior wives, N'dora. N'dora used to visit Bintu at her place. This was how N'dora and Brima met for courtship. Gibao thought it would be a good idea if he and N'tuma could meet at Bintu's place in order to possibly fall in love.

When Gibao first saw N'tuma, he surveyed her features. He was particularly impressed with her delicate frame and her sensuous movement. He noticed N'tuma's sizeable bouncing breasts. It occurred to Gibao that many other women he had seen in Njama lacked N'tuma's beauty and intelligence. Gibao pretended not to see Alhaji's wives the night they had come one after the other kneeling to greet Kemoh. None of the wives greeted him. It was at that kneeling exercise that he managed to scan N'tuma's body. He promised himself then that he would act upon the thoughts he had about her. He felt desire for N'tuma from that very moment.

On a day when Gibao and Brima went to visit Bintu, Gibao told Bintu about his burning desire for N'tuma. He said she was the only woman he wanted in Njama. Bintu warned Gibao that she would not like to involve herself in a situation whereby she, as an intermediary, would be ashamed of herself in the future. She said that she knew that young men including her brother were not satisfied with one woman. Gibao swore by his ancestors that there was only one woman he loved and itchingly desired—N'tuma, the wife of Alhaji, his employer.

After more urging, Bintu consented to play the role of intermediary, but, still, only after she got the blessing and tacit approval of her brother, Brima. Bintu did not want to jeopar-

# THE DIAMONDS

dize Brima and N'dora's relationship by involving another Alhaji wife in an affair.

This process of courtship could be protracted and painful, and one had to be patient. The use of a female emissary in such a matter was based on the belief that women understood each other better than men understood women. So Bintu could therefore be more persuasive on Gibao's behalf.

Social custom dictated that there was always an interval between the intermediary's contacts and the prospective boyfriend's receiving the message of acceptance or rejection. It could be an agonizing interval, especially if one was not sure of oneself. Rejections were as frequent as acceptances.

The women had built around them a ritual of courtship. First, there was the common feeling among women that men would appreciate them better the more protracted the negotiations. The girl who was approached by the intermediary would hold the prospective boyfriend to an emotional ransom for a long time by denying an answer to become his girlfriend to see if he would remain interested. If the girl did not do this and instead consented immediately after she was approached, the man would consider her a cheap commodity. Holding off on an immediate answer served to inflate a girl's ego and give her the upper hand. In the future, if any misunderstandings arose, the girl would be quick to remind the boyfriend how difficult it had been for her to consent. N'tuma would have the excuse that it was only because Bintu had forced her that she had consented.

The interval of waiting required that Gibao put on his best clothes. This was part of the game. He had to create an irresistible image. He took time to polish his shoes and made sure his hair was well cut and neat at all times. These were trying times for him, no matter how successful he was in his diamond work.

Gibao asked his friend, Brima, if he thought N'tuma would answer. Occasionally, when doubts about N'tuma's interest in him surfaced, he would talk openly with his friend. Brima thought about the question for some time and said, "My brother, I cannot vouch for her. She is supposed to know the white man's book they call the Bible. This was the reason I ignored her initially. You see, I did not go to school and I don't know book, and I am afraid of book women."

"Well, you should have discouraged me, too, because I do not know the white man's book either. Now, see what you have done to me," Gibao lamented.

"Do not misunderstand me," Brima reacted. "Just because I feel that way does not mean she will reject you. Here in Sewa women love for various reasons. N'tuma had a boyfriend who was a student, but the boy left. Now, I thought I could not rival the boy. So, I went to one of Alhaji's other wives, N'dora."

N'dora was slim and lighter in complexion. She was not as pretty as N'tuma, but had enviable assets. She was much more intelligent, more emotionally mature than N'tuma, who was flamboyant and sometimes juvenile. She had a very conspicuous gap in her upper teeth, set against her beautiful black gums. She was slightly taller than N'tuma, more elegant. She walked in an easy flexible manner, making sure every part of her body was in motion. This display of physical movement produced an emotionally paralyzing effect on men.

Before Gibao's arrival, N'tuma had threatened a few times, or boasted even that she was going to run away and get married to her educated boyfriend, who had left to go back to the Gambia. She used to think about the boy for hours. She would torment her co-mates about her lover from Gambia, often by singing his name in the kitchen while cooking.

Gibao continued to undergo emotional torture, while awaiting the outcome of N'tuma's decision. He complained to Brima how he had exhausted all his good clothes in the process of trying to look good in N'tuma's eyes. He wanted Brima to tell him what else there was for him to do.

"If a woman loves you, you can put on rags, and she will still love you," Brima told him.

## THE DIAMONDS

"Brima, you don't sound encouraging in this affair, though you give your tacit approval. Is it that you know the outcome will be negative and that I will be ashamed for a long time? Then, you will laugh at me?" Gibao asked seriously. "Let us assume everything will be all right. What about the possibility that Alhaji would have the power to make us go mad if he finds out we were in love with his wives?"

Brima laughed at the question. Gibao never liked people laughing when he spoke or asked questions.

"Yes, madness," Brima answered half seriously. "They say that Alhaji's are capable of making people go insane. I have been in love with N'dora for over a year. Here I am," Brima boasted. "I am still as sane as Alhaji himself," Brima said in a condescending tone.

"But, that is because he does not know about it," Gibao said.

"I have never known an insane man who came to be that way by an Alhaji making him so," Brima said.

Gibao was not very happy about the way Brima had analyzed the situation for him.

There were persistent rumors that Alhaji and those learned in Arabic literature could make people insane. This was the reason people didn't want to antagonize them, let alone go near their wives. Their wives and property were always safe while people believed the rumor. This was a disturbing thought to Gibao, who wanted to maintain his sanity. Insane people were treated with scorn, ridicule and distaste. Arab people, who were alleged to be capable of making others insane, were feared, and their presence alone could be frightening.

Brima went on to say how grateful he was to N'dora who had been of much help to him since they were in love. He told how N'dora had sometimes provided him with money. This was unusual in Sewa because it was the women who expected money from the men. N'dora had even extended her kindness to Bintu, in the form of money and small decorative gifts.

Bintu always kept food for her brother each evening in case he showed up. If he did not come, the food would be heated the next morning and eaten for breakfast. N'dora was already at Bintu's, as arranged, to meet Bintu. Since the place was wet and cold, Gibao had on a new and attractive cardigan. He had wished N'tuma would be at Bintu's by chance, but she was not there. Gibao hoped N'dora would tell N'tuma how she had seen Gibao in a beautiful cardigan. He had many such fantasies.

Alhaji's wives paid close attention to their husband's movements. The moment Alhaji was out of the house they took to the streets. N'dora was making pillow slips for Brima, which were kept at Bintu's place. Each time she came to Bintu, N'dora would spend time embroidering love messages on the pillow slips. The fabric was white with beautifully designed inscriptions. N'dora had requested an educated person to do the inscriptions. The resultant embroidery was full of romantic sayings and requests. Though one's lover may not be able to read, it was always understood that the decorative messages expressed the woman's deep love. These gifts were always appreciated. If a girl was in love with two men, she could show her preference for the one she loved more by making such gifts for her preferred lover but not for the other.

N'dora's four pillow slips bore the following embroidered inscriptions: "SLEEP TENDERLY TONIGHT"; "SWEET KISSES ARE WHAT I ASK FOR"; "LOVE ME FOREVER"; and "I WILL ALWAYS BE YOURS." It took N'dora six months to finish the embroidery.

Gibao was anxious to find out whether Bintu had seen N'tuma and spoken to her. He pulled Bintu to one end of the living room to talk to her quietly. N'dora was almost laughing at Gibao's frantic impatience.

"Have you seen her since I talked to you last?" Gibao asked Bintu. He tried to calm himself by smoking the *Woodbine* cigarettes he had begun using.

# THE DIAMONDS 123

Bintu could almost hear Gibao's heartbeat. "Yes, I saw her when I went to their compound, but there was no chance for me to talk to her about it," Bintu said.

Gibao's heartbeat returned to normal. He was still hopeful. Adding to the drama was the fact that Alhaji was showing serious interest in Bintu as a potential eighth wife. Thus, whenever Bintu visited N'dora in the compound, Alhaji kept her busy by talking to her. Bintu would then have little time to attend to N'dora. Alhaji had made his intentions known to Bintu, but had not had enough time to develop a coherent strategy. He was too busy with his business. Meanwhile, Alhaji gave generously to Bintu without attempting to have an affair with her. Bintu, for her part, never declined Alhaji's generous gifts.

N'dora had tried a few times to tell Alhaji she was going to visit Bintu, and because of Alhaji's interest in Bintu, he always assented, not knowing or thinking that her brother, Brima, might be involved in the meetings.

Bintu had vowed she would have nothing to do with an old man who had so many wives. It scared her to think that she would be wife number eight. It was also morally difficult for her to marry Alhaji or have an affair with him, while knowing full well that her brother was in love with N'dora. The idea of both her and her brother involved in affairs in the same household was not acceptable to her. Bintu always said she wanted to start out with a young man. Until Alhaji made up his mind, she would adopt an open-door policy toward him. She would continue to take any gifts he gave her, but not think too much about it.

Gibao and Bintu continued talking in the corner of the room while Bintu watched N'dora embroidering.

"Do you think I stand a chance?" Gibao asked hopefully. He inhaled nervously on his second cigarette.

"Let me be frank with you. I do not know N'tuma very well. She is not easy to know. I will try to talk to her and see what comes up," Bintu said. Bintu did not explain that N'tuma would often make a fuss over Bintu's lack of any formal education, which would only serve to deflate Gibao's ego and continued interest.

Gibao did not realize that it was a case of the blind leading the blind. If he had known that it would be difficult for Bintu to relate to N'tuma, he might not have bothered.

Gibao had considered not pursuing N'tuma, but he suppressed the urge. He had suffered too much to withdraw. He wanted to know the outcome. He did not want N'tuma and Bintu to accuse him of feeling inferior. N'tuma was also the only one of Alhaji's wives at that time who did not have a boyfriend among the workers. If Gibao wanted a woman among the wives, N'tuma was the only candidate available, and so he continued his appeals to Bintu.

Bintu had promised Gibao that she would do her best and that the next time N'dora came to her she would request that N'tuma come along, if Alhaji was away. The fact was that Bintu knew Alhaji would be away on two visits somewhere because he had told Bintu before he mentioned anything to his wives. All his wives would be looking forward to a social feast in his absence.

Gibao looked forward to Alhaji's departure with mixed feelings. As the time approached, Gibao became less sure of himself and more worried about the outcome of his enterprise. A failure could be socially catastrophic since Gibao was going to be working for Alhaji, he hoped, for some time to come. The incident with Nyahawa flashed in his mind, and filled him with doubts about this his first romantic test since arriving in Njama. He finally prepared himself, mentally, like a gladiator about to enter an arena, ready to pursue his chosen love interest and win her over. On this he was firmly resolved—he would succeed or fail, yes, but never would he withdraw.

The workers were to continue prospecting in the new plots Alhaji had acquired. This was their second plot in the new diamond-rich area. Njama was flooded with new people by

# THE DIAMONDS

this time because of these new sites. The living conditions deteriorated at an appalling rate. All sorts of afflictions beset children and adults every day. By July, the rains had taken over the skies and the earth. Food was becoming scarce, drinking water grew dirtier, yet the population of Njama and its environs tripled.

These human afflictions were offset by the incredible material abundance of those who survived and enjoyed acquiring it, even if it was all so temporary. There was plenty of money, and there were many more vehicles. Young men were making quick fortunes, and Gibao along with Brima and the rest of those working for Alhaji were part of this avaricious group. Gibao's fortunes had quadrupled. It was said that men in vulgar displays of their opulence used to wrap currency notes around tobacco to smoke. This was the reckless way the people were living with the diamond money now.

Gibao realized how much he had prospered. Though he was by no means rich by the standards of Sewa, he was far from being poor. He convinced himself that he was now more affluent than Pesima, but he still felt it was too early to go home. He had no thoughts of returning just yet. The diamond boom continued, and Gibao worked harder to get more money.

Gibao's friendship with Brima became stronger each day. Mulai would occasionally join their company, but Mulai was more comfortable when he was alone. He was not as sociable as Brima and Gibao. Gibao thought it was because he had no girlfriend among Alhaji's wives. Mulai was almost the only one of Alhaji's associates who was opposed to the idea of pursuing any of Alhaji's wives. He made this known to them whenever the topic arose.

Mulai had tried to explain on one such occasion that he saw no need for men pursuing married women. He said one was not really free in such relationships because such a couple spent all their time hiding from the woman's husband. He argued that there were many single girls floating around, who posed fewer problems than the married women. He mentioned the moral implications. What about the possibility of being caught eventually by the woman's husband and subjected to paying "woman damage" to the husband for the adultery or for causing a divorce? What Mulai did not appreciate was that even married men, like Alie, went on making love to Alhaji's wives. Would Alie, a married man, approve of similar activities? The whole moral structure of this romantic practice was not conducive to social harmony and communal solidarity. Sharing without consent is not sharing at all. Indeed, he remarked how he had noticed serious social tensions arising from this kind of behavior taking place in his own village and also in Njama since his arrival. "Aren't all these goings on simply evidence of human weakness and folly?" Mulai liked to ask. Mulai pursued unmarried girls and left married women to their husbands.

But Gibao did not listen. He went on with his quest for diamonds and his new equally exciting quest for N'tuma.

# Chapter 12

**■ ■ ■ ■ ■ ■ ■ ■ ■**

"The first time I saw you, something in me told me both of us will fall in love," N'tuma told Gibao. They were at Bintu's place. Alhaji was away.

N'tuma and Gibao lay in bed. N'tuma's body was warm and soft and responsive to every touch from Gibao. She was radiant, and the aroma of the latest fashionable perfume was wafting from her, as she coiled and recoiled her body. It was the end of July, and the rains had become defiant, even to the pleadings of the ancestors.

They enjoyed every bit of that first long encounter. The moment was special, their first meeting, made more pleasurable by the rhythmic accompaniment of the rain in the background, resonant and exhilarating. They had arrived in the rain to meet at this prearranged place, while the husband was away in search of more wealth.

"I was almost going to give you up. It took such a long time for you to make up your mind," Gibao told N'tuma.

"These things take time, you know. I don't think one should just plunge into them just like that. Besides, Alhaji is a very jealous man. Then, there is another point. I used to have a boyfriend from Gambia, but he went away. So, it is not easy for me to take a lover. Again, you young men are not reliable. Today is fine, but tomorrow it might be something else. Heartbreak…" she told Gibao.

Gibao asked for his cigarettes, which were on the table. He lit one and started smoking in bed. There was no ashtray, so he dropped the ashes on the floor.

"So, in other words, you are saying I am just lucky," he asked N'tuma.

"Well, if you want to call it that, yes. Because, if my other boyfriend were here, I would not consent. I love only one man at a time. I don't like headaches," N'tuma said with a smile.

Neither of them wanted to move. They hoped the rain would continue to pour down. Of course, most people prayed to God to hold the rain so they could venture out in order to get something to eat, or so that their makeshift buildings would be safe. N'tuma and Gibao were praying for the opposite, oblivious to those in danger of being made homeless or hungry by the rain.

"When do you intend on bringing your family over?" N'tuma's question struck a sensitive nerve in Gibao. She looked straight into Gibao's eyes as if putting him to a test. She mesmerized Gibao with her eyes. He was not prepared for that question, so he asked for another cigarette to summon the courage to answer her.

"Oh, I have never given it any serious thought, you know?" he said rather absentmindedly, like someone under the influence of hypnosis.

N'tuma knew he was not telling the truth. However her smile gave a clue to Gibao that she would not contest his statement just yet.

"I have heard from reliable sources that you have made up your mind about it. I am just curious," she told Gibao.

Gibao knew he had mentioned bringing his family to Njama some time ago. The only serious constraint from bringing them was the lack of decent accommodations.

"You said you have a daughter in Harford School?" she continued. This was a welcome digression for Gibao. He confirmed that his eldest daughter was a pupil at the school. N'tuma told Gibao with delight and a sense of nostalgia that Harford School was her alma mater.

"But, why are you married to Alhaji?" Gibao asked, suggest-

# THE DIAMONDS

ing that literate women had no business marrying Alhaji or his kind.

N'tuma thought about the question for a while. She knew it was a good question, and she wanted to explain so that he would understand. N'tuma came from a family that did not believe in educating its daughters. Her parents felt it was a waste of time, energy, and resources. Educated girls who marry usually ended up as compliant wives who spent most of their time in the kitchen. In N'tuma's case, it was sheer luck that she ever went to school, where she had studied Arabic. That was supposed to be sufficient for her. The Arabic was to enable her to conduct her prayers.

Her marriage to Alhaji was due to a singular event in her father's life, such a long time ago. When her father had gone to the Holy City of Mecca on a pilgrimage, he had ended up encountering financial difficulties. No one had helped him but Alhaji Jimoh, who was also making the pilgrimage. Her father's financial situation was said to be very precarious at the time. On their return, her father was profoundly grateful, but had no means of expressing this to Alhaji Jimoh. He, therefore, decided to give N'tuma in marriage as an expression of his gratitude. She was taken from high school, where she was in her second year, and was forced to marry the old man. Though N'tuma was opposed to the marriage, she had had no way of expressing her opposition. This was the story N'tuma told. At its conclusion, N'tuma and Gibao made love again, glad to be in each other's arms.

■ ■ ■

One day the diamond miners, Alie and Buya, met by accident at the hut in Tokpombu for their favorite wine. As they walked home, the rain gave warning with the dark clouds that it was going to pour some time during the night.

"Buya, you know what I have been thinking about these past days?" Alie asked.

There was no answer. Buya thought it unnecessary to answer such a question.

"Our brother Gibao is now in love with N'tuma. So, seven workers are in love with each of Alhaji's wives. We are, as they say, sitting on a powder keg," Alie pointed out.

Buya cleared his throat, took out a kola nut and broke it in his mouth. Alie heard the sound and requested a piece, and Buya moved towards him and handed him one.

"I never see you buy kola nut, Alie, but you are always asking for a piece when someone is eating it," Buya told him, apparently ignoring what Alie had said about Alhaji's wives. But as Buya continued walking, he said, "You are right. You have made a good observation. But does it matter what will happen when he asks us to leave his compound and tells us he will not employ us anymore? There are many people looking for workers. Really, I am not worried about it," Buya concluded.

Alie was in fact married and had his wife staying in the compound. At one time, Mulai had had the courage to point out to Alie that he did not see how Alie could justify his behavior since he was married and his wife was with him. Mulai had said it in a joking manner, but he knew Alie would not take his comments kindly.

Buya said to Alie that he did not like the way Brima and Gibao were carrying on with N'dora and N'tuma. He did not think they were being as discreet as they should be. Moreover, Buya added, a reliable source had told him that Gibao was also in love with some single girl in Njama named Fudia.

As for Alie, he was a mature man. He had been having his affair for a long time now. The possibility of Alhaji or his own wife catching him was remote. He did not see why he or Buya should be involved, even if Brima or Gibao were caught by Alhaji. In the end, everyone involved with Alhaji's wives continued on with no interference, and, seemingly, with no negative consequences.

Alhaji was to embark on a second trip. He could not be at

# THE DIAMONDS
131

the site when the gravel was washed, so he asked his brother Kemoh to act as his deputy. Kemoh agreed as usual, and Alhaji left again. Kemoh was to supervise Buya's group, but Alhaji had made arrangements with other relatives so that the other workers were also supervised.

Each day of work was hectic but in the end rewarding. It was August, which meant the summer rains poured down for days and nights at a time. But the rains could not stop people from going to work. Nothing would stop them as long as they continued to find the gems.

While everyone was busy prospecting in the new sites and making fantastic finds, infidelities and jealousies continued to grow in Alhaji's compound. N'tuma had developed a new jealousy over Gibao. She suspected for some time that Gibao was having an affair with another girl. The name of Fudia had been brought to her attention. She had expressed her concern to Gibao, but he denied such a thing each time she introduced the topic. N'tuma had threatened to withdraw from the relationship, but Gibao maintained that her concern came from sheer, unfounded jealousy.

Gibao had begun to secretly see Fudia even before he had expressed his romantic feelings to N'tuma. In fact, he had developed feelings for Fudia over time and had continued to enjoy Fudia's sexual companionship until N'tuma made up her mind. Besides, Gibao rationalized his love for each woman as two different types of love, which complemented each other. He knew any such confession to N'tuma about knowing Fudia would destroy his relationship with N'tuma.

N'tuma suspected Gibao was seeing Fudia who was the mother of two children, each fathered by a different man. It was rumored that she was a pretty girl, so that men were known to desire her. Fudia was one of hundreds of girls who had drifted to Sewa in response to the diamond boom, and the calls of men and money.

Fudia had been informed time and again by various friends

that N'tuma had stated that she did not intend to be a rival of Fudia, since Fudia was a prostitute. All N'tuma wanted was to ascertain from Gibao whether he was in love with Fudia.

Fudia in her way knew that Gibao was in love with N'tuma. On the other hand, Gibao had convinced Fudia that N'tuma was a married girl and that their relationship was not as serious as that between him and Fudia. Fudia thought there was logic in his statements, and she felt less jealous than N'tuma, though she was extremely unhappy to think that Gibao was seeing N'tuma.

On a few occasions, N'tuma and Fudia met, either at the market or at the butcher's. Both of them had looked at each other with evil, suspicious eyes. They were both convinced that someday their mutual dislike would burst open. They never spoke to each other, but each knew that a state of undeclared war existed between them because of Gibao.

Then the gossip mongers said that N'tuma was singing Fudia's name in Njama in reference to her profession as a prostitute. Fudia found it difficult initially to go and ask N'tuma in person about the remarks, while at the same time she was finding it increasingly difficult to continue to bear what she considered to be her gratuitous insults. The best thing to do was to go and confront N'tuma straight in her compound and damn the consequences, she thought. She was going to do that, even if Alhaji was present.

Nande, Fudia's friend, warned her not to resort to such a measure. She cautioned her that the implications could be far-reaching. She told her that the best place to attack N'tuma was when they were in the marketplace or at the butcher's. At a marketplace, there would be a large crowd. Fudia would be able to humble her as a married woman and, if need be, even beat her until she took her lappa or waistcloth off so that N'tuma would retreat naked to her compound. Nande thought this confrontation would teach N'tuma such a lesson that she would leave Gibao.

Fudia understood what her friend had told her, but she

# THE DIAMONDS 133

could not wait any longer. She was boiling with rage at the insults. Fudia told her friend that each time she went to bed at night she hardly slept because she constantly thought about the issue. People in the profession of prostitution did not take kindly if they were openly pointed out. This was the paradox of the whole trade. Prostitutes felt emotionally naked and empty when people referred to their work. Fudia, therefore, refused to accept the location of the marketplace or the butcher's as Nande suggested. She did not want any more comments made publicly about her profession.

"I will end her gossip. I will go to the Alhaji compound and beat N'tuma until her tongue falls out!" Fudia said furiously.

"Fudia!" Nande pleaded. "I have warned you not to go to that compound!" Fudia and Nande were not cooking for anybody, so they had time to talk.

"Listen, Nande. I am going to teach N'tuma a lesson. I will tell her that God did not make Gibao for her alone. Nothing will stop me," Fudia vowed.

"But you have no right to invade someone's place just to insult or assault her. Wait until you are both in a neutral place. Don't be stubborn. God does not come down from above to warn people. So, I am warning you!"

Nande and Fudia had been friends since their time in Njama. They had been able to stay together much longer than many other girls. They influenced each other greatly. Of the two of them, Fudia was the more unpredictable. As for Nande's advice, which was abundant and always ready, sometimes Fudia would heed it, but more often she would not.

"I won't wait for any neutral place. I will go straight to her house. That is the place where I understand that she spoke about me. So, I will attack her there," Fudia said.

"I suggest you warn Gibao to talk to his Mrs. You can threaten to expose the whole affair if he does not take steps to put an end to her behavior. This is more sensible than the confrontation you have planned," Nande insisted.

## J. SORIE CONTEH

"Listen, Nande. If I do not go and confront N'tuma in her place today, that means I am a child." Fudia's remarked.

Nande knew from this that the confrontation was inevitable. Fudia had spoken, she had taken a firm oath to defend herself, an oath which could not be breached.

In Alhaji's compound, all the women were busy preparing food for the workers. One could sense a general atmosphere of euphoria in the stuffy kitchen. The same euphoria was evident everywhere in Njama. Children sensed the happiness, and they joined it, too.

The rain had stopped briefly, but the clouds were gathering again for another downpour. No one took notice. N'tuma and other women were still cooking, while Gibao and the workers were busy bending their backs sieving diamonds from the gravel. The kitchen where N'tuma worked was full of smoke and the clanging of spoons, plates, calabashes and other utensils. Everybody moved about in a hurry. The workers would be expecting their lunch very soon, and the clouds looked like being in a hurry to deliver rain.

N'dora, Brima's own girlfriend, had left the kitchen briefly to go to the toilet. On returning to the kitchen, N'dora saw Fudia entering the gate to the compound. N'dora was startled and shaken. She nervously adjusted her lappa. N'dora smelled of smoke from the kitchen fires, but she sensed other fire coming from Fudia. She knew about the undeclared state of war between Fudia and N'tuma, but she had never imagined that Fudia would pay a visit to their compound. N'dora walked up to greet Fudia cordially, but with obvious apprehension.

Fudia answered stiffly. She did not believe that N'dora could claim ignorance of what N'tuma had been saying. They belonged to the same sisterhood of hypocrites. They smiled to your face, but tore you apart verbally the moment you were away. Fudia's face looked grim and serious. Her eyes were red. It was easy to see that she had been drinking, which meant she must have needed extra courage for the meeting.

# THE DIAMONDS

N'dora could read in those red eyes that something was amiss, something that could involve everyone, unless sheer luck intervened. She herself had told N'tuma to wash her hands of Gibao the moment she realized Gibao was messing around with a single girl. There were many girls like Fudia in Njama. They were the desperate ones and did not give a damn which young man they seduced. Fudia had nothing to lose by causing trouble for them, N'dora had told N'tuma time and again. But, like Fudia, N'tuma never heeded advice from friends until it was too late.

Since their marriages to Alhaji, each wife had been unfaithful, but, thank God, there had been no open scandal. A few times Alhaji had suspected them, scolded them, and even threatened them, but mostly he had left them in peace, because the outside world was not aware of the suspicions. What guarantee was there that Fudia would not involve all of them? N'dora often asked N'tuma. She knew that once the truth was out Alhaji would come to know about it.

In her mind, N'dora could see the total collapse of her own marriage, which, despite her infidelity to the old man, she would not like to see happen. She knew how kind and generous he had been to her parents, and these reflections haunted her as she stood before Fudia and absentmindedly took off her head tie.

It had been some time now since N'dora had left the kitchen, so N'tuma decided to go out and look for her. She stepped out of the kitchen and looked in the direction of the toilets. Her face was hit by the cold, rainy-season wind. Her eyes were sore from the kitchen smoke, and she squinted. She took one end of her lappa to blow her nose. She had not taken more than four steps out of the kitchen door when she heard a sharp aggressive voice calling her. N'dora, whose back was toward the kitchen, turned and saw N'tuma. N'dora and N'tuma looked at each other and sensed something was wrong. N'tuma did not answer Fudia's call, but simply walked toward her and N'dora.

"It is you I have come to see, Mrs. Alhaji Jimoh!" Fudia shouted at her. She walked away from the gate and a little bit more into the compound.

"Have I offended you?" N'tuma asked naively.

"You don't know you have offended me? You don't know me? Yes! I am a prostitute! You have been singing my name all over this town. So, I am here today, this day, for you to tell me what makes you think I am a prostitute but not yourself!" Fudia said angrily.

N'tuma and N'dora knew by the tone of that acid voice that the bubble was going to burst. Alhaji's compound was fenced, but the fence was not high enough. Even people of average height could see inside. Moreover, before Alhaji left for his trip, he had allowed four important visitors to remain in his house until his return. They had been waiting patiently for his return for the past two weeks. They were assembled in the living room, drinking coffee as usual, and noticing that it was going to rain.

"N'tuma, believe me. You will kill me today. I realized that, each time we met at the market or the butcher's, you looked at me contemptuously. Of course, you know I returned the same look. We have been at that for a long time, but today, it will be decided once and for all. If you beat me, then I will leave Gibao in your hands forever," Fudia said, and ended by clapping her hands twice.

N'tuma was not sure whether to accept the challenge. The important guests heard the commotion and were alerted to what was happening in the compound, but they remained seated. People outside were beginning to gather around the fence near the gate. From the disturbance caused by what had happened up to this point, Alhaji was bound to find out the truth. He would know that Gibao's name had been mentioned in connection with N'tuma.

*N'tuma's marriage will be wrecked, and Gibao will be fired. What a pity.* N'dora thought. She was happy that Fudia had

# THE DIAMONDS

restricted herself only to N'tuma. *But, what if madness overtakes her and my name is mentioned?* N'dora worried. N'dora thought about Gibao, about the deceit of all men. She was careful not to behave in any manner that would give Fudia cause to mention her name. She kept hoping that God would intervene and end this madness.

At this point, Kema, Alhaji's first wife, appeared on the scene after emerging from the kitchen.

"Ah, Mama Kema, I have come to visit you today in your compound," Fudia said. "I am your visitor. Your mate will beat me today. N'tuma will beat me for Gibao, her second husband. She said I am a prostitute." Fudia spoke with increased vehemence.

A crowd swelled around and gathered momentum. It was typical of Njama. There were always happenings like this and people were always ready to stop whatever they were doing to watch them. This one would be the talk of the town for the next few days.

It must be said in Alhaji's favor that his compound had never been associated before with this sort of social turbulence and female anarchy.

"What is the matter, Miss Lady?" Kema asked. She had never really known Fudia. Fudia, like many other women and girls, knew Alhaji's first wife, because she was a very well-known member of the female community. But her romantic relationship with Alie did not make her any different, morally, from the rest of her junior co-mates. And Fudia knew this, too.

Kema was in her mid-forties, but still well-preserved. She and Alie had been in love for almost four years without Alhaji knowing anything about the romance. Alhaji had never suspected her of infidelity. She was sexy without being particularly beautiful. She was an expert at pursuing her interests without letting the world know about it. Kema acted as a mother to all her co-mates. They liked the way she comported herself.

"Miss Lady, I say, what is your problem?" Kema asked Fudia a second time. Her voice was conciliatory.

"Mama Kema, I have no problem. It is your co-mate that has problems. She said she does not want to be the rival of a prostitute. Can you imagine, a woman married to an Alhaji saying that? Well, I am going nowhere. I am determined. Ogiri de kos kenda for smell, the kettle calling the pot black!" Fudia fumed loudly.

Kema realized the matter was serious. She gauged Fudia's mood. She knew Fudia had decided to come to confront N'tuma.

N'dora went to the kitchen to attend to the food, but she did not stay long and rushed out with the rest of Alhaji's wives to watch. They listened and prayed Fudia would not let loose with all she knew about their affairs. Some co-mates felt N'tuma deserved her fate for not controlling herself better. She had no business calling Fudia a prostitute. Kema, a few weeks before, had taken time to lecture N'tuma about how to go about her extramarital life, but she didn't heed those warnings.

"Who told you I called you a prostitute?" N'tuma asked Fudia, more courageously.

"Your mother who bore you, yes, your mother who is a prostitute. That is the only reason you know who a prostitute is, how else?" Fudia answered simply, insulting N'tuma.

N'tuma was frightened by Fudia's audacity. Kema realized that she could not defuse the crisis, and she would hate to do something that may lead Fudia to drop hints about her own infidelity to Alhaji. Kema chose to disappear into the kitchen and leave N'tuma and N'dora with the volatile Fudia. The other wives followed her example and decided to listen from the kitchen.

N'tuma told N'dora that they should go inside the kitchen and continue their work. "Fudia, it is not worth my time to exchange words with you. You are drunk and idle," N'tuma told her.

As N'tuma tried to move, Fudia blocked her way.

"Yes, I am drunk with your mother's urine. It has alcohol in it," Fudia hollered, almost spitting the words into the dust.

# THE DIAMONDS

There was great laughter from those listening. Other women were embarrassed.

"You don't know who is a prostitute, you bastard! You don't know? Ask mi wes (ask my ass!)" N'tuma answered insultingly.

There were shouts of "fight! fight!" across the fence. However women rarely resorted to physical battle. Instead, they fought with their mouths. A larger crowd was now gathering around the compound. This was the effect Fudia wanted, so that there would be no way to escape Alhaji's attention when he came back.

"N'tuma, it is enough," N'dora whispered. "Let's go inside. The workers may be waiting for the food."

"Madam!" Fudia called N'dora. "Why don't you go your way so that I don't involve you in this case. Leave me and this dog. I want to teach her a lesson today!"

N'dora became frightened and melted away into the kitchen. There, in the temporary safety, N'dora found her mates talking about the possibility that Fudia would let open Pandora's box.

"See who calls me senjago, a bad prostitute. How dare you?" Fudia asked N'tuma. She took two steps towards N'tuma.

N'tuma's feet felt heavy. She did not move. She was not afraid of Fudia. If Fudia was bold enough as to touch her, she was not going to give her the physical superiority easily. She would defend herself. She took off her head tie and belted her slender waist to reinforce her lappa. She did not want to be taken unawares.

Fudia continued her taunts.

"You are not a prostitute, but you don't even have a child. You know why? Yes, you know. That is something that should engage your attention Mrs., rather than talking about me. When you were younger and going to school, you specialized in having abortions. Now you have become permanently childless. Yes, that is something that you should talk about!" Fudia said furiously.

"You can say what you want. I know it is not true. It is the work of God. I am not yet past child-bearing age," N'tuma said, defending herself.

"Keep quiet, you child of a harlot! Don't call God's name in vain! Don't call upon His name in connection with your immoral life!" Fudia spat on the ground, clapped her hands, turned around and stood firm.

There was laughter around the fence. N'dora wished the show would end then. The prayers of the other wives had been answered so far because their names had not been mentioned, but the anger outside was becoming fierce.

"Believe me, Fudia, you should be ashamed of yourself! You Kafiri, daughter of evil, you are not ashamed? All men know you in this town!" N'tuma said firmly.

"Yes, that is because I am beautiful!" Fudia answered. "Despite my prostitution, have I begged from you any day?"

"You won't dare, Fudia! You won't!" N'tuma said. She raised her hand and slapped her hip. N'tuma did not change her position. She stood firm.

"What is the difference between you and me? What is the difference? Tell me before I put my foot through you!" Fudia badgered. "God has cursed you. That is why you go to bed with your husband's workers. Woe on you!" Fudia continued. She was ready to fight. She turned to the crowd to tell aloud what she knew about N'tuma's life.

But N'tuma would have preferred a fight, although she was not sure that she could beat Fudia. She had worked out a strategy. If Fudia assaulted her in this drunken state, she was going to try to strip her naked so that she would have to walk home that way with people following her and shouting. N'tuma knew there was no guarantee she could succeed. The opposite might just happen. Fudia was a fairly tough woman. They continued to pour insults on each other, with ferocious venom and acidity. At some point physical confrontation was imminent. But then there was divine intervention.

## THE DIAMONDS

A heavy downpour succeeded in dispersing everyone, including Fudia and N'tuma. Fudia called back to N'tuma and promised she would come back sometime. She met Nande at the gate, and they walked home in the downpour.

# Chapter 13

News traveled swiftly in Njama, like lightning, as people used to say, but by the time it arrived it was always distorted. Somewhere along the way, it seemed to gain embroidery, like one of N'dora's pillowcases. It was not surprising that the news soon reached the workers at the new site. The gist of the news remained intact, but the story was that two of Alhaji's wives had fought physically for a man named Gibao, an employee of Alhaji. No one from Alhaji's compound had visited the workers. It was much later that the more accurate story filtered out to the effect that a certain girl named Fudia and N'tuma had had a verbal confrontation, which had nearly resulted in a physical battle but for the timely intervention of pouring rain.

It was the news of the town. Alhaji was such a prominent member of the community that anything of a scandalous nature that touched his household was bound to have widely spread around.

Kemoh was shocked when he learned about what had taken place in his brother's house. He was concerned with the effect it would have on Alhaji's reputation. Kemoh recalled that when Alhaji married N'tuma he had said to himself that N'tuma looked like a girl who was more suited for outside life than for housekeeping. He was convinced that N'tuma would not make a good wife. However, the news about Gibao shocked him even more. He had advised Gibao over and over not to have anything to do with his boss's wives. He knew he had recruited him for his brother because he believed in Gibao, which was why he was so disturbed by Gibao's misbehavior.

## THE DIAMONDS

If Kemoh was shocked, the important guests who witnessed the fight were embarrassed. One of them was a reputable Arabic and Muslim scholar. It was even rumored in Njama that this scholar's occasional presence in Alhaji's house brought divine influences which were responsible for all the gems Alhaji's workers collected. It was also rumored that he had predicted to Alhaji that by the time he came back there would be an unpleasant situation waiting for him, but he told Alhaji not to worry since the event would not have anything directly to do with his business. So Alhaji had decided to go, which was apparently why the fight had occurred at Alhaji's compound.

The guests discussed the issue very seriously. They agreed that the world of today was radically different from their own world of years gone by. These things, they said, were unheard of in their own day. They unanimously dissociated themselves from the present-day events in this different world, implying that those that occurred during their own days were not nearly as serious, or as dangerous, than what they had just witnessed. Each of them recounted familiar experiences. They agreed that, what they witnessed in Njama, the fact of marital infidelity, the boldness of young men having an affair with wives of their elders now, sadly, was not that unusual, and occurred everywhere.

The Arabic scholar said that the confrontation between the two women was frightening and he attributed this to the evils of money and avarice. He believed that Alhaji should not forgive N'tuma and Gibao. They should be severely punished, which would serve as a lesson for others.

"Somebody, whom you have fed and lodged, can never escape your curse," The scholar told his colleagues. "Marriage is a sacred union and no outside person should interfere with it."

The scholar went on to deplore women who remained single. Why should they presume to be respected? The presence of too many single women in any society undermined social cohesion and harmony. Fudia's language was the work of the devil, to say the least, he asserted.

His colleague, Alpha Ibrahim, agreed with him and observed further that what was happening was a clear manifestation that the world was coming to an end. The consensus of the scholars was that such events had been predicted and they were now witnessing the end of the world. Indeed, all this evil showed the patience of Allah, but Allah would destroy it all. Moral degeneration was increasing, respect for authority and morality was lax, children were not afraid of their elders, wives indulged in infidelity. Alpha Ibrahim was sad as he made these observations. What was even worse was the growing indifference toward religion. They had been to the mosque several times and it was always the same. It was empty. Sad, indeed, he commented. These were the signs of the end. When people behaved by abandoning the spiritual for the material, this was the time Allah would destroy the people. Piety could not be relegated to a second place. The guests were unanimous on this observation. The Njama that they saw was a town of infidels.

Kemoh was morose even though he had just come from the new site where diamonds were being found. He felt personally responsible to some extent in the N'tuma-Fudia-Gibao matter. He held a bag with many diamonds, which Gibao and the others had collected that day. His face was sour and there was pain in his heart.

When Kemoh got home, one of his wives informed him that, if he wanted to wash, hot water was ready for him. He entered his room, took off his dirty clothes, wrapped a towel around his waist and proceeded to the bathroom. After he finished, he felt clean, but he was still troubled. Before being served his evening meal, he sent one of his sons to run and call his friends to join him. Kemoh had no appetite. He longed only for the collective support and wisdom of his friends. He sat on the veranda wearing a morning gown, as he tried to relax after his bath. All his wives knew his mood had presumably been the result of what had happened at his brother's com-

## THE DIAMONDS                                        145

pound, so they tried not to upset him in any way. They were
prepared for any scolding he might want to give them because
he often thought there was a female conspiracy going on in the
case of such infidelities.

"Kumba!" Kemoh called in a coarse voice, to his first wife.

Kumba scurried rapidly, with a hand held on her chest, as
far as the veranda door and announced her presence.

"Don't you see people have started coming? Bring food,"
Kemoh ordered without looking at her.

Kumba left and returned quickly with food, water, spoons,
and plates.

Sahr, Kemoh's friend, was the first to join him. None of the
other friends who were arriving spoke about what happened at
Alhaji's. They wanted Kemoh to start the talking. So, to pass
the time, Sahr commented on the weather.

"You know, I don't like eating tonight. My mind is not
good," Kemoh finally started.

There was no reply from anyone. They chewed their food
and sat silently. They were waiting for him to give the reason
for his unhappiness.

"You see how daring young men are these days," Kemoh
added. There was still no response, since he had avoided a
direct mention of the subject. "Was there any one of you in
town today during the commotion at my brother's place?" he
finally asked.

"We heard about it at the site," Sahr answered for the rest.
"In fact, at first, they said the two women fought, but, when I
came to town, my daughter told me there was no fight, only
the use of bad words."

"What will Alhaji do when he comes back?" Lebbie cut in.

"I don't know what Alhaji will do," Kemoh answered.

"N'tuma is his favorite wife. He should drive her away. If
the favorite wife behaves like that, can you imagine what the
others will be up to? He should fire Gibao, then take him to
court," Sahr put in.

"Oh! People are not afraid these days. You cannot trust young men," Lebbie remarked.

All of the men felt Kemoh's pain. They also had young girls as wives, some as young as only seventeen years. It was particularly worrying because these young women could not be kept under lock and key. It was hard to impose sanctions on wives, considering the laxity of the social situation in Njama, made worse by the presence of diamonds. For this reason, most of Kemoh's friends spent their time at the mining sites and away from their wives.

Lebbie had some personal experience in such matters. He used to have a work force of five. One of his workers had had a love affair with his youngest wife, Katuma. One day this worker feigned illness and had not gone to work. Lebbie had not been told about his illness until he got to the site. Since that particular worker was his favorite man, Lebbie decided he would go to town, buy some medicine and take it to him. When Lebbie arrived at the man's house, he found the bedroom door ajar. He tapped and then pushed the door open. There in front of him was Katuma and the man in bed, both nude. Lebbie said he had almost collapsed. That was a long time ago. Kemoh, Sahr and even Lebbie himself started snickering about this until Sahr almost choked on his food. "Please don't tell these stories to Alhaji," Kemoh said.

The men soon left Kemoh's since they all had other serious business engagements. Sahr was expecting a Lebanese friend, so he left as soon as he had finished the food.

Alone now on the veranda, Kemoh summoned his four wives. They came in and sat with him. There was silence. The only noise was that of children playing in the back yard.

"Nana, go tell them to stop the noise. Otherwise, I will bruise their backs," Kemoh directed with a stern look. Then he spoke to his first wife. "Kumba, tell me what happened at Alhaji's place today," he ordered.

Kumba was the most daring of the lot. She burst out laughing violently. The others joined in the laughter.

# THE DIAMONDS                    147

"All of you think I am mad?" Kemoh asked with growing annoyance. "Don't you!"

"But, what makes you think I should know something that happened so far away?" Kumba asked, stopping her laughter.

"You will swear, all of you, that you did not go there when you heard the commotion?" Kemoh challenged.

They all answered they would take the oath. Kumba was the first to give a strong "yes!".

"You, Kumba you have a witch in your belly. Nothing can touch you. If you the others follow her, you will die," Kemoh warned.

There was more laughter among his wives, bordering this time on derision.

"All of you cheat. That is why you don't treat the matter seriously. I have sent for a medicine man from Mongereh. You all know him. All of you will come and take an oath, as to whether you are faithful or not. That is the only way to control you now. You will have to tell the truth to the medicine man!" Kemoh threatened.

The wives appeared still unmoved.

"Do you know that Gibao boy who stayed with us was not a good boy. He saw no woman in Njama for his sexual appetite except my brother's wife, N'tuma," Kemoh said, with disgust.

The wives were fully aware of everything. They knew all the male friends of Alhaji's wives, just as Alhaji's wives knew their own male friends and lovers.

"You, Kumba, can you take an oath that since Gibao came here you had nothing to do with him?" Kemoh persisted in the cross-examination.

"Why do you always pick on me?" Kumba asked.

"Because you are the least afraid and you are a fox," Kemoh told her.

There was laughter. This annoyed Kemoh. He felt sorry himself because of their apparent lack of respect. Age was catching up on him. Years ago, none of his wives would dare cough when he spoke. Now they made fun of him. He was a victim of arthritis, rheumatism and other ailments associated with old age and the diamond trade he had indulged in for a long time.

Kumba was indignant at Kemoh's accusations. She asked him how many times since their marriage had she been caught with a man or had confessed infidelity. Her questions now were turning serious.

In the end, Kemoh dismissed his wives, having accomplished nothing by assembling them. However, he felt much better that he had spoken about their possible infidelity. It was another warning that he would not keep any wife who was found out to be unfaithful.

■ ■ ■

When Gibao and N'tuma met at Bintu's, N'dora and Brima were also there to try to discuss what should be done next. Gibao and N'tuma started the meeting by blaming each other for what had happened. N'tuma heatedly accused Gibao of being responsible because of his promises to Fudia, and said that he should be prepared to accept the consequences of this transgression. N'tuma concluded her ranting by saying that she was shocked that Gibao had had anything to do with Fudia, an obvious prostitute.

Brima intervened and told N'tuma to stop referring to the girl that way. It was not right to think, just because Fudia was unmarried, that she was a prostitute. But, N'dora remarked that the word prostitute was right for Fudia, who had two children by different men and not by a husband.

Gibao tried to explain his actions to the group. "Listen, people. I never knew that Fudia was a prostitute, and I still don't know if she is. She has no label on her back to say so. Let us consider that."

"You are still defending her! Bintu, you see? It was you who brought us together. You remember when I told you I was not

# THE DIAMONDS

that much interested in this relationship, you see now?" You, Gibao, when I asked you about Fudia, you lied to me by saying you had nothing to do with her. Yes, you lied!" N'tuma scolded furiously.

"Oh! You expected me to truthfully answer such a question?" Gibao asked.

"If it was not because I am shy of saying what I think before the people here, I would give you a piece of my mind. But I don't blame you. I blame myself," N'tuma added shaking her fist at Gibao.

The women agreed that Gibao and N'tuma were in serious trouble. N'tuma's marriage was wrecked. Gibao was going to lose his job and perhaps be taken to court by Alhaji for "woman damage." Alhaji, they all agreed, could tolerate many things, but not anything relating to infidelity on the part of his wives. In fact, they said, it was only old age that had tamed Alhaji's jealous instincts. When he was younger, he humiliated any of his wives caught in an extramarital affair. They said he would catch the couple, tie them up, shave their heads and give them a merciless beating. In time, many women had deserted Alhaji, but he was not deterred by this. He continued to mete out what he considered justice to his wives until he was too old to do so. Now, he could not run after his wives and had no energy to beat them. But once caught, any unfaithful wife would be sent away immediately and without support.

N'dora and Bintu told N'tuma to start packing in readiness for Alhaji's arrival. Gibao needed no one to tell him what his situation was. Since the commotion, he had stopped going to work. He was only waiting for Alhaji to come and pay him off. He planned to move and rent a place in town.

As lovers, Gibao and N'tuma made a truce and reaffirmed their devotion to each other. They would not let Fudia or Alhaji destroy them or their love. N'tuma agreed that she and Gibao could plan future meetings at Bintu's place, but he would have to wait for her return before they married. They had no doubts that they wanted to marry. N'tuma would become Gibao's fourth wife. Arrangements for the marriage were sealed between them before N'tuma left for Bo.

# Chapter 14

In the aftermath of the Gibao-N'tuma-Fudia imbroglio, Fudia felt triumphant. She was convinced she had accomplished her mission. She had got the public show she wanted, and she had succeeded in humiliating N'tuma. There was one thing she was positive about. Alhaji would know about the incident and he would take appropriate action against N'tuma and Gibao.

Fudia and Nande were in Fudia's room that evening, drinking and smoking. The Aladdin lamp's cozy glow in the room had faded out with the last drops of kerosene. Nande got up and tugged at the crumpled handkerchief she had tucked near her breast. She pulled it out, untied the knotted end and took out some coins. She carefully picked up an empty pint bottle and went out to buy some kerosene. Fudia remained seated in the partially dark room.

The room was fairly small with a sofa that could only accommodate two average-sized people. The whole room was served by two chairs infested with bedbugs. When Fudia's friends visited her, as they did frequently, they preferred sitting on the sofa. Near the only window in the room, against the wall, stood a rickety table which was always creaking under the weight of numerous items: Bintu el Sudan powder, tins, half pieces of mirror, a badly framed picture of the King and Queen of England, and many more items. Under the bed were pots, pans, spoons, calabashes, and many empty bottles.

Fudia sat on one of the chairs and stretched her legs onto the other, smoking one cigarette after another. The door remained ajar just as Nande had left it when leaving. Suddenly, there was a tap on the door. Fudia did not move. She knew it would not be Nande. Nande had no reason to knock at the door so soon after she had left, unless she was drunk. There was another tap.

"Udat? Who?" Fudia finally asked. She took her feet down from the chair. There was a brief moment of silence, then the person entered.

In the darkness Fudia asked with a slightly intoxicated voice, "Who do I have to pay this night?"

Gibao had already come inside without saying a word. Fudia recognized his figure in the dark. Since the confrontation with N'tuma the other day, Fudia and Gibao had not met to discuss what happened. Gibao stood silent. He did not sit down. He did not talk. He did not move. He just stood there. The only light available came from the window. Fudia took the matches from the table and lit another cigarette. Gibao adjusted his posture. He stood with one hand akimbo and rested the other hand on the wall so that his hand was above his head.

Then, Nande entered with the kerosene. She almost bumped into Gibao.

"Tenki ya my sister, thanks for the kerosine," Fudia said. Nande quickly poured the kerosene into the lamp and lighted a match, so that there was light again.

"Hey, Mister, so you still think about us?" Nande asked, now recognizing the person she had almost bumped into. Her voice broke the tense silence in the room.

"It is because you are idle that is why you are talking to him," Fudia remarked.

"How, you want to malice me, not to talk to me?" Gibao asked naively.

"Don't you dare talk to me this night, you hear! Have less to do with me," Fudia warned.

Gibao raised his brow.

"Things were very peaceful here before your arrival," Nande told Gibao.

"Let him go to his Mrs.", Fudia said, ignoring Gibao. "As for

# THE DIAMONDS
153

us, we are prostitutes. We like it that way. Please go to your Mrs. and leave me alone," Fudia said, waving the hand that held her cigarette. She turned away to talk to Nande. "Nande, do you know that new song that's just out? They say it is the talk of the town."

"Oh, yes, Mambu has it in his club. We should go there tonight. Just to go and shake the body," Nande said, laughing. She shook her breasts, expressly to tease Gibao.

"I came to find out what happened between you and N'tuma. I did not come to make a palaver," Gibao tried to explain.

"Gibao, let me say today, you big fool, you no get common sense. You are only big fool man." Fudia spat out her sentences in her anger. "Why don't you go and ask your Mrs. damn fool. As for me, our relationship is finished. So, leave me alone. You men are so dishonest. Didn't you tell me you had no business with the fucker. Lie to me again, damn hog," she ended abusively.

Gibao didn't know what to say. He felt guilty and could not bring himself to engage in a war of words with Fudia.

"Alhaji will make you either mad or impotent, or both! That Alhaji will not miss you! I only hope by the time you are mad you would have got out of Njama so that people will not say I had anything to do with a mad man. So! Go to your home town!" Fudia screamed.

Gibao believed what she said. It was widely rumored that Alhaji and his Muslim friends had certain spiritual powers. Which was worse, he wondered, to be insane or to be made sexually impotent? The two choices were unimaginable for Gibao to contemplate.

"Nande! Tell him to leave this room. He does not pay our rent nor does he feed us," Fudia said. She continued to drink her Guinness Stout while puffing on a new latest cigarette.

Gibao felt defeated. He lost interest in trying to calm Fudia. He accepted that he was responsible for all the commotion because he had lied to both women. Deep in his heart he had not said goodbye to Fudia. Many times he had told Fudia he loved her, though it was unusual for men to develop such a feeling for prostitutes.

Fudia remained sitting, smoking, and vowing that she would never have anything more to do with Gibao. Even if she were a prostitute, why should she listen to a liar like Gibao?

"Nande, please talk to your friend on my behalf," Gibao implored. He wanted Nande to negotiate peace, to accord him moral amnesty, to encourage reconciliation. But his request fell on deaf ears. Nande had already come to agree with Fudia that it was necessary in the name of peace to close Gibao's love chapter once and for all.

"Nande, tell him to take his shirt—the one over by the window—as he leaves this place. Let him not come here anymore," Fudia said resolutely, looking only at Nande.

"Well, well, mister man, lonta, that's that," Nande told Gibao.

"Nande, I'm asking you to help and you tell me that?" Gibao asked. He was still convinced that an emotional cease-fire could be worked out if tempers cooled.

"In any case, as of this night," Fudia said, "anytime you come here now, you do so at your own risk. You will find a man here." Fudia said, putting an end to Gibao's attempt to reconcile with her.

Fudia, her cigarette still in her fingers, opened up a piece of gum and stuck it in her mouth. She started chewing on the gum and cracking it violently. She knew Gibao hated the sound. She was doing every thing she could to irritate him. She got up and took Gibao's shirt, which was hanging on the pole supporting the mosquito net. She threw it at Gibao. "I don't want you to come here again using the shirt as an excuse!" Fudia hollered.

"So, you will not accept apologies?" Gibao asked.

"Mister, I don't vomit and lick it! I have told you. I'd rather starve than have anything to do with you. I was surviving here

# THE DIAMONDS

155

very well before you came. I will continue to survive after you vanish from my life. Just leave me in peace!" Fudia blew a big bubble then drew it in and cracked it. Nande was humming a popular song. Fudia turned her back to Gibao and joined Nande. They started singing:

> Yu say mi na senjago-oo
> (You say I am a prostitute)
> Yu say mi na senjago-oo
> Mi mami de, mi papa de,
> (I have a mother, I have a father)
> Yu say mi na senjago-oo

Gibao felt humiliated. He walked out with the shirt Fudia tossed at him, dangling from his shoulder. Fudia and Nande did not take any notice of his exit. They continued reveling in their song. Then the sound of his footsteps disappeared in the distance. The two women stopped singing as the footsteps faded.

"If we had our gramophone, it would be a good night for us to celebrate the departure of this creature from my life," Fudia sighed. She now appeared more relaxed, and her mood turned jovial and cheerful. Fudia had a gramophone, but it was overused and the poor thing had just stopped running. They were unable to rewind it.

"Nande, believe me. Men think too much of themselves. This man comes right up to me to apologize and then he expects me to forgive him. You know it is the lie that I hate more than anything else," Fudia talked excitedly and lit up another cigarette. "Each time I brought up N'tuma, he would deny everything, tell me he has had nothing to do with her. Something kept telling me I should not believe him." Fudia blew smoke into the air.

"Well, I know Gibao will lose his job with Alhaji, but what about N'tuma?" Nande inquired, only to prod Fudia to talk some more.

Fudia opened another pint bottle of Guinness Stout. "Listen, dear, for all I know she could go down and drown herself or she could be strangled. What the bloody hell do I care?"

"Men are unpredictable. Alhaji may not even do anything to her. In any case, I think that Gibao will marry her if Alhaji gets rid of her," Nande said.

"Well, she will be wife number four with Gibao, not wife number seven with Alhaji. That is promotion," Fudia sneered. They laughed heartily.

"Ha! Tell me, Fudia. They said N'tuma knows book. How come she is married to a man with so many wives?" Nande asked.

"Bo, lef me ya, da King Jimmy book, that her cheap education from the waterside!" Fudia said, contemptuously.

They continued making fun of N'tuma and Gibao well into the evening. They said that Gibao did not even know the local lingua properly, but yet he wanted an educated woman.

■ ■ ■

Gibao walked the streets that night regretting that he and Fudia could not make peace together. He still felt he wanted to talk to Fudia. Even though he had no intentions of marrying her, he thought it was nice having her. But, he had to resign himself to the fact that Fudia had told him in no uncertain terms that she was not willing to serve as a substitute for N'tuma or for his wives any longer.

Previously, Gibao and Brima had discussed Fudia. Brima had suggested then the possibility of Gibao marrying Fudia, but Gibao countered that that was impossible for him. He explained to Brima that some women were good material for marriage, others were good only as girlfriends, and there were those who were good just for casual encounters, to alleviate tension. Gibao did say that some girlfriends could indeed be nurtured into the roles of wives. But Fudia, he thought, was

# THE DIAMONDS

the girlfriend type who could not be nurtured to that point. She was destined to be a girlfriend and no more.

After the turn of events between N'tuma and Fudia, Gibao had finally decided that he wanted to marry N'tuma. He planned to buy a spacious compound for her and his other wives where everyone could live peacefully, while he himself continued to grow wealthier in the diamond fields.

After leaving Fudia and Nande, Gibao finally arrived at Bintu's place. Brima was there with his lover, N'dora. Gibao was not expecting N'tuma to visit that night. The mood of the other three was gay, so Gibao tried to pretend that he, too, was happy, despite his problems. Fudia was never discussed. Brima informed Gibao that he and N'dora were spending the night there at Bintu's place. Alhaji, he said, would be expected in two days and they wanted to make use of their time together.

"To tell you the truth, I cannot have N'tuma with me now;" Gibao told them. "I am not mentally at ease. I think I must go and try to sleep." He left, feeling as alone as if this were his first day in Njama.

■ ■ ■

People said that Alhaji knew about the incident the very day he arrived in Njama. Alhaji had become predictable with age. His baser and more aggressive instincts had mellowed with time. This time he called all the leaders of his workers and paid them so they could, in turn, pay the diggers in their groups. It was said he did this to avoid seeing Gibao.

After being paid, Gibao left the compound, unnoticed and unaccompanied, the same way as he had once entered Njama, except that now he carried two big beautiful portmanteaus filled with his valuables. He left late in the morning when all the workers had gone to work, so as to avoid speaking to anyone. He had a transistor radio under his arm. As he walked away, he thought about Fudia. His memories of her ached him. The rhythmic gyrations of her hips still fascinated him, the whole center of her being seemed to be on those hips. He walked on to his new dwelling, thinking about her.

Meanwhile, Alhaji's wives were on the alert. They were waiting to be summoned by Alhaji just as Kemoh had summoned his wives. N'tuma, on the other hand, was packing. All her co-mates had spoken to her, encouraging her and telling her all sorts of things to guard against in the future. N'tuma had decided she was going home first to report to her parents what had happened. She had decided to do so at Kema's strong suggestion. She would tell her mother why she had left Alhaji's home for good. Tears fell from N'tuma's eyes as she packed.

"Stop crying," Kema told her abruptly.

N'tuma said she was not weeping because she was leaving Alhaji. The reason was personal. She knew her mother was going to bear the brunt of her misbehavior, according to Muslim tradition. Her father was going to scold her mother forever. This was the reason she was crying. N'tuma would be expected to stand silent before her father. Indeed, the choice as to whom to marry and when to marry was the well-defined prerogative of the father. She was determined, if the opportunity presented itself, to tell her father that she had never wanted to marry Alhaji. Of course, she knew her father would be shocked to hear that. She imagined him saying that she was getting such nonsense from the White Man's book. It was only the White Man who taught such blasphemy. N'tuma planned to tell her mother that Gibao, whom she would marry, was also well-to-do financially, though not as successful as Alhaji.

N'tuma left for the lorry park after Alhaji had gone to visit the workers. Since his return, he and N'tuma had never spoken to one another. N'tuma also avoided Alhaji, not even bidding him good morning, as all of them did each day.

Rain was falling when N'tuma left the compound. N'dora and Kema came to see her off. As they walked, N'dora was crying. She was very sorry to see N'tuma go. N'tuma, on the

# THE DIAMONDS

159

other hand, did not feel that sorry. She told N'dora to stop crying and only pray that she would come back safely. Two of N'dora's children followed behind the three women. They carried some of N'tuma's belongings.

As the lorry apprentices saw them coming, they rushed towards the women to tell them which lorry N'tuma should take and which one was ready to leave immediately. N'dora, Kema, and the two children could not wait in the rain. They bade N'tuma farewell and a safe journey, and then turned to run back to the compound.

N'tuma knew she and Gibao had reconciled their problems and she would be returning again as soon as Gibao bought a compound for her and his wives. In facing her mother and father, N'tuma felt uneasy as to how her life had taken such an unexpected turn and so quickly.

N'dora's tears mixed with the rain on her face. She looked back to see N'tuma being offered a place in the front seat of the Bedford lorry truck. Minutes later the lorry, with the inscription "BAD BUSH NO DE FOR TROWAY BAD PIKIN, THERE IS NO BAD BUSH TO THROW AWAY A BAD CHILD" left Njama, speeding for Bo, the next town some twelve hours away.

# Chapter 15

Gibao bought a house in Njama in readiness for the arrival of his family and his mother and grandmother. He had secured the house when he realized that his fate in Njama was in jeopardy. It was a big house with five bedrooms, a living room and a large veranda. A shop that sold mining supplies and household items was attached to the house. There was a big kitchen, detached from the main house, and some extra bedrooms adjacent to the kitchen.

One of Gibao's achievements in Njama was securing a mining license. It was a remarkable achievement. His Lebanese friend was very instrumental in helping him towards this. The license enabled Gibao to become a boss, a very different status from that of an employee. He had to set a new goal for himself in order to be a successful boss in the diamond business. He had to learn to monitor his workers day and night. He had to ensure that good luck was on his side. All these things meant lots of sacrifices to the spirits.

He knew from experience that in the mining business some men prospered more quickly than others. Brima and others had told him many times about the cases they knew of people who had become successful very quickly compared to others who took many endless years toiling away. Gibao knew he had to learn a host of other things, if he wished to prosper in the mines. He knew that mining was a competitive, savage business, with a ruthless savagery where weaker bosses were eliminated.

But although Gibao had made progress by acquiring a house and a mining license, he had other formidable domestic tasks

# THE DIAMONDS                                           161

to cope with. He had told N'tuma that she would be responsible for the shop. When he gave her that assignment, it meant by implication that the other wives were relegated to the kitchen where they would cook first for the household and then for the workers. Gibao knew his other wives would not like this arrangement, but they would have no choice. Any one or all three of the wives could therefore initiate hostilities towards N'tuma. Teneh, in particular, could be angry for having lost her coveted place in the marital hierarchy, having been the last, youngest and most favorite of the wives.

Gibao had convinced himself that he would reason with Teneh by telling her that she was still his favorite wife. He planned to tell her that she was younger and more beautiful than N'tuma. Moreover, they would have a child. N'tuma was also divorced. All these reasons, he thought, would convince Teneh to keep peace with N'tuma. What if Teneh asked the reason for her not being assigned the shop? Gibao considered all possible questions ahead of time rather than be caught tongue-tied in front of his wives. He was also sure Yebu would poison Teneh's mind. That was one of his biggest fears. Manu and Yebu would use the shop assignment as evidence. Gibao feared there would be domestic chaos in his house. How am I going to preside over a house that is in a state of female anarchy? he wondered.

■ ■ ■

The ride on the lorry allowed N'tuma time to reflect on her future. What would happen to her now that she had left Alhaji Jimoh? She wondered. She was extremely disturbed over the fact that her mother would bear her father's anger about what she had done. Fathers always scolded mothers for the bad behavior of the children, as if fathers had no responsibility for their children's upbringing. Poor mother, she thought, as she braced herself on the bumpy ride home.

She had suffered for Gibao and wondered if life with him would make her happier. He was a man with three wives. How many more would he choose? How would her co-mates react to her when they came and found her in the house and operating the shop, a coveted assignment as compared to the kitchen chores? Gibao, she recalled, had described the personalities of all his three wives to her in order to prepare her for their meeting. Of the three wives, Yebu was described as unfriendly, rude, and dangerous. Yebu feared no one. N'tuma could only hope to neutralize Yebu's caustic personality by an outward show of friendliness. That would be her strategy. N'tuma knew that she and the other wives could not last forever in a perpetual state of war in the house. It would take Gibao a long time to build a separate house for her. She knew Gibao had no plans to buy or build any more houses, just so as to accommodate his feuding wives.

◼ ◼ ◼

N'tuma sat with another lady by the driver. They had spoken briefly when she boarded the lorry at Njama. After their short conversation, there was a long silence as the lorry sped for Bo. N'tuma's thoughts were scattered. She always came back to the disturbing thought of what would happen to her mother. She knew her father had sent away one of his wives and her daughter, who had gotten pregnant by a boyfriend, never to be seen again. N'tuma was ready to tell her father that she was against having had to terminate her studies prematurely to get married to somebody of his own age. But of course, she knew it was very rarely that her father would allow her to speak her mind.

"Madam, do you live in Bo town?" the driver asked N'tuma. That was the first he had spoken to her since she boarded the bus.

"Yes," N'tuma replied after collecting her thoughts.

# THE DIAMONDS
163

"Oh! What part of Bo?" he continued.

"Sewa Road."

"Oh! Who are your parents?" the driver asked again.

"Alhaji Baba." N'tuma's father was a prominent man on Sewa Road and many people did business with him.

"Oh! I know the man. I know all his wives. Ah! You see this is a small world. This is why it is not good to be bad," the driver said while N'tuma and the other woman listened. "Why were you crying when you boarded the vehicle in Njama? I saw that some of the people who accompanied you were also crying. I hope it is not a funeral," the driver observed, quickly glancing at N'tuma. The two pretty women sitting next to him had stirred his curiosity.

N'tuma looked at the other woman, as if it was she who had asked the question. They looked at each other and smiled.

The driver turned away as he began negotiating a dangerous curve. Once past the curve, he relaxed and waited for N'tuma's answer.

"It's a long story. My husband and I had a misunderstanding and I have to go home to my people. My husband is Alhaji Jimoh. I was weeping because I don't know what my father will do to my mother," N'tuma said with a frown.

"I know Alhaji Jimoh. I have known him for a long time. He is a very jealous man. But the man himself (bump) see how old he is and with so many young and beautiful wives! They provoke young people (bump) that is why they run into such problems," the driver said, as he kept his eyes on the road before him.

The other woman listened with keen interest before speaking.

"My dear, I have gone through such problems (bump) for a long time." She tried to speak as the lorry ran through more bumps in the road. "What can you do? With men these days (bump) only God can help (bump) us women. The young ones are as bad as (bump) the older ones. It is difficult (bump) to find a good man now."

Unperturbed by the woman's comments or by the bumps, the driver replied, "You always blame men. What about (bump) you people? You do not see your faults. It is always (bump) men you blame. You are never satisfied (bump) with what we (bump) do for you, especially you women of Sewa."

This remark did not satisfy the two young women. They looked at each other to determine who should reply to the driver.

"Eh!" N'tuma uttered with exasperation. "What do you (bump) do for women? Tell us. When you have two (bump) three (bump) four or five wives, how much can you really do (bump) for each of them? You also have girlfriends (bump) to care for. My dear, we know the secrets of men. How much does a man get to satisfy so many (bump) women?" N'tuma looked at her female companion whose face showed anger.

"Right!" the woman added.

"Right!" the driver came back. "This is precisely the reason (bump) you can never satisfy women. They want (bump) every piece of cotton material in the market (bump) every type of shoes (bump) headties (bump) and many other things." Each bump in the road served to dramatize the list of things that women always wanted.

The other woman could not let this pass. "Women are just different (bump) and I am not sure we are as greedy (bump) as you paint us. Men don't understand us. You see (bump) you men want to be proud of your wives (bump) to show them off as beautiful, decent, well-dressed and well cared for (bump) but you don't want to provide for them. That is why we also look for boyfriends. Don't you know the saying these days in Sewa (bump) that one man cannot fill a suitcase?" She paused to look over at the driver who continued to look at the road ahead. "Anyway, tell us how much we are going to pay. Let us forget about this subject. No one will win. We always talk about it anytime we meet."

"How much do you want to pay?" the driver asked as he glanced at both of them.

# THE DIAMONDS

The young women looked at each other and smiled. There was silence.

"Okay. We will talk about it (bump) when we arrive in Bo," the driver said, to close the topic.

The vehicle made a stop in a small town to discharge a passenger. The driver stepped out to collect his fare.

"How much do you think we should pay him?" N'tuma asked the other young woman.

"I think he will not take anything from us. Don't you see he is trying to make contacts?" the young lady asked.

"Men! They can be so foolish. I have enough problems already, my dear," N'tuma said impatiently.

"If he wants me to spend my nights with him when he is in Bo, I will accept his offer," the young woman said, and then added a smile. "But, I will always deceive him and have other boyfriends. When I want him to find out, he will leave, but I will have gotten my free rides on his bus."

"But some men are very stubborn. Once they have started spending on you, they will chase you to the bitter end," N'tuma warned.

The other woman laughed, causing N'tuma also to laugh.

"How long are you going to be in Bo?" N'tuma's companion asked.

"My dear, I am just going to inform my parents about what happened between me and my husband. Then, I will leave and join my boyfriend, Gibao, who is going to marry me." N'tuma hesitated before answering directly, "It may be a week or two after I return."

The driver got in and continued the drive on to Bo. He spoke less frequently and concentrated on the bad road.

When the lorry arrived in Bo, it was already night. The lorry park was full to capacity. N'tuma had gotten off a few streets earlier along Sewa Road. She did not pay a single penny for the trip, neither did her traveling companion.

# Chapter 16

N'tuma had rightly gauged her father's mood and reaction. He was implacably opposed to what had transpired between his daughter and his friend, Alhaji, who had at one time rescued him from financial disgrace. What her father considered more unfortunate was that N'tuma left Alhaji without having conceived a child, and that therefore, a bond no longer existed between him and Alhaji.

"What has become of children these days?" her father moaned, wandering about the house.

N'tuma had made things even worse by abandoning Alhaji for someone like Gibao whom her father considered an infidel, a sinner, a non-Muslim. Her father walked around the house, crestfallen, with sagging shoulders, burdened by the shame N'tuma had brought to his household. Despite her father's annoyance, N'tuma refused to alter her views. She would never go back to Alhaji, the old man she did not love, even if Alhaji was willing to forgive her.

The time had come for N'tuma and her mother to receive their punishment.

"Hawa!" N'tuma's father shouted for her mother. N'tuma and her mother knew what form of punishment was coming, because N'tuma had informed her mother about the incident. N'tuma's father was an orthodox Muslim and a fanatic about following Muslim religious laws. N'tuma stood in front of her father.

Hawa came and stood by the door. She announced her arrival in a low voice. Her husband was sitting in a hammock. It was

## THE DIAMONDS
167

the only hammock in the veranda and he virtually monopolized it. He motioned for Hawa to come in and stand by her
daughter.

"I have told you several times over that your blessing will
depend on your children. Now look at your eldest daughter,"
he started scolding Hawa. "You have no blessing with her.
That is why Satan can succeed in misdirecting your own
daughter. You are all infidels! Let me tell you. The fire of hell
will consume you all! And I have warned you before, the fire
of hell is ten times worse than the fire on earth. So! You and
your daughter should prepare to be consumed by that fire.
Believe me. When that time comes and I am called to rescue
you, I will disown you. You, daughter, leave my house today. I
cannot accommodate sinners, and my word in this is final!"

■ ■ ■

That day N'tuma left and joined Gibao in Njama. When
N'tuma met Gibao, she told him about her mother's plight
and suggested the necessary steps to be taken to help her. The
mother was fairly old. N'tuma planned to pay periodic visits to
her at times when her father was out of home.

N'tuma was pleased with the efforts Gibao had made in
buying a house and opening a shop to sell a variety of household items, fabrics and beads. She prided herself on having an
enviable position of shopkeeper in a household with so many
wives.

Of course such a position should normally belong to a
senior and favorite wife such as Teneh. Brima had called
Gibao's attention to this anomaly, and suggested it would be
preferable to delegate N'tuma to a subordinate position until
such time as Gibao would be able to find fault with Teneh to
make the switch, replacing N'tuma with Teneh as shopkeeper.
But Gibao explained that N'tuma had proposed this arrangement as a condition for marrying him. Brima did not accept

this argument. He argued that Teneh was much younger and even had a young baby. Gibao had met Teneh fresh from her initiation into the women's secret society and Gibao was the first man in her life. These reasons, Brima thought, were enough considerations for allowing Teneh to run the shop. In the end, Gibao brushed aside Brima's advice and put N'tuma in charge as prearranged.

When Gibao's family arrived in Njama, a heavy downpour soaked everyone, leaving Gibao's mother and grandmother wet and shivering in the rain. N'tuma played the role of hostess effectively, making sure that everybody was taken care of. Rooms were allocated to each wife, while the mother and grandmother were taken to the separate small building adjoining the main house. Gibao's mother was pleased to meet the new wife, N'tuma, and they embraced warmly.

In the process of getting settled, Teneh dashed into Yebu's room to chat and gossip.

"I told you what Gibao would do, remember?" Yebu whispered to Teneh.

Teneh nodded her head affirmatively, and seemed impressed by Yebu's predictions. They discussed the arrangements of the shop, which they had learnt about earlier from N'tuma herself. Teneh felt great disappointment with her husband, but Yebu consoled her "People do not get disappointed when they do not expect too much, you know?" Yebu said.

Teneh found it hard to talk and fell into a prolonged silence. She had a feeling of emptiness in her.

"I have every reason to be indebted to you, Yebu," Teneh admitted. "I am happy I have never antagonized you. You are a sister to me, an elder sister. You have helped me grow, I have learned much through you. This our Gibao had told me in confidence that he would never have another woman in the house. Three wives he said, were enough," Teneh lamented.

Yebu smiled. "My sister, that was a long time ago. Never trust men. They have two tongues." Yebu went on lecturing

## THE DIAMONDS    169

Teneh about men. Gibao's name and actions served as fuel for the anger the two were generating.

Teneh had a habit of resting her right index finger on her lower lip as she thought about something. The finger rested there a long time as Yebu talked to her. Teneh was deeply shocked and saddened by Gibao's broken promises to her.

"This whole affair explains what I told you, that when you have the opportunity you should do your own thing," Yebu asserted. "This is not the time to believe men, my sister." Gibao's arrangements in Njama had further convinced Yebu of his deviousness and hardened her heart against all men.

Teneh left the room dejected. She went back to her room to finish unpacking. Her little son was trying to help but was mostly scattering things all over the room.

"Gibao-wo, little Gibao! What are you doing? You are giving me more work," Teneh complained to the little boy. "I am going to change that name," Teneh added, resentfully. "I don't want you to be like your father. Otherwise, if you come across a tough woman, she will kill you." Teneh continued hissing and talking to herself, cursing and regretting that, all the time Gibao was away, she had lived without another man's pleasures. Now she has come to Njama to find that Gibao had another wife and would keep Teneh at kitchen duties. She wished she had accepted Yebu's suggestions back home and had not worried for Gibao. Teneh vowed it would never happen again.

Gibao knew that somewhere Yebu and Teneh would be gossiping intently about him. He remained busy, talking things over with his mother and grandmother. Both of them were happy about what Gibao had accomplished: acquiring a new house, a new shop and a new wife.

Mama Yatta's affection for N'tuma served to fuel Teneh's hate and extreme scorn for N'tuma. From that first day in the house, Teneh was the enemy of N'tuma. Teneh made it clear that Yebu was her ally and considered Yebu her guru pertaining to any subject. Teneh accepted Yebu as the herald of truth, not Mama Yatta nor N'tuma, and certainly not Gibao. Teneh happened to overhear Mama Yatta ask N'tuma when she was going to give her a grandchild. At that moment, Teneh felt an intense urge to strangle N'tuma.

Manu, the eldest wife, was in her room trying to see how she could make space for her three children. She decided she would sleep with her eldest daughter, Jeneba, while her two boys would sleep on the floor by the sofa.

By now, the whole house resounded with noise from children jumping and shouting everywhere. The young ones were less interested in what their adults were feeling towards each other and more interested in exploring their new house. The sound of raindrops rhythmically beating on the zinc roof increased the noise. N'tuma came from the shop with toffee for the children, which they grabbed at gleefully.

Teneh sulked when she saw her son with the toffee. She was bitter, but even in her bitterness her beauty did not disappear. She stayed in her room much longer than anyone, actually doing nothing, just wanting to be alone to think about her future in Njama. Her anger started to turn against her father. She wished she did not live in a society where marriages were prearranged by fathers. Teneh felt she would have been happier in another part of the world. Indeed, she thought how much she would have preferred to make her own choice of mate. If the marriage went wrong, then she would have had only herself to blame. She remembered how men had vied for her when she first came out of the secret society that initiated her into womanhood. She and her mother had had a favorite choice, a younger man. Her father had made the final choice of whom to marry without ever thinking of consulting the mother or young Teneh. Gibao was his favorite and nothing would stop the father from making the marriage arrangement. Teneh reflected on her father's selfish reasons. He had been told that Gibao was a genius in farming, a good hunter and

# THE DIAMONDS

fisherman, as well as a good dancer. This was the type of man the father wanted. A man who would supply him occasionally with meat and fish for him and his workers. It was these considerations that had led her father to choose Gibao. Teneh now came to understand Yebu's and Manu's infidelities as regards Gibao. They, too, had been forced by their selfish fathers to marry him. She concluded that these prearranged marriages might have been ideal a long time ago, but were no longer acceptable.

Gibao, meanwhile had other concerns. He had contemplated seeing a soothsayer about why his neighbor had started to find more gems than he did. He was, therefore, prepared to do something about the situation in order to become one of the richest diamond prospectors in Sewa. He saw himself someday equal to Alhaji, and he talked impatiently to everyone about his future wealth. He had developed the attitude that he would obtain great wealth as predicted for him and that nothing could stop that prediction. Gibao also had an ally in his Lebanese friend, who was willing to support him in his ambition. He walked about Njama with an air of new confidence and happiness over the fact that he had found someone he trusted in the diamond business. He also owed his success to the wise diviners who had guided him in his search.

Gibao firmly believed that divination can predict the future. Divination and future-telling are known in every society. Gibao was like every man who wanted to know what he should do to make his millions of dollars. Every society has people who claim to have special powers to see into the future. In Sewa, these people came with various names. The people said these psychics were endowed with third eyes. They were believed to see much beyond the ordinary man's vision.

Besides the psychics, there were those who claimed further powers. They claimed they could alter natural phenomena and change situations according to their wishes. These were the Alpha-men, the manipulators of peoples' destinies.

It was this quest to probe ahead into the future, to see ahead, to predict events and to manipulate coming events that had reinforced the social value of the diviner. These Alpha-men diviners became an important part of Sewa society because they could foretell fortunes and intercede to increase someone's fortunes. Like the diamond adventurers, these diviners also came in response to the boom. They knew their so-called expertise would be required and inevitably they found their way into Sewa by the dozens. They professed they could work wonders. They attracted clients in abundance, who wanted assurance and security to match their greed. Many of the Alpha-men claimed that they had acquired their skills as a result of prolonged studies and acquaintance with Arabic literature. Indeed, there were a handful of diviners whose names and reputation impressed the most hardened cynic. Their clients spread the word of the powers of these prophets.

There were also diviners who operated as quacks and made money from the ignorance of their clients. These quacks had developed a mass psychology of their own, which they used effectively to dupe innocent victims every day.

The diviners who typically had proven themselves capable of foretelling the future knew how to make contact with prominent people in the diamond business. They knew equally well prominent local and national citizens. Because of their store of civic contacts, they were quick at dropping names to prospective clients. It was commonplace for a diviner to be heard to say he was a friend of well known citizens and had helped this person reach his present status, that he helped such and such a person win an election, win a power contest, win a court case, get a promotion or discover a big gem stone. And the people came in their masses and paid good money to the diviners and Alpha-men of Sewa.

The diamond dealers would do anything to enhance their prospects for making money. Some dealers had secretly gone to the extreme of sacrificing human beings as part of the pre-

# THE DIAMONDS
173

scription for success offered by the more extreme soothsayers. A dealer engaging in human sacrifice would be promised by such a soothsayer that his ultimate sacrifice had appeased the diamond gods and that he would become a millionaire. Strangers walking about in Sewa were at risk of becoming someone's sacrifice, as dictated by one or other of the local diviners.

People also came to the Morieman or Alphas for many other reasons: Students came to them for help in passing their examinations; civil servants came seeking help with a promotion; and women came seeking help with fertility. People afflicted with chronic illnesses always made their journeys to the diviners. People rushed regularly to the diviners with their personal needs and greedy desires.

Within this social climate of people and diamond dealers meeting with diviners and Alpha-men to foretell and manipulate their futures, Gibao in his impatience, could not resist taking advantage of one of the best diviners to ensure his continued success with the diamonds.

# Chapter 17

▓ ▓ ▓ ▓ ▓ ▓ ▓ ▓ ▓

The departure of Gibao's family from Semabu did not cause the people of the village any emotional distress. The pulse of life continued throughout the rainy season. Even the chicken and goats were not fully aware of the family's departure.

There was only one creature that was extremely and immediately affected by their absence. That was Elongima, Gibao's dog and traveling companion. He almost went mad. Elongima was the only member of Gibao's family household that did not make the journey to Sewa. He had behaved the same way when Gibao had left him and had gone away. He cried all day long. Elongima seemed very distressed. His home was now gone. He no longer had a place to go to warm up when it was rainy and cold. Mama Yatta's hut remained closed. Elongima cried and made all kinds of noises, searching for his lost family. He would follow the main road, smelling the ground as he went along. When he got to the river, which was swollen with rain water, he would come back and try another road. He roamed all over the village. He would start out on different routes, but would always come back and stand barking at Yatta's hut. He would then go to Gibao's grandmother's hut and stand by the door, smelling and sniffing. Thus he stayed in Semabu, alone and abandoned.

Someone else as well was left behind: Maada, Gibao's old godfather, who kept praying for him every day.

Maada was lying by the fireside. He turned his face towards the wall, giving his entire naked back to the fire. He wore only a loincloth. He breathed slowly. Maada was not well. Old age

# THE DIAMONDS

175

was treating him roughly. One could count the ribs on his back with accuracy, they were so conspicuous and prominent. The fire was not bright enough to give sufficient warmth, and the room was full of smoke.

"Good morning, Ndiamu, my friend," a voice softly called out to him.

Maada was unmoved. "Good morning," he responded with much effort. He recognized the voice as that of Kinawova. He did not attempt to get up, but continued lying on his side.

"Maada, you are not well," Kinawova observed.

Maada coughed painfully, his ribs expanding and contracting with each heave. He could not say a word.

Kinawova seated himself on a bench made of raffia fronds. "Maada, you have been ill several times, but I think that this is serious." There was a pause of silence. "It is very serious," Kinawova observed as he surveyed Maada's body.

"Yes ... you are ... right," Maada said, breathing deeply with his words. "This whole night ... I did not ... sleep. It's my ... sides and chest. Kinawova ... I'm not well. I know that," Maada finally admitted. Maada slowly turned towards Kinawova.

Kinawova gave his friend a penetrating look. "Maada," he said patiently. "The world is not good, eh? It is you who are lying down here today like this. Maada, it is you that Yatta has left lying in a sick bed and gone to Sewa. You, Maada, you who would do anything for the family. It is you they have abandoned. Maada, my friend, human beings are not good, I tell you."

Maada's eyes were red, perhaps because of the smoke in the hut. Kinawova attended to the fire to keep it glowing. He put more logs into the dying flames.

"When I recall how much sacrifice you have made for that family, when I recall not too long ago, that you accompanied them to your friend in Kpetewama, and, now, they have left you in a sick bed. Ah, Maada, the world is not good. People can use you at any time, even on your death bed, for their own benefit. Tell me. You call this a good world? Believe me. The whole world is represented here in Semabu, here in this small village. Here you find men of virtue and men of vice. Here you find witches; men of greed and boundless ambition. Here you find friends and enemies. This small town is full of all sorts of people," Kinawova said knowingly. He turned toward the wall of the hut, pressed his right thumb on his nose and emptied phlegm on the wall. Tears were forming in his eyes because the hut was filling with smoke.

Maada had by then struggled to sit up. His breast bones showed bare and visible. "All you have said is true, Kinawova. It is true," Maada spoke slowly and breathed carefully with each sentence. "But what can I do? Can I fight people because they are not good to me? Let me tell you." Maada paused to breathe deeper. "We all have to go and answer for our deeds in the next world. So, let everyone play his own part here on earth. That is why I have been kind to them. What they have done for me they will answer for. When Mama Yatta came to say goodbye to me," Maada paused to take another breath, "I told her I will pray for them and I mean it. I will do it. Kinawova, you see me as I am. My mind is clean for people. I do not hold hate. I do not have a bad mind." He breathed some more. "That is why I think I have grown to be this age." Maada spoke his mind, while his friend watched sympathetically.

Kinawova listened respectfully and replied to Maada. "You will recall when Yatta's husband was sick, the sickness that ultimately took him to his grave. We put him in a hammock. We all went, traveled the whole night, no one slept. We took him to the medicine man at Falaba. Can you imagine the distance? That is what friendship means. But the world of today is different. People's eyes are very dry with wickedness. That is the trouble," Kinawova concluded.

Maada felt too ill to respond. He was tormented by physical pain. The pain in his body took away the gift of oratory for which he was known. But despite the pain, Maada felt com-

# THE DIAMONDS

pelled to tell Kinawova what was in his heart. "Sometimes, I wish I was not born into this troubled world. Believe me, Kinawova, I do not know for certain, but sometimes deep down in my mind something keeps telling me there is another world, much better than this. This world seems to defy the very existence of God and all the attributes of his divine perfection." Maada was not trying to teach his friend anything new, but sharing his feeling because he felt inspired by Kinawova's conversation.

Kinawova replied, "You see, Maada, I look at this world around us. Things have become progressively worse. Our own times were better. You know that. But, now you can even see that on the day children are born, they struggle to open their eyes. What do they want to see in a hurry? Some of them talk early, some walk early, everything is fast. This is the reason we move too fast to our destruction. Maada, I tell you this is the reason the world is not right," Kinawova offered in strong complaint.

Maada listened, enjoying his company and the chance to take his mind off his old bone and muscle pains. His face became more animated and his eyes more alert.

Then Elongima entered briefly, sniffed around, went out, stood by the doorway, raised one leg, sprayed the wall with urine and left. No one bothered him.

"Let me have some snuff," Kinawova asked.

Maada reached for the snuff tin under the pillow and handed it over to his friend. "That is all I have," Maada said.

"So, this town is going to go without good snuff for sometime. Oh, God!" Kinawova exclaimed. "If I have to go over the river to buy good snuff, I will do so, Maada, but I will not eat snuff in this town if you don't have any for us. Their snuff is not good. They do not put enough ingredients in it and the ties are small. Do you know that child of a slave? She sells the worst snuff in this town. She is a witch. Do you know the chronic ulcer on her foot? It cannot be cured. What is the reason? Nothing but the witchcraft in her stomach. It is a very potent witchcraft," Kinawova said caustically.

Maada just smiled, his first such smile since Kinawova came in to see him. "Kinawova, I think I will overcome this illness," Maada said with a subdued voice. His facial features looked yellowish. Despite their alert brightness, his eyes looked weak, but he had a determined voice. He still had the will to survive.

By this time, his friend was busy grating some kola nuts for Maada. That was the only way Maada ate kola nuts. His mouth had few teeth left.

"Let me go. I will come back to check on you, if the rain will allow me." Kinawova made a final attempt to attend to the fire. He put more wood on it, then got up and grabbed hold of his walking stick by the doorway. People recognized Kinawova by his tall walking stick which he customarily held in the middle, as he walked along, with a slight stoop. Though he was nearly as old as Maada, he was much stronger and still had plenty of energy. He talked a lot, offering mostly wise, pithy advice. Because of his opinions and complaints about the way society was deteriorating, he had few friends. People simply found it too difficult to argue with him. Maada was one of the few friends.

Kinawova stood outside Maada's hut for a while, holding fast to his walking stick. He looked up at the clouds. "Rain, ump! Rain again today. This one is going to pour heavily ... heavier than yesterday." He then walked away. "Ungrateful people. See how they have left him there to die. No consideration for old age these days. Chai!" he mumbled to himself in disgust and spat as he walked. Before he got to his hut, the rain was pouring down on Semabu. The rains would come for the day and, sometimes, for whole nights and continue into the morning.

People went on with their lives, paying little heed to the abandoned dog Elongima, and equally abandoned old man Maada, the only two living reminders of Gibao's life in the village.

# Chapter 18

■ ■ ■ ■ ■ ■ ■ ■ ■

Gibao and his workmen had found some valuable gems. The quality of the gems brought Gibao fame and notoriety. Lebanese dealers and Moroccans flocked to his house. He was offered a Bedford lorry as a gift by one of these prospective customers, but Gibao was unwilling to sell to anyone. He refused to breach his contract with his Lebanese friend, and he gave to the man the biggest finds. Gibao kept some of the smaller pieces and sold them privately, and his friend went off on a two-week trip to Antwerp to cash in on the gems.

Gibao's Lebanese friend had been in Njama for a long time without having to travel. He had not been able to get enough of gems of quality to justify his taking a trip outside of Njama to Antwerp. Gibao now provided him with that opportunity. He was unable to convince himself he should go through Lungi Airport without being caught by customs officials for smuggling diamonds. He carried four different passports identifying himself as having four different nationalities. On such trips, he used passports that camouflaged his Lebanese identity because the Lebanese people were the most suspected of being in the diamond smuggling business. He made his way to Antwerp via London, carrying with him some of Gibao's finds, to cash them in.

With the help of this friend, Gibao paid his workers handsomely, more than they would normally have expected. He was generous in his payments so as to let them know that a better future lay ahead for all of them. He organized a big party at his house with an abundance of food, drink, and music. He invited

Ndoinjeh's friend, the man who sold roast meat, to bring enough of it for the occasion. Gibao never told his family about the story of roast meat in Njama, as it was revealed to him when he came, for fear that none of them would eat it.

Brima and his sister Bintu joined Gibao at his party. Since it was not raining, Brima provided two gas lights in the veranda, which illuminated the surrounding area during the night. The children, who were confined to the living room, wriggled their hips to the beat of the music and peeked out of the window to watch the adults. Occasionally the children shouted, their voices blending in with the music radiating out into the cold night air. While the children moved to the music, the adults were content to sit and listen, sipping pints of beer or Guinness Stout. They walked over occasionally to the man with the roast meat to refill their plates. The people tended to bundle themselves into groups, all of Gibao's friends in one group, his three wives from Semabu in another. Bintu and N'tuma sat together in a third group, and Gibao and Brima in yet another. Jeneba was in the shop supplying music from the gramophone with the help of N'tuma, who would periodically go into the shop to suggest the next song to be played. Other people came in, gate crashers were always looking for pleasure especially where they heard music playing. Gibao was in a good mood and took no action against them.

N'tuma and Bintu occupied themselves with analyzing and gossiping about each of Gibao's wives. They eagerly discussed one wife after another. The two of them concluded that Teneh was the prettiest of them all. N'tuma thought that Jeneba was too pretty to be the daughter of Gibao and that she looked more like her mother. They agreed without any reservation that Jeneba was pretty and had good potential, if she did not get married too soon. As for Yebu, N'tuma criticized her as aggressive and hostile, which was obvious from the very first day the family arrived in Njama.

The gossip was not monopolized only by Bintu and N'tuma.

# THE DIAMONDS 181

Gibao's wives were also busy gossiping about Bintu and N'tuma. There was a unanimous dislike of N'tuma. Manu was passively opposed to Gibao's marriage to N'tuma, not so much because she was another wife, but because of the way he had assigned her a place of honor, which should have belonged to Teneh.

The party continued late into the night until people finally got tired and went to bed.

■ ■ ■

Jeneba found ways to help N'tuma in the shop, so she would have something to do when she was between semesters at school. Teneh and Yebu were assigned to the kitchen where they cooked for the workers and the rest of the household. Manu would periodically supervise cooking the sauce. At the end of cooking Manu served the food. Both Yebu and Teneh did not enjoy this kitchen work knowing that N'tuma was right next door taking care of the shop. The cooking chores sometimes meant preparing four meals a day or working late into the night. By the time they left the kitchen, Yebu and Teneh would be too tired to be useful even to themselves.

In the morning, they would be the first to wake up to ensure that the workers had food to eat before going to work. Their assignment was laborious and monotonous. It did not matter to them that most women who were married to diamond entrepreneurs did the same thing. The normal staple of the country was rice, but rice was always scare during the rainy season. So on this particular day Yebu and Teneh were cooking fufu, which required a great deal of energy. The preparation of fufu was dreaded by most women. Yebu sat in front of the pot. Her lappa was securely gathered in between her legs. She put a paddle-like spoon into the pot and started stirring the fufu. When it was hardening, she strained her arm muscles to stir the thickening mixture. She felt as if she were paddling a canoe against a strong tide. The heat and the muscular effort caused her to perspire so that, eventually, her body became drenched in sweat. Teneh held the pot to keep it steady.

"Let me take a turn," Teneh suggested. She and Yebu exchanged positions. Teneh soon became drenched in sweat. The women worked at the fufu while the kitchen grew smoky from the fire.

"Ah! See how we are struggling and that infidel N'tuma is sitting in the shop," Teneh complained. Teneh had by now acquired enough training from Yebu to be just as vicious and aggressive. She became harder, more rigid. She had learned to be wary of men, because of Gibao's trickery. She continued to mix the fufu for some time, becoming angrier as she did, wanting to kill Gibao with each difficult stir of the fufu. Teneh suggested they add more water to the mixture to make the stirring a little easier and Yebu complied by pouring some in.

"I don't know how long this slave work is going to last," Yebu said in a tired voice.

Teneh stopped for a while. Sweat dripped into her eyes. She wiped it away and let out a violent hiss. She started again on the difficult stirring.

"Yebu, if it was not for my child, I would just quit and damn the consequences. I can always get someone to marry me. I am young yet. How can I be a slave to my co-mate? To labor for her to eat!"

Yebu gave a cynical smile and laughed. "Well, they say the baboon works, the monkey eats." They both laughed at the thought of the proverb.

"If someone had told me this would be my fate, I would not have believed it," Teneh told Yebu. "I recall when you said this to me in Semabu. If it was your intuition, I must confess I admire you. Everything you said is now happening. You know this dog of a Gibao so well. See. We smell of smoke everyday, even when we use perfume," Teneh snarled bitterly.

"Teneh, I told you I know this man well. I did not want you

# THE DIAMONDS

to think, just because you were the favorite wife, that I was trying to spoil his name. I was confident you would find out about him for yourself in time," Yebu said, smiling in spite of the perspiration dripping off her face. She put her hand into the pot and collected a bit of the fufu to see if it was properly cooked. "A little bit more, then it will be out of the fire," she added.

"Tell me, Yebu. Has such a man the right to be jealous? He has no time, no energy to make you happy. It is useless labor we are engaged in. And, that mother of his is terrible," Teneh observed with exhaustion.

Yebu smiled with satisfaction. Her lectures to Teneh had produced their desired effect. She had an understanding co-mate in Teneh who knew what her grumbling and suffering was all about in this so-called marriage.

Teneh continued. "Let me tell you something. That woman was trying to put fire between us. Remember the time we were in Semabu when her son sent the money? Well, when she called me into her hut to give me my share, she told me I should not let you know how much my share was. She gave me the idea I had more than all of you," Teneh said.

Yebu laughed loudly. Teneh joined in. Mama Yatta had told each of the wives the same thing, letting each one think she had more than the others. The truth was that each wife was given the same amount, fifty pounds sterling.

"I told you the woman is a big witch. I told you this a long time ago. She knows me and I know her, too. Don't you know the saying that witches know themselves? That is why she will never bring her nonsense to me. I will always tell her about her daughters," Yebu said.

Yebu and Teneh had now finished stirring the fufu. They had to take a few minutes to relax outside in the fresh air. They happened to see Mama Yatta standing by the door of their outhouse, but they pretended they did not see her. Yatta, in turn, did not say anything to them. She didn't notice that

Yebu and Teneh had become allies and that Teneh's personality had changed: she had become remarkably rude and uncompromising compared to the quiet Teneh back in Semabu. Yatta might have guessed that Yebu had had an opportunity to contaminate Teneh's mind, but she did not seem to notice the extent of Teneh's change in attitude. She thought that Teneh was a child and that she would rethink her position and complaints after a while. Mama Yatta thought Teneh was just going through a phase. The only thing that Mama Yatta thought important was that Teneh should have a baby boy for Gibao.

Teneh and Yebu had grown beyond being mere co-wives to the point of being close friends. Being responsible for most of the heavy work in the operations of the house, they considered themselves mutually troubled by the plague that was spreading in it. This mutual self-interest by the two wives became so strong that Gibao felt threatened. He worried about a female conspiracy leading to a coup de foyer. He noticed that each time it was Yebu's turn to sleep with him, Yebu complained of an illness. Teneh did the same thing. Manu never treated him seriously. Gibao wondered how he was going to cope with this state of affairs. He realized that Brima was right when he had told him not to elevate N'tuma to the shop position right away.

Yebu and Teneh went ahead to secure boyfriends in Njama to satisfy their physical and romantic needs. Manu had no problem organizing her extra-marital life. Gibao knew nothing about these developments, yet he suspected things were not right. He began to worry.

But if Gibao felt tormented, N'tuma felt worse. Gibao was fortunate to be able to spend most of his time outside the house and away with the workers. N'tuma had the discomfort of staying home and enduring the looks of her co-mates. She made every effort to be polite to them, but her overtures were not welcome. Yebu and Teneh would gossip about her and speak directly to her to cause a reaction, but N'tuma tried to contain herself. Sometimes the hints took the form of songs.

# THE DIAMONDS 185

While Manu did not overtly show any liking for N'tuma, she did not resort to the sort of harassments exhibited by Yebu and Teneh. Sooner or later, Gibao would have to deal with what was becoming an explosive situation concerning his wives. However, now, he was too busy with his diamond business to allow the females to dominate his time and mental energy. He decided to ignore them as long as he could. He resolved to take no action unless the situation within the house became unbearable. Meanwhile, he dismissed any thoughts that his wives might start looking for happier relationships with new boyfriends.

Instead, he devoted more time to his work and his future. Some may have called it dedication. Kinawova and Maada would likely have called it greed. Gibao planned to go to a faraway town called Pelewahun, where it was rumored that there was a leading Morieman, or Alpha-man, who could perform magic wonders.

He went on the secret journey to find out from the Morieman what his future would be in the diamond business, but he never informed anyone at home exactly where he was going or why he was making the trip. Whenever people wanted to make such trips, secrecy was always the rule. Likewise, the Moriemen were like medical doctors who never revealed to others what they knew about a client or the client's future. Most of the visits to the Alpha-men occurred surreptitiously late at night. The nature of the visit was held in strict secrecy by the Alpha-man and by the client.

On his way to Pelewahun, Gibao came to the big river and stood at the edge, afraid to cross at first. He had to canoe to the other side. He had heard that once a year, especially in the rainy season, someone who was not a citizen of Sewa would drown in the river. The gossips said that there was a river spirit who had to take a human being as a sacrifice. Gibao also hesitated out of fear of being told negative things by the Morieman. However, Gibao summoned up his courage and stepped into the canoe to cross the river. The desire to find ways to make more money in the diamond mines was stronger than any of his fears.

Gibao had chosen to make the journey at night because he did not want any of his colleagues to see him. However, other colleagues always had the same ideas, so that people ended up meeting each other at the Alpha-man's hut at night much to each other's surprise.

When Gibao left Pelewahun, he continued on to another Morieman for his advice, so as to compare this with the predictions of the first Morieman.

Gibao returned home confident that the information he got from his two visits was not too different. Both Moriemen were said to be extremely good. But the best of the Moriemen was said to be close to Gibao, right there in Njama. He was named Alpha Finoh. If the others whom Gibao had consulted were said to be extremely good, Alpha Finoh was said to be excellent and a paragon in his trade. The only problem about him perhaps was that his services were expensive. However, once his costs were met, no one dared to doubt the outcome of whatever he would do. He was known to have plenty of money and he drove about Njama in a Mercedes Benz. It was rumored that Alpha Finoh and Alhaji were good friends, besides his having many other important friends at the national level. He also had five pretty wives and many children in his compound.

Although Gibao had been given encouraging news by the soothsayers, Gibao decided to be the customer of Alpha Finoh, with the hopes that this famous Morieman would help him hit the jackpot in the diamond business.

■ ■ ■

When Gibao returned home he found that Miatta, his sister, had arrived unexpectedly with her three children to stay at his home, because she had run out of money. She had been

# THE DIAMONDS

married to a Lebanese merchant, but the man had run off with another woman.

Miatta arrived with Lilia, who was fifteen, and two other girls who were thirteen and eleven. Back in Semabu, Yebu had been an enemy of Miatta and they could not tolerate each other. The arrival of Gibao's sister only increased Gibao's domestic difficulties, because both Yebu and Teneh would not welcome the extra cooking to take care of these unwelcome relatives.

Though the sister arrived at midday with the sun shining, everyone knew it was a deceptive sunshine. A storm was brewing inside Gibao's house. The situation wasn't helped when Gibao had to pay the driver because his sister had no money to pay. The sister was lucky to find Gibao home after he had been away on his secret visits to the Moriemen. Many times people told the lorry drivers the same story that the relative they were going to would pay for the trip, only to find out the relative could not be found or had moved to a new house at an unknown address. When such situations occurred, drivers would take the passengers' luggage from them until they had retrieved their money. Though it was an embarrassing experience, this happened very frequently.

Mama Yatta was glad to receive her daughter and grandchildren. Now, there were nine grandchildren in the house and four of her son's wives. Under normal circumstances, they should have been accommodating to each other. But, now, Gibao had to deal with an imminent crisis in his household, in spite of his continuing obsession with his diamond work. All these things were testing his position as the head of both his home and his business. Though he greeted Miatta with smiles, he was not pleased at the thought of his growing domestic chaos.

# Chapter 19

For two days, a stale, foul smell had lingered in the air, permeating the neighborhood, from the remains of a dead dog nearby, which had been hit by a lorry and left to die. The whole neighborhood was suffused with the stench of the carcass. It started rotting and oozing with maggots, attended by a swarm of flies and occasionally by a cluster of vultures. Scenes such as this were frequent in Njama.

The turbulent situation brewing in Gibao's household, coupled with the acrid stench, distracted Gibao from tackling his various problems with good wisdom. With the heat of pressures around him, Gibao found it difficult to find emotional tranquility or peace. He wavered between dealing with the problems directly or simply pushing them away.

Gibao found out that Miatta had come to stay permanently with her three children. His mother informed him that she would have to stay until she found another husband. Without her Lebanese husband, Miatta had found life too difficult to endure on her own. Her husband had left her with a relatively decent house and a shop stacked with goods. She was not able to manage the business, so the goods ran out and the house came under siege from the bugs and elements. She was not able to make even minor repairs to the house, and so the place became a physical liability.

Miatta also suffered psychological problems when Lilia, the eldest daughter, lost her virginity to a retarded man. She was faced with the shame of having to initiate Lilia into the women's

# THE DIAMONDS 189

secret society, not as an innocent girl but as an experienced woman. The rapist was not worth bringing to justice because he could not afford the offerings for the ritual cleansing of Lilia. Miatta could not seriously scold her daughter. Her conscience would not allow it, because she had also had the same experience of having sex before being initiated. Lilia thus presented her mother with a bundle of problems because she could not be presented as a virgin to the secret society. First, Miatta decided to keep it a secret. For this reason, Miatta decided to leave town. But she could not afford to live on her own without a husband.

Miatta thought that going to her brother was the only solution. She planned for the initiation of her three girls into the secret society in Njama and taking all precautions that Lilia's secret was kept.

Gibao had no choice but to accommodate his sister and her three children. His initial impulse was to give Miatta money to start a business such as the money Brima had provided for his sister, Bintu. However, Gibao saw how his sister had made it abundantly clear that she had no business acumen. Gibao saw only a remote hope for his sister: marriage to another man. He privately evaluated his sister's situation: she was overweight, not particularly beautiful, lacked business skills, worked herself into being a near alcoholic wreck, and had three children from her first husband. He concluded that her chances for finding a husband were quite remote.

Miatta told Gibao that she had had problems with the shop because she could not collect debts from her customers. Collecting money and debts was necessary for doing business. People asked for certain goods and promised to pay later. At one time, Miatta said, a man threatened to beat her because she had gone too early in the morning to collect her debt. The man accused Miatta of blockading his house. He had taken a substantial number of goods from Miatta's shop. But when the time came for him to pay, he took to playing hide and seek. He was usually never at home. His wives would say he had gone on a trip, or he was still in the farm. There was no end to the problem of collecting from the man and others like him.

Mama Yatta exuberantly accepted Miatta and her daughters into the family. What else could happiness mean for Mama Yatta but to rule over this assemblage of wives and grand-children? She felt like Mama Queen.

Gibao's grandmother was equally happy, having the host of great grandchildren around her. She felt the fulfilment of ripe old age, seeing the great grandchildren happy and feeling con-tentment in her grandson's new house.

The missing member in this game in Njama was Njabu, Gibao's other sister. Mama Yatta wished she would come too. But Njabu was still married and had no problems on the scale of Miatta's, so Njabu had no need to live with Gibao.

Since the arrival of Miatta and her children, Mama Yatta and her mother kept an open-house policy, meaning that the children could come into their rooms at any time, which they did, at all times of the day and night. When they fought, Mama Yatta would be the one to mete out justice. When they wanted sweets, they would come to her. They summoned her for virtually everything. Their own mothers were always too busy what with the chores and cooking for everyone, to tend to their children.

One day Miatta was with her mother, Mama Yatta, and her grandmother. Yebu and Teneh, meanwhile, were working laboriously in the kitchen while the other three women talked leisurely.

"I wish Njabu was here," Mama Yatta said. She was not aware of and had no concerns about the economic considerations of supporting a household that might end up with more than twenty people in it.

"Maybe she does not know of Gibao's success. I am sure she will come when she knows her brother is in Sewa," Miatta observed.

Mama Yatta tilted her head, thinking about Njabu. "I will

# THE DIAMONDS

tell Gibao to send some money for Njabu and her children. We can send Lilia there sometime after her initiation. I know that Njabu must be suffering this rainy season."

"What does her husband do for her?" Yatta's mother asked.

"Granma," Miatta called out, "men these days are very callous. One has to be very lucky to come across a good man who will do something worthwhile for you."

"Well, I guess that is why most of you are not faithful to your husbands. Our own time was different," the old woman said in her trembling voice. Her jaws had sagged and her eyesight had worsened in the past year. Her hair was as white as Jeneba's teeth.

Mama Yatta touched on a sensitive subject."When are you going to initiate these girls into the society? They are big now. See Lilia. Her breasts are almost falling. She is ready to be married and have children. I want to see her child before God takes my life."

Miatta was not prepared for the subject of marriage and tried to put it off by replying, "We have to wait for the dry season."

"You people. You always change things. During our own days, a child like Lilia would have been initiated by now and in a man's house. But, now, you wait until their breasts have fallen," the elderly grandmother remarked. Her memories were about a previous time when life was wonderful and every woman was either married or a potential wife.

"I see that my brother has married a new wife," Miatta remarked.

Mama Yatta smiled. She approved of the wife. "They have been together sometime now. No signs of pregnancy," But then she arched her eyebrows. "It is not just marriage, it is getting children that is important. It does not matter how beautiful you are. You have to have children before they consider you a woman. I wonder what they are waiting for."

"But, Mama, it is God that gives children. When the time

comes, she will have them," Miatta said, consoling her mother. A childless mother was considered an unhappy woman, a social outcast. She represented evil and bad luck to other women and would be shunned by other mothers for fear of what she might to do their children. A childless woman was supposed to live a forlorn life.

Mama Yatta swished away the flies that had intruded on her comfort. Since another dog had died in the neighborhood, the compound was full of flies. It was the same thing in the other houses nearby. Dead dogs and cats lay rotting in the streets. They were not disposed of by anybody, but were left to decay. They would decompose and foul the air until the whole carcass became a skeleton. Nobody took the responsibility of removing the carcasses. People would do nothing because they believed that there were persons employed by the government to dispose of these creatures. They still would do nothing even if the animal rotted in front of their own houses. Someone might push the remains a little away from the house, but the carcass was never disposed of. Instead of correcting the situation, the people would spend time holding their noses to arrest the smell. This was life in Njama. Life was void of a sense of civic responsibility. Life was dedicated to only one thing: making quick money, even at the risk of an early death.

■ ■ ■

Although N'tuma remained the only wife who cooperated with Gibao, he held certain reservations about her. He was beginning to suspect N'tuma of infidelity, a case of the monkey worrying about another monkey's tricks. He had gotten N'tuma as a result of her infidelity to Alhaji. Does one infidelity lead to another? Gibao wondered to himself.

The possibility of N'tuma engaging in an act of infidelity seemed remote at first, but Gibao's imagination kept growing the wealthier he became. He never assumed he might feel guilty

## THE DIAMONDS                                    193

over what he did to get N'tuma. His mind had started to
wonder about Mustapha, who had come from Bo like N'tuma,
one of Gibao's better workers.

By sheer coincidence, Mustapha and N'tuma had known
each other in Bo before N'tuma married Alhaji. They never
had a romantic attraction for each other. Gibao knew these
things and never had grounds for his suspicions that N'tuma
and Mustapha might try to get together. It was only his own
jealous mind at work. People say thieves know why they are
always so suspicious of others.

Gibao's suspicions started to torment him. One thing was
certain, and perhaps natural: Mustapha did get occasional considerations and little gifts from N'tuma. These would be in the
form of cigarettes, milk, coffee and sugar. Gibao was never informed about these free gifts. The reason for the gifts is that
Mustapha had known N'tuma and her family, including her
younger sister, Tewoh. Mustapha even used to say half-seriously
that he would marry Tewoh, though he was illiterate and defi-
nitely not Tewoh's choice. N'tuma and Mustapha had joked
many times about this marriage idea. He often asked N'tuma
when she thought Tewoh would come to visit her in Njama.
But apart from the friendly jokes and the gifts, nothing serious
developed between N'tuma and Mustapha.

As a wife, N'tuma measured up well, becoming a most
favored wife and enjoying a place of honor in her new home.
Despite her loyalty and hard work, Gibao's mind was not at
rest. He was becoming a victim of his own earlier infidelity.
The friendship between N'tuma and Mustapha was too much
for him to ignore, even though he lacked the evidence to
support his growing suspicions and fantasies.

Manu, Yebu and Teneh had never contemplated having
anything to do with Gibao's workers. N'tuma's case was far
different. She had not fully recovered from the Fudia-Alhaji
drama. Since her return to Njama, N'tuma felt her feet to be
too heavy with shame to venture into town. She was still

recovering from the painful emotional wounds she had sustained over the Fudia affair. Bintu had once asked N'tuma to come to pay her a visit, but N'tuma said she needed more time. She was waiting for the whole incident to blow over. She feared that her feet would give way if she ventured into town. N'tuma had become a captive of her own conscience.

On the night that Teneh slept with Gibao, he planned to discuss with her the issue of N'tuma's infidelity and try to learn anything she might know about it. As was the evening custom, Teneh was supposed to heat water for Gibao to wash before going to bed. Teneh flatly refused to do this. She told him to tell his niece, Lilia, to do it instead. Teneh said the nieces were old enough to do these things. The teenagers should not just stay in the house and eat and, play without doing something worthwhile. Teneh believed that Lilia needed the practice of work to prepare for marriage. She repeated her refrain that she was tired and did not want to kill herself. That was the way she had begun to see her life in Njama.

Gibao was surprised. He knew that his hold on Teneh had become tenuous. He was learning to be careful with her, as he had been with Yebu and Manu. It was only N'tuma who was amenable to his commands at this point. If he could not diffuse the explosive situation brewing in his house, he was not prepared to create more tensions that would just add to it. He chose to ignore Teneh's belligerence. Feeling very tired, he went to bed early, hoping that Teneh would join him for what they called "bedtime talk," the discussion of domestic issues, without being distracted by third parties. Teneh deliberately went to bed late enough so that Gibao would already be asleep. When he was awake enough to realize her presence, it was already morning.

"Now, why do all of you ignore me?" Gibao complained to her.

There was no response. Teneh felt disgust for the man, nothing but hate for his changing his promises to her and

# THE DIAMONDS 195

making her work harder in Njama. Her heart was full of bitterness.

"I know all of you have male friends. But, be careful about my workers," Gibao taunted, provocatively.

Teneh smiled more from pity than annoyance. "Listen. Let me tell you today. If I want a man, I can choose one from those that benefit me. I don't marry a driver and then make love to his apprentice. I know what is good. I have the blessing of a child. I am a good woman, if you don't know that by now. Please. Don't provoke me this morning. The wives you brought here from Semabu are now the slaves. So, leave us alone, us your first real wives from Semabu, and let us do your dirty work," Teneh said in an acid tone.

Gibao, sensing trouble in the early morning air, abandoned the topic and backed away from Teneh. By the time he was up from his bed, Teneh was out of the room, hissing as she went out.

Gibao thought Teneh however had made a point that pleased him. She would not engage herself in an affair with one of his workers. This soothed his emotions, and he redirected his mind to the day's activities.

Every morning, Teneh, Yebu and Manu would be engaged in the first activity of the day, cooking breakfast for the family members and the workers. The breakfast was a ritual in the diamond areas. Teneh had to rush away from Gibao to help her co-mates with this household burden. They were in control of all that related to cooking and feeding in the house. N'tuma waited until all the others had finished and her co-mates were no longer there having their breakfast, so she would not suffer their harassment and very unpleasant comments.

Breakfast was served in an orderly fashion and, yet, everyone at the table knew who hated whom. For his part, Gibao considered that N'tuma was now his only ally, even if just temporarily. The other wives, he felt, were ready to gang up on him and to make his life miserable in many ways.

# Chapter 20

N'tuma had found an ally in Miatta. This bond did not help in improving N'tuma's relationship with her other three co-mates. The dislike which Yebu and Teneh had for Miatta only made N'tuma the avowed enemy of the other three wives, who wanted to isolate N'tuma. Anybody who contributed to reversing this plan was not treated kindly. Jeneba was the only exception, mostly because she was not a wife and just wanted to spend time in the shop.

Strangely, Miatta had taken to calling N'tuma "my wife" and N'tuma would call Miatta "my husband." This familiarity was not appreciated by the co-mates. Miatta was ignorant as to how strongly the other wives disliked N'tuma. Miatta innocently continued her familiarity with N'tuma, not suspecting what the consequences might be. In order to give Miatta some work to do, Gibao agreed that she could help in the shop. This involved less work in the kitchen, and it only made the other three wives angrier at Gibao and his other relatives.

One day, during a heavy downpour, rain seeped into the shop. N'tuma and Miatta closed the shop and sat inside, waiting for the wind to subside.

"Ah, my husband, I have been longing to ask you some questions," N'tuma started. The shop was dark, but a candle gave off a faint light.

"How did you manage to know that your brother was here in Njama? He used to talk about you a lot and about how your husband was helpful to you at one stage in his life," N'tuma wondered.

# THE DIAMONDS

Miatta sat, indulging herself by eating her favorite sweet, toffee, and drinking a pint of Guinness Stout. Several variations of toffee were stored in big white bottles on top of the counter, and Miatta was always sure to try one of each. Leisurely, as she chewed, she launched into an extended explanation.

"Only luck, my wife, only luck. I always wanted to come when I heard my brother was in Sewa. I even sent Lilia to Semabu to Mama to find out if he was here. She came back and told me that Mama did not know where he was. Then there used to be all sorts of news about what might happen to people in Sewa. One day a lorry driver came asking for somebody in our town. He said he came from Sewa, that he was sent to someone, but he did not know the person who'd sent him. I helped him. In our conversation, I told him I had a brother in Sewa, but I did not know the precise town he was living in. My wife, you will not believe me. The man said he knew my brother very well and that at one time he had made a delivery of money to Mama at Semabu. He called Mama's name. I jumped with joy. He then told me the name of the town. Could you believe it? He gave me two pounds that very day. That was how I found my brother." This was her version of the story and she smiled at the supposedly joyous luck of finding her brother.

"What did you do with your house?" N'tuma asked.

"I sold it. It was leaking all over."

The rain and wind continued outside. Some children were making noise out in the rain as they washed and played.

"You don't plan on going anywhere, do you?" N'tuma continued.

Miatta smiled. "Where can I go? I have brought all my things. Unless I get a husband, I will stay with my brother."

N'tuma smiled, gladly accepting Miatta as a new companion and friend. She did not want to be alone. Miatta provided comradeship and confidence that she needed so badly. N'tuma remembered being happier with Alhaji's co-mates, a total of seven wives, but without the friction and envy that Gibao's wives brought with them.

"You are lucky you don't have to be in the kitchen," Miatta remarked. She looked around to make sure no one overheard her.

"Ah! My husband, when I was with Alhaji, that was my lot. We used to cook separately for the workers," N'tuma explained. "We used to cook for your brother's group. That was how I met him. But, that was when everything was different. When he had made money, there were always hired women who cooked for the household."

Miatta moved her jaws quickly, chewing the toffee candy.

"I must confess it is a difficult job. We could be in the kitchen until late at night. Sometimes, we had to take the food to the workers," N'tuma continued.

"Since I came, I have not seen you and the other co-wives much together," Miatta said as her eyes glanced about for any strangers.

N'tuma smiled. She came close to Miatta and whispered into her ears, "JEALOUSY! JEALOUSY!"

They both laughed, and N'tuma relaxed in her seat.

"Well, I must confess. They do not seem to care about me either," Miatta said as she chewed diligently on the toffee. She sipped her Guinness Stout. She was always used to be drinking something. Prior to the shop, she drank either the cheap local liquor or palm wine back home. It was her dependence on the bottle that made her physically and morally anemic. She came to her brother in time to be rescued from further physical and moral degeneration. "They think I have come to take away all of Gibao's money," she said.

■ ■ ■

Meanwhile, Jeneba and Lilia had become the talk of Njama. They were both teenage girls and close friends. Many visitors started flooding into Gibao's house to see Lilia. Holiday-makers

## THE DIAMONDS                                        199

were trekking to the place. The male competition was ferocious.
Many young men wrote her love letters. To try to win over Lilia,
many boys enlisted the services of Ndoleh, Jeneba's childhood
boyfriend, since he had already established a place in the house
over the past eight years. In the end, all the boys failed to attract
Lilia because she was not interested in schoolboys. They had
nothing to offer her. She had decided on the things she wanted
from men: money, good clothing, and expensive food. Boys
her own age were merely poor, glorified beggars in her eyes.
Lilia wanted diamond men.

Her cousin, Jeneba, was rather disappointed by Lilia's attitude. Jeneba was surprised that Lilia was still not yet initiated
into the secret society. She may have been the only person,
apart from Lilia's mother, who suspected that Lilia's apple had
been harvested before the right time.

Whenever Jeneba's friend Ndoleh came to visit, Lilia felt
uncomfortable in their presence because the other two spoke
about books, comic, magazines, the news from Freetown, and
such things that were of no interest to Lilia. Lilia wanted to
hear about the latest cowboy film, the next party or dance and
the latest news in women's fashions. Lilia eventually began to
avoid Jeneba and Mustapha and to go to Njama on her own,
instead of sitting uncomfortably in their presence and listening
to their conversation.

One day Jeneba told Ndoleh that she had seen her cousin,
Lilia, with an expensive gold watch. She wondered where Lilia
got the watch. Certainly, Jeneba's father Gibao could not have
bought it for her. In time, the other two came to ascertain that
Lilia had a Lebanese boyfriend. What depressed Jeneba was that
Lilia's mother knew about all Lilia's activities and might have
even been a willing accomplice in their design and execution.
So much the worse for her aunt Miatta, who was hoping to
marry Lilia off to some rich man in Njama.

"I see that you are concerned about your cousin," Ndoleh
once remarked to Jeneba.

"Yes, because she is my cousin. We are related by blood. One must be concerned about one's relatives. It is family. As the people say, a family tree may bend, but it never breaks. I think Lilia would be happier if she were at school. But never mind." Jeneba added.

"Yes. You're right, " Ndoleh said. He had his usual pint of Vimto cordial beside him. "But, why is she not at school?"

"Honestly, I don't know. All I know is that her father is alive and doing well."

Ndoleh looked at Jeneba and thought, a concerned cousin. Very few of them around these days. "Does she visit her father?" he asked.

"That I don't know. It is a subject I don't discuss with her. She is very sensitive about it. She almost hates her father for abandoning her mother for another woman. Isn't that painful? Maybe that is why she does not want young men her age. I'm interested in seeing how the other sisters will end up," Jeneba replied.

"Well, even I can see that Lilia wants nothing to do with students like me," Ndoleh observed.

They both laughed. As they talked, they saw Lilia in the distance, delicately holding on to an umbrella with one hand and carrying a beautiful basket in the other hand. As she came towards them, they saw that her basket was filled with Lebanese bread, salad and all sorts of fruits.

■ ■ ■

Teneh and Yebu left the house on their way to the market. They always went to the market together. The rain continued in a steady drizzle. The roads were muddy and full of potholes. They walked by the side of the road to avoid the mud and pot-holes as much as possible. Their mutual dislike for N'tuma was now deepening and was moving toward paranoia. N'tuma's presence, coupled with her elevated status as shop-

# THE DIAMONDS 201

keeper and favorite, dashed any hopes Gibao might have had of his wives living peacefully in his household.

It was inevitable that Teneh would react negatively, and often she had to hold herself back from acting violently. The whole N'tuma affair was troubling her constantly. Teneh started eating very little and could not sleep well. She began to lose weight as a result of her own mental torture. The only thing that kept her from breaking down totally was her association with Yebu, who encouraged her. Yebu was Teneh's pillar. Teneh ended up needing Yebu more than ever. Each day their mutual dislike of N'tuma increased dramatically like spring rain. Teneh and Yebu regarded the close friendly relationship that developed between N'tuma and Miatta as part of a well-orchestrated family plot designed by Mama Yatta.

They spent the time offering greetings to the other women going to the market, until they were alone to talk more about the N'tuma affair.

"Miatta has joined hands with her mother. They are all for the new wife now," Teneh said.

Yebu fumbled with her wrapper and then laughed her usual contemptuous laugh whenever the names of N'tuma and Miatta were mentioned. "Don't you know that we Mende people like new things?" Yebu joked. "Ha! You take Miatta seriously. Wey-yah! Don't you see God has started punishing her already? See her children? They are all useless like their mother."

Teneh listened silently to this verbal attack.

"Wait. Omole is going to kill her," Yebu went on, with a tug at Teneh's arm. "But now she drinks stout. That's why she's keeping her wife's company ... to beg for stout! SSHEEORRR!" Yebu laughed.

Teneh spoke now. "To my living God, Gibao is the most ungrateful man I have ever seen. He treats us as if we have never done anything for him. Yebu, believe me. God will fight our cause. We have burned our hands, been cut by thorns, bitten by insects. We have toiled under rain and sun. But God will fight our cause. Each day we cook, I will curse his name to the fire," Teneh hissed.

However as Yebu and Teneh approached the market, they detoured to the left and went to a prearranged place to meet their boyfriends. For the next hour, the four of them would be there eating roast meat, drinking stout, and making love. The four had planned secretly to meet there three times every week.

The boyfriends were traders, smuggling diamonds on the side. They were fairly well-to-do and serious, apparently much in love with the two women, lavishly providing them with food and drink in the style of diamond smugglers.

Yebu and Teneh treasured the few hours each week with the boyfriends, from whom they derived greater physical, material and emotional satisfaction than from Gibao. They would dress beautifully and put on perfume. Gibao could not monitor his wives' movements since he had to oversee the work in the diamond fields. Yebu and Teneh continued their three visits a week, using the undercover of going to market.

■ ■ ■

One day while Ndoleh was away, the cousins, Jeneba and Lilia, teamed up to go window-shopping in Njama. Jeneba, not trusting what Lilia might do with the men in town, was cautious in her agreement to go. Lilia or Jeneba, individually, could attract attention from all the young and old men wherever they went. Lilia usually dressed purposely in a provocative fashion. Her skirts would be far above the knee, exposing her smooth, soft legs. Her pronounced breasts would be clearly visible through her puffy blouse. Men often spoke among themselves about how she provoked their appetites. Her provocations seemed to be quite deliberate.

Miatta and N'tuma as usual were in the shop. Most of the children were playing in the living room at home because it was wet outside. The two girls left for the heart of Njama.

# THE DIAMONDS

They moved from shop to shop, constantly attracting attention everywhere.

"Do you like keebe?" Lilia asked her cousin.

Jeneba thought keebe was a type of dress or shoes.

"Hey, so you don't know keebe?" Lilia teased.

"You don't expect me to know everything, do you?" Jeneba replied.

"Keebe is a Lebanese food. It's like stuffed cake. The difference is, this one is stuffed with meat. It's very good. You must try it. You'll like it," Lilia said excitedly.

"Lilia, how am I supposed to know about Lebanese food? I might know it if it was food from this country. But, Lebanese food?" Jeneba asked with a smile.

"Would you like to taste it?" Lilia continued.

"Yes," Jeneba answered to appease Lilia.

"We'll get some today, Jeneh" Lilia promised.

Jeneba listened quietly.

"Do you notice anything in the house?" Lilia asked with feigned innocence.

"Like what?"

"About uncle's wives...N'tuma seems isolated," Lilia remarked.

"I wouldn't say so," Jeneba replied. It was a white lie, but Jeneba was afraid of offering an obvious agreement. She suspected Lilia might say the wrong thing to someone else later. "Teneh and Yebu are overworked, but cooking is like that. All the same, I feel sorry for them."

Lilia thought about Jeneba's reply, and decided to drop the topic and indulge in the pleasures of window shopping. They walked along, ignoring the remarks of men they passed. The girls reached a well-stocked shop and went in.

Lilia went up to a Lebanese man about thirty-five years old. "This is my cousin I have been talking about," she said glancing back to Jeneba.

Jeneba stared in astonishment at the man, whom Lilia evidently knew.

"You are all beautiful in your family," the man observed as he looked from Lilia to Jeneba. "How are you, Lilia's cousin?" He was surveying Jeneba with a look that hinted that he was attracted to her. He had told Lilia that his father had a chain of such shops like this all over Sewa. He was managing this shop while his father traded for diamonds.

"I am fine," Jeneba answered.

"So, you go to school at Harford at Moyamba?"

"Yes," Jeneba answered, giving Lilia a quick glance and wondering what else she had told the man. "I go to Harford. It's a wonderful school." Jeneba looked directly at the man and asked, "Do you have sisters at Harford?" She was trying hard to remember if she had ever seen the man at her school.

"No, but I used to pass through Moyamba a couple of times. I have an uncle there," the man replied.

Jeneba did not say anything further. The shop became crowded with customers, so Lilia and Jeneba prepared to leave. The man called one of his shopboys who came immediately.

"Yes, massa?" asked the shopboy.

"Go bring de pasul," the Lebanese ordered.

The shopboy went round the corner and brought back a parcel immediately. The Lebanese man took the parcel and handed it over to Lilia with a smile. Lilia smiled in return, and the girls left.

Lilia considered the parcel her "Saturday gift," something the Lebanese man gave in exchange for enjoying Lilia's kisses and certain sexual favors. When the girls got home, Lilia unwrapped the parcel in front of the other children, her mother and N'tuma. She already knew there would be keebe inside, along with other diverse foods and candy. The other children watched as Lilia put a hot keebe into her mouth and handed another one to Jeneba. Jeneba managed to put a small bit into her mouth, but she did not like the taste or smell. She gave the rest to Lilia's two sisters. They devoured the keebe in a minute and looked at Lilia for more. Lilia felt disappointed that Jeneba did

## THE DIAMONDS

not like the keebe, so she offered Jeneba some fresh apples, which Jeneba liked much better. Lilia gave a keebe to N'tuma and offered one to her mother. N'tuma loved it, but Lilia's mother would not have any. Miatta had never liked keebe meat, and now she disliked it even more because it reminded her of her former Lebanese husband. But the mother said nothing about Lilia being given a parcel of gifts by a strange Lebanese man, and no one else made a comment.

# Chapter 21

Gibao had made an appointment to see Alpha Finoh. He had been looking forward to this appointment and considered it more important than the one he had made with Ndawa. Everyone he spoke to, including Brima, told him that Alpha Finoh was the best of all wizards in the art of divination. His predictions were considered sacred. People from all walks of life came to see him for many reasons and very few complained of being disappointed. The only complaint they had against him was that he was expensive. His charges were based on the law of supply and demand, and he never compromised on his price. Whatever his fees, his services were highly valued. Alpha Finoh had acquired a sound reputation in his profession.

Gibao's need to see Alpha Finoh had become more urgent because some time had passed since he had made any significant gem discovery. He felt that others were making finds at his expense. He could not stand being behind in the competition. He did not know whether it was God who was against him, or whether the ancestral spirits were upset, or whatever else was happening. At one stage, he even blamed his bad luck on the misbehavior of his wives. If he were still in Semabu, Gibao would have assembled the wives and asked them to confess their infidelities, because he believed that this could change his luck. But in Njama, Gibao had to approach his problems differently. He was told that others in the diamond trade, like him, were not sleeping well either.

Gibao began to worry greatly that he might be facing the end of his diamond days. The worries caused him more and more sleepless nights. They increased as the time approached

# THE DIAMONDS 207

for him to see the old diviner. The other two diviners he had consulted had given him identical information. But Finoh was their master, so for that reason he was going to see Finoh and would accept whatever he said. Gibao often had dreams of fighting with others who were trying to steal his money and gems. He was going to tell Alpha Finoh about these dreams, his nightmares, and everything else he was experiencing. The matter of how much he was going to pay Finoh did not bother Gibao. Gibao had saved money.

Gibao also worried about the near state of anarchy existing in his house. He recalled that, when he was celebrating the opening of his home, the Muslim priest who officiated at the ceremony had told the gathering that a house divided against itself could not stand. That celebration was a long time ago, but Gibao easily recalled the saying. How am I going to ensure that my house would not fall? He asked himself. Are my wives going to desert me? Will I lose my standing and my respect before my workers and others in Njama? He would also bring these issues to Alpha Finoh. The arrival of his sister had not eased his burdens. If anything, she and her daughters served to increase the tensions among the wives. Gibao could only conclude that some sinister force was behind all his problems.

At one time, Gibao had thought to call Teneh and Yebu to ask their forgiveness and bribe them each with one hundred pounds sterling. But he had dismissed this thought, thinking that Yebu would probably turn down his offer. Teneh and Yebu would probably not settle for anything other than driving N'tuma out of the house. He was sure they would not compromise. These worries gnawed at him. He could not go to his mother and grandmother to settle his domestic problems because Mama Yatta herself was not neutral in the matter. She was a target, and the wives would not be prepared to listen to her advice. Gibao saw his domestic situation depending upon the unholy alliance the wives had formed, while Satan waited for an ideal moment to sink and destroy the household boat.

Alpha Finoh's compound was fairly large. There were always numerous relatives coming and going, and there were always guests in his house. Clients who had traveled long distances and had nowhere to stay in Njama would stay with Finoh.

Finoh's own abode was separate from the main house, a round house. Visitors or clients were escorted into the main living room of his house and then were ushered into his own private meeting room. Many people would come and find friends seated waiting for their turns to be ushered in. Sometimes people would be embarrassed at meeting others they knew, because they did not want their association with Alpha Finoh to become known.

There was a time when two men, both contesting to be chief of the region, met at Finoh's place. The old man Finoh had devised a way of getting over what was certain to be an embarrassing confrontation. Two contestants for one post could not both win. Finoh charged an exorbitant sum for the particular contestant he did not think would win. That was his way of telling the man to withdraw. The man could not raise the money to pay him, and so would have to go to another Alpha man.

There was an aura of solemnity about Finoh's place. In his round house, one felt surrounded by almost supernatural forces. Alpha Finoh's art of divination permeated the whole environment. His house, his dress, the odor in his room, the mirrors, handkerchiefs, feathers and skulls were all manifestations of his trade. They all played a part to ensure that his supernatural powers were efficacious. The room where he consulted with his customers was like a holy sanctuary. The room's talisman decorations intimidated any who remained skeptical of his powers.

Before Gibao entered Alpha Finoh's sanctuary, he took off his shoes. This was the rule. Alpha Finoh was seated on a beautiful carpet, a gift from a client who had brought it to Finoh after

# THE DIAMONDS 209

making a pilgrimage to the Holy City of Mecca. Finoh sat with his legs lamely crossed as if he were practising the art of Yoga. Gibao was surveying the room, gathering in its spiritual aura, so as to feel confident before the Alpha man. But his heart pounded with excitement, and he fumbled nervously at his hair. This encounter could not but enable him to achieve his long held ambition to become a diamond tycoon.

Alpha Finoh was as calm as still water. "You say you live here and prospect in diamonds?" he asked.

"Yes, Kaamoh, teacher," Gibao answered. "I have lived here for some time now. I was working for Alhaji Jimoh before I started my own business."

"Eah! Jimoh is my friend. Ask him. He knows me well. I have known him from the time he himself started in the business."

"Kaamoh, who doesn't know who you are?" Gibao observed, smiling.

In the next few minutes, the old man took time to name several characters whom he claimed he had helped into prominence, both socially and financially. "What is your name?" he asked.

"Gibao Semabu."

"And your mother's name?"

"She is called Yatta."

"I know what your problem is. You diamond men, it is always the same."

Gibao felt relieved he did not have to go through a long explanation of his hopes and fears.

Alpha Finoh took out a fat book written in Arabic. It was bound in animal skin supported by strings. Finoh opened the book and appeared to concentrate all his thoughts deeply into what he was reading. "Your father is dead, not so?"

Gibao was impressed. The old man told him many things that were revealing. Gibao stared at Alpha Finoh in astonishment.

"My son," Alpha Finoh said slowly as a start to new revelations.

Gibao looked on alertly. He could not afford to miss one word.

"You have a bright future."

Gibao opened his eyes wider and sat stock still at this pronouncement of good fortune.

"One of the brightest I have seen for a long time," Finoh said with confidence. "I like to help young men because of their future. I am now an old man, but I have sixteen children. Who knows tomorrow?" the old man asked.

Gibao was happy.

"You have two genies behind you. We have to get rid of the bad one. Then, we have to appease the good one." There was a moment of silence. "A big sacrifice! You understand? A big sacrifice!"

Gibao listened intently.

"After the sacrifice, seven days later you will come to me full of happiness. Your name will be mentioned in this town for weeks," the old man predicted.

Gibao felt like jumping up and down. "Kaamoh, anything you say! I am ready. I need your help!" Gibao exclaimed as his body relaxed.

"Let me tell you. You may have heard. The whole project is one thousand pounds sterling. That is for the work I am doing. You give me five hundred pounds sterling, then I start the work. When you get what you want, you come and give me the rest. As for the sacrifice, it is two thousand pounds sterling. The cost of the sacrifice is not negotiable. It involves several people. If you can provide all the items—the knife and shovels—then you can go ahead without my help. Then you don't have to pay the other five hundred pounds to me. I can tell you who to see and where to go. It is left for you to decide."

The *sacrifice*, Gibao understood from its high cost, could only be human sacrifice. Gibao considered the cost. That was

# THE DIAMONDS 211

no problem. All he wanted was to ensure his shining success in the diamond fields. He looked around, impressed once again that this man could appeal to the spirits to help ease the conflicts in his home and ensure his success. "Kaamoh, everything is left to you. I will give you the money," Gibao agreed.

"The sacrifice has to be performed when the first cock crows," Alpha Finoh pronounced.

"Yes, I think I know that," Gibao answered.

Finoh was now carefully closing his big book. "Let us finish this assignment, and you will see the results," he assured Gibao.

Gibao was satisfied. The machinery was set in motion. Gibao remained itchy and expectant from then on, to improve his prospecting and the circumstances of his household. Already, he was imagining himself as one of the big tycoons in Njama. He would direct all his energy and time to becoming this tycoon. He left Finoh's place beaming with confidence. The die was cast in his favor, and for him there was no turning back.

# Chapter 22

Gibao and his workers were to start prospecting in a new plot he had recently acquired. His workers had embarked on the laborious task of clearing it by cutting shrubs, felling trees and removing the stumps. In the process, they accidentally discovered that there were several graves in the plot, which had evidently been plowed under. One of the graves was marked with the name Mana Kposowa. Other workers around the sites became curious about the graves. Gibao became worried about the discovery. Who were these dead people? Would they pose a problem for him? He put aside his concerns and instructed the workers to continue preparing to mine the whole site with such thoroughness as to leave "no stone unturned." The remains were moved to a new site and buried. Among them was the remains of Kposowa, one of the unlucky victims of the diamond boom.

No one knew who had inhabited the other graves, their stories were buried with them. The diamond adventurers came from all walks of life, but farmers formed the majority of them. These adventurers were men and women who left their towns and families to go off to work in Sewa. Nothing in the world had a more dynamic or magnetic force than the quest for money, the urge to get rich quick. Money to these workers was the sum total of human existence. Their own world was dominated by the prospect of acquiring as much as possible of the things that money could bring. It was a world where the acquisition of money took priority over the quest for the spiritual. It came down to the basic logic of wilful acquisition: the diamond logic. It was a force. Just as gigantic forces of nature formed the

# THE DIAMONDS                                    213

diamonds, so other gigantic social and greedy forces shaped
the lives of the people who sought the diamonds. These forces
took people beyond normal reasoning, and especially Gibao
who thought diamond wealth was automatically his for the
taking, as if his future were already fated that way.

The boom continued in Njama and other parts of Sewa.
Every day people would hear names of prospectors who had
hit the jackpot. These successes were evident in the way Njama
was booming with money coming from all directions and
from all kinds of people involved in prospecting, stealing, and
smuggling. People who hit the big money found ways to live
in garish and reckless opulence. Horrible accidents such as pits
collapsing and burying people increased tenfold in the rainy
season, but had no apparent effect on the rabid pursuit of
more and more diamonds. Gibao was an active participant in
this social wave with a growing desire to make even more
money. Greed begat more greed.

■ ■ ■

One evening, when the night had a dark charcoal thickness
where people could not identify each other, N'tuma and Gibao
went to visit Bintu, knowing that they would meet N'dora and
Brima there. When they arrived at Bintu's, as expected they
found N'dora and Brima relaxing with Bintu and everyone
already in a happy mood.

Gibao had cause to be happy after his visit to the Alpha-man.
He thought himself as a soon-to-be wealthy man in Njama. As
soon as he achieved this status, he intended to buy a Bedford
lorry to take his daughter, Jeneba, to the Christian school, a
secret ambition he had held for a long time. There was jubilation as the five friends reunited. N'dora and N'tuma embraced
each other and remembered their roles as co-wives and partners
in infidelity.

"It is a long time since we saw each other," N'dora said,

smiling at N'tuma. The last time they had seen each other was when N'tuma had left on the lorry to go back to her parents.

"Ah, N'dora, you are looking so good and well," N'tuma remarked.

"My sister, it is Brima who takes good care of me," N'dora said with a broad smile.

N'dora realized something had changed. "N'tuma, you have lost weight? Why, Gibao?"

"Maybe the new married life does not suit her," Bintu interrupted in jest.

"Don't say that Bintu," N'dora said.

"My sister, this marriage is not easy for me. Too much jealousy. My mind is not at rest. How can I put on weight?" N'tuma explained, seriously.

"I hope it will end soon. See? Your good features have all changed. See how prominent your collar bones are now? Isn't it a shame," N'dora lamented, sounding full of pity. "Gibao, you should do something about my sister. You know she was not like that when we were together. Please try and do something," N'dora implored Gibao.

Gibao smiled. "You just wait. I know what I have planned. It will not be long. I'm going to kick the whole lot of them out. I know what is happening in my house. I shall clean it out thoroughly. If they don't want N'tuma, it is they who will have to pack up and go away," Gibao's voice was determined as he spoke, making N'tuma smile.

Brima intervened. "No, no, no, Gibao! You can't say that. Think of God. You can't! You should be able to bring peace without such drastic action. Remember, whatever happens, they are the wives you have had before you and N'tuma met. They cannot help being jealous of N'tuma. Wouldn't you have been the same if you were in their position? Please, let us think about tomorrow, not today."

"Yes, you want to be their lawyer, not so?" N'tuma asked aggressively.

# THE DIAMONDS 215

"Bintu, warn Gibao," Brima responded. "I am saying this because, like Gibao, I also have sisters."

"Listen, Brima, if you want to talk case, go to the police," N'tuma said.

"N'tuma, you have to realize that we all favored your marriage to Gibao, but for goodness sake imagine yourself in their position. Imagine yourself," Brima pleaded.

"Bo, lef me, wetin na de tin, what is the issue?" N'tuma lashed out at Brima.

Gibao listened. He was enjoying the give and take as a man confident of his future. Bintu supported what her brother was saying, but refused to endorse it verbally. However, she did not like N'tuma's hardness of heart and unreasonableness.

"Misef bin de kuk if na dat, le dem leave wi do, I used to cook too, what's the big deal, leave us alone." N'tuma continued without mercy. Her selfishness and disregard for her co-mates was not understandable to the others, except to Gibao.

"How is work, Gibao? When are you going to make the next hit?" Bintu asked, turning the conversation away from this unhappy topic. The issue of the co-wives was apparently too hot to handle.

"I shall make it soon!" Gibao shouted with overflowing confidence, although he had not told anyone about his visits to the Alpha-man.

"It is said that Alie, Buya and Mulai have left. I feel so sorry," N'dora said.

"Ah, my sister, even I was sorry the day they came to say goodbye to us in the house," N'tuma replied. "But, they had all said they would leave after a year. They are lucky. They are among the few who made a decision and kept to it."

N'dora promised that night that she would visit N'tuma at the shop before Alhaji came back from his trips. The rain was falling steadily by the time Gibao and N'tuma left late. Gibao held the umbrella with his left hand and his torch in the other. N'tuma held him around the waist so as to fit herself under the umbrella. They appeared to be the perfect image of a loving couple.

"I don't like Brima's attitude," N'tuma said. She seemed not to have recovered from Brima's spell and feared his remonstrances might have had an effect on Gibao.

She wanted a peaceful household without jealousies, and could not conceive of any reconciliation with her co-wives in the immediate future. Gibao's pronouncement that he would cleanse the house of any troublesome wives sounded like good news since it was her co-mates who had started all the animosity.

"Yes, Brima always thinks he's wiser. That was the complaint we all had against him. One might think he would have changed by now. But, don't mind him. He was just bluffing. When I am ready for action, I don't have to consult him for approval." Gibao leaned over to keep himself under the umbrella.

Once N'tuma heard Gibao's last comment, she concluded that her situation was temporary. She felt grateful that N'dora had brought up the topic. She wished that Gibao would act soon to rid the house of the fighting dogs. If Gibao wanted to marry more wives after dismissing his co-wives, N'tuma promised Gibao on the way home that she would recruit the new wives for him. Her plan would be to avoid recruiting any enemies. N'tuma smiled in the rain, thinking about these upcoming changes in the house. Gibao and N'tuma arrived back home when everybody else was asleep, and they went to bed and enjoyed making love.

■ ■ ■

N'tuma's mother had been ill for sometime. The illness was becoming more serious. Because of a sudden change for the worse, it was decided to send for N'tuma. Tewoh was to take a letter to N'tuma and inform her about her mother's condition.

Tewoh was about fifteen years old and had been initiated into the secret society, but she was found out not to be a virgin.

# THE DIAMONDS          217

Her loss of innocence was the cause of her mother falling ill, mostly because Tewoh's and N'tuma's father constantly badgered and blamed the mother for Tewoh's moral transgression. Tewoh and the mother had brought irreparable shame on the family, the father would say, and he could not live happily with what he considered a defilement of the family name and reputation. And this, in addition to the disaster of N'tuma's marriage to Alhaji. Tewoh had not met Gibao before because she had been away at school in Mongereh when he had come to pay the bride price for N'tuma.

Tewoh was pretty and fair in complexion. It was this very girl that Mustapha had half wanted to marry. He was always asking N'tuma when Tewoh would come to visit. Tewoh had never been to Njama nor had she traveled such a long distance before. But she was an intelligent girl, so she was chosen to take the letter to N'tuma about their mother. Leaving her mother bedridden and gravely ill, she wept bitterly, afraid that she would not see her alive by the time she came back with her sister from Njama. Luckily, she was able to get a direct lorry from Bo to Njama. It was a Bedford lorry with the inscription "YOU NEVER KNOW TOMORROW."

When Tewoh left for Njama, she was told by the lorry driver that the easiest way to contact N'tuma was to find Alhaji Jimoh's house and ask there for N'dora, who would then direct her to N'tuma. The rains were heavy and the roads were dangerously bad. The lorry had constant engine troubles on the way. By the time Tewoh arrived in Njama, it was about 2 A.M. on a Sunday morning. It was a time when virtually everybody was asleep. The rain was pouring heavily.

Tewoh and all the other passengers got off the lorry after a long, tiresome trip, but they were quite wet from the persistent rain that was still falling. She had on a light blouse and a lappa. Because the fabric was so wet and clung to her body, the contours of her breasts were prominently displayed. She shivered as she started looking around for where to start her search.

A man approached her and asked her if he could help. She told him she was looking for the house of Alhaji Jimoh. The man told her that he was one of the workers of Alhaji and knew where Alhaji lived. There would be no problem getting there. The man called over two others to assist with her portmanteau, and he even paid her fare to the driver. Tewoh shivered from the cold but followed the men as they headed towards Alhaji's home. The only light they had was a torch that one of the men carried in his hand in front of the procession.

■ ■ ■

Gibao left N'tuma in bed that morning a couple of hours before the sun rose. She was still sleeping and did not notice his absence. Whenever she had some alcohol in her system, she would sleep a long time because the alcohol affected her like sleeping pills. Gibao took with him two of his four workers, Mustapha and Kaanja. The workers knew no one could leave for diamond digging this early, unless he wanted to steal someone else's gravel, and this they thought was the purpose of their early start. It was not considered wrong to steal gravel, as long as nobody got caught. Stealing anything, especially gravel that held diamonds, and getting away with the theft was all part of the game played out in Sewa by both the workers and the diamond bosses.

Mustapha and Kaanja trudged along in the darkness behind their boss Gibao. They were going through a forest bordered by a large swamp which was rumored to contain rich deposits of diamonds. The swamp was yet to be allocated for any prospecting, though people made occasional forays into the swamp land to dig, in spite of the strict security measures. The forest at night was totally silent. Nature seemed to be fast asleep, but creatures of the night were silently at work.

Suddenly the three men met up with Alpha Finoh, who was already at the appointed place. Mustapha and Kaanja were

# THE DIAMONDS

made to take an oath, which was administered by the Alpha-man. They were to be entrusted to keep a secret, and they swore in the name of their secret societies. The oath would have to be kept or they would face certain death, the Alpha-man gravely warned them. Then, Mustapha and Kaanja heard a distant sound which they couldn't identify at first. It turned out to be the sound of the first cock crow echoing in the forest. The four of them walked nearer to the swamp and there they were joined by three other men, unknown to Mustapha and Kaanja. No one greeted one another. They behaved exactly like people going to steal diamond gravel. They talked only in whispers.

Mustapha and Kaanja were curious and wondering what it was all about. If it was gravel they had really come to steal, how could they do so without any containers to put the diamonds in? How come Gibao had chosen to bring only two of them while the others slept? Why had Gibao not informed them about it earlier? Then they heard the second cock crow. They were made to walk a short distance, and in great haste. Finally, they all arrived at their destination.

Without wasting time, Alpha Finoh pointed the torch at an object. It was lying there wrapped in white cloth. It was not a pile of diamond gravel. The object was the corpse of Tewoh, the sister of Gibao's wife, N'tuma. The three men were those who had led her from the lorry park when she came from Bo to deliver the letter to N'tuma about her mother's serious illness. They had made Tewoh the *sacrifice* of a virgin that Gibao had planned with Alpha Finoh in order to secure his success in his diamond fields.

Alpha Finoh knelt down and carefully examined the body, like a pathologist performing a postmortem, while Gibao held the torch. His examination took a long time. Then he stood up and, with a grim face, he announced that the sacrificial lamb had not met the elementary requirement of the ritual. The dead girl was not a virgin. Something had gone wrong. The sacrifice had failed. Gibao's blood ran cold. Time was running out with the coming dawn, but Gibao's thoughts were only on the threat to his success in the diamond fields. Gibao suggested to Alpha Finoh that the men look for another sacrificial lamb even at this early hour. The three men who had brought Tewoh were delighted because that meant another contract for them. That was how they made their money, delivering such sacrificial lambs to a select few customers of the Alpha-man. But not immediately. By now it was well past even the second cock crew. Alpha Finoh and Gibao decided to meet again to make sure that the next sacrifice would not fail.

Mustapha looked at the corpse with a frown. It looked very much like someone he knew all too well. The resemblance was too perfect, no two people could look exactly alike, unless they were identical twins. He looked around, but did not say a word for fear that he would be killed on the spot if he admitted to knowing the girl. But he vowed he would do something about this. He would have no part of this type of sacrifice. How could one spill so much innocent blood just to get rich? He felt like crying, and the hair rose at the back of his neck. But for the moment he had to hide his reactions.

Kaanja had heard about such sacrifices even before he came to Sewa. But he had never thought he would be asked to be present at one of them. If Gibao had told him earlier that he was bringing them for that purpose, he would have flatly refused to come. He would not be involved in blood money. Despite the oath to secrecy that they had taken, Kaanja was prepared to give evidence against Gibao and the others if they were caught.

That morning all seven men helped bury Tewoh in the swamp. The three strangers left Njama temporarily, waiting to be summoned again by Alpha Finoh and Gibao for a second virgin. Gibao took his men home to join his other workers for breakfast. He had no knowledge that he had been a party to killing his wife's sister. Mustapha was the only one who knew the truth.

# Chapter 23

■ ■ ■ ■ ■ ■ ■ ■ ■

Alpha Finoh had been in this divination profession, as he claimed, for over twenty years and in Njama for a longer time. He had practiced his profession all over Sewa and all types of people of high social standing knew him. He was revered by many and feared by others, since he could predict or break their fortunes. However, he could not recall anytime during his professional practice when he had gone wrong. That was why he was baffled by the recent fiasco of Gibao's situation. After he and Gibao hired the three men to carry out the sacrificial mission, he had divined that, whoever the hired men were, they would be right for the sacrifice. He had done this several times before and it had always proved right. The case with this young girl proved to be different. She was not the right creature because she was not a virgin. This mistake tormented Alpha Finoh greatly. How could he, Finoh the master of masters, make such a mistake at such a crucial moment?

Had Finoh's plan worked out as anticipated, he was convinced that within seven days of carrying out the necessary rituals, Gibao would be the talk of the town. His client would make a wonderful diamond find. Finoh had planned to give Gibao a special talisman that he would tie around Gibao's waist and Finoh would give him incantations to recite at the diamond site, after which everything would be all right. Gibao would hit the jackpot. Finoh had informed Gibao about these plans. Gibao had believed Finoh and remained expectant about what was to come.

Mustapha felt saddened all day. Nothing could change his

thinking that the dead body was not Tewoh. He just could not comprehend the reason for the butchery and the senselessness of the whole act.

Kaanja, while he did not know Tewoh as a person, viewed the whole incident with utter disgust and pity. The idea of human sacrifice for wealth or power was something he found distant, unreal. He knew that in his own home town people used to disappear occasionally. But the situation at home was different, radically different, Kaanja thought. There the spirits of the river and of the forest were in the habit of demanding fealty from the community as a whole. It was only when the community disregarded the spirits that the spirits would demand retribution. Thus, a member of the community would drown or be missing in the forest, as the sacrifice to the spirits. This was a community affair and everyone knew what would happen. But he could not recall individuals resorting to such a brutal sacrificial murder with an Alpha-man as he had witnessed, just so as to ensure someone's diamond wealth.

How could Gibao, a man who had told them some time ago about his disgust and dislike for the callous attitudes of people towards the dead, engage in the same thing he had condemned? Gibao had at one time told his workers about Ndoinjeh's death, and also about another terrible incident where a man had disemboweled a boy because he suspected the boy had stolen and swallowed his diamonds. Gibao had vehemently disapproved of such behavior and actions. How could Gibao now participate in what he once hated? What had happened to Gibao in Njama? Kaanja wondered.

That very morning Gibao and his four workers went to work. Gibao showed no sense of remorse. Mustapha felt weak and tired by the hour, exhausted by the sadness of the truth. He tried to conceal his emotion by not talking to the others.

By lunchtime, Mustapha took a break. He went to inform the police about the morning's event. He was promised a pardon at the conclusion of the case in return for his cooperation.

# THE DIAMONDS

The police officers went straight to the diamond pit in search of Gibao. When he could not be found, they went to the shop and started talking to N'tuma.

"Mrs, where is your husband?" one officer asked N'tuma.

"He is not around. He came from work and went out again," N'tuma answered.

"Where did he go?"

"Well, he never tells me where he is going or when he is returning," she answered.

The police waited inside Gibao's compound for his return. They were waiting unobtrusively for Gibao, but their police van was clearly visible and it drew a crowd of idlers to the veranda. Gibao's mother and grandmother rested in the living room. Lilia and Jeneba were out in the town. Manu, Yebu and Teneh were at work in the kitchen.

"Ah! That is him coming," someone on the veranda hollered.

Gibao had spotted the crowd at his house and he wondered what was happening. He never thought that his complicity in the ghastly *sacrifice* was the real concern. He approached his house feeling confident that the assemblage of people had nothing to do with him. In fact, he had just come from Alpha Finoh to design another mission that would secure another *sacrifice*.

"How are you, Mr. Gibao?" the police inspector asked politely.

"I am very well," Gibao replied.

"Please, we want to talk to you. Accompany us to the station," the inspector said firmly.

Gibao did not argue. He merely told N'tuma he would be back soon. He entered the police van and was driven off.

The gossip was that they must have taken Gibao away in connection with a diamond theft. Everybody on the veranda came to that conclusion. Diamond thefts and such arrests were a common thing in Sewa. Maybe someone was trying to implicate him.

Maybe it is the Lebanese dealer trying to implicate my

husband, N'tuma worried as she stood watching the van disappear.

The gossip continued to swirl around N'tuma. Maybe he was taken away in connection with his residence permit in Sewa, one man suggested. Maybe he refused to renew his shop permit, another man suggested. New theories and suggestions kept appearing. The only person who knew the truth was Mustapha, but he remained silent on the veranda. At one point, N'tuma thought she had hit on the answer. She thought that Alhaji and another man had finally succeeded in plunging Gibao into trouble for the divorce. N'tuma vowed to the others that Alhaji would not succeed. Even though she was a young woman, N'tuma said, she would go to Alhaji and warn him that his plot to hurt Gibao would not succeed.

"I am going to see the top men in the police station and kill the case!" N'tuma angrily bellowed. "Why is Alhaji still pursuing us to our destruction?" N'tuma was confident she could divert Alhaji's anger away from Gibao.

When Gibao's mother learned about her son's trip to the police station, she asked N'tuma to leave Miatta in the shop and accompany her to the station. Mama Yatta, like some others in the country, never took police matters lightly. She worried herself into such a state of anxiety that she was perspiring in the cold air.

Mama Yatta and N'tuma entered a crowded police station. The police officers would not let them see Gibao and they never gave any explanation as to why they were detaining Gibao. The two women reluctantly gave up and returned home to wait for Gibao's release.

Gibao was being held in an interview room. The police investigators planned to ask him questions all night if necessary or until he confessed.

"Your name is Gibao?" one officer asked him.

"Yes," Gibao responded confidently.

"You have been living here for long?" the other officer asked.

# THE DIAMONDS 225

"Yes, for about four years," Gibao replied.

"You have a permit to reside here?"

"Yes."

"Where do you come from?"

"From Semabu in Moyamba District."

"You are married?"

"Yes, I have four wives and six children."

Gibao answered the questions respectfully but proudly. He was sure that the policemen knew nothing about the sacrifice, which he knew to be a capital crime. He refused to let his thoughts dwell on what had happened that morning.

"How old are you, Mr. Gibao?"

"Ah, I do not know when I was born, no paper."

"But you can guess approximately how old you are, like most of us. I myself don't know the time I was born, but, if you were born when they farmed a bush, you should be able to know how many times since your birth that same bush has been farmed."

"I think about forty years."

"Mr. Gibao, I want to know, where were you this morning at the time the first cock was crowing?"

There was silence from Gibao. He feared for the first time they might know something, but he wasn't going to give anything away.

"I mean by four o'clock this morning, to be precise, Mr. Gibao."

There was silence from Gibao.

"Mr. Gibao, I have many things to attend to. You are not the only person in this station. You have been answering all the questions I put to you quite clearly. Do you now want to say you don't know where you slept?"

"In my house."

"Are you sure Mr. Gibao, or are you trying to play tricks," the inspector asked more aggressively.

Gibao eyed the inspector and observed his stern look.

"You were sleeping with who?"

"With my wife."

"Mr. Gibao, are you sure that by four o'clock this morning you were sleeping in your house? When the first cock was crowing, you were in your house?"

Gibao nodded yes, though he knew it was a lie.

"Do you know that old Alpha-man down the road?"

"Yes."

Gibao was jolted into the growing awareness that the police may be after him directly as well as the Alpha-man. His stomach grew nauseated and his bowels weakened. He asked to use the toilet. He was granted permission, but he was accompanied by a police officer.

"These people can be wicked," the inspector sighed to his companion as they waited for Gibao to return. "Here is a man with children, and he may actually be murdering someone else's child."

"If they are guilty, Justice Wyse will ensure justice," the other inspector responded.

Gibao returned to the room accompanied by the officer and the interrogation continued.

"I hope you now have all the answers to the other questions I am going to put to you. I hope you have thought about these questions while you were in the toilet. You are all right now, I gather," the one inspector said in a slightly mocking tone.

Gibao looked back solemnly.

"How did you get to know this Alpha-man?"

"We are just friends."

"When did you last see him?"

It was another painful question. He knew his answer might differ from what the Alpha-man might say. There were some questions that would reveal his lies, but Gibao chose not to answer.

"Mr. Gibao, I am suggesting to you that you and your Alpha-man were together somewhere at around four o'clock this morning, right? Near the swamp to be specific."

# THE DIAMONDS

Gibao took a deep breath. He felt like breaking down. He was being presented with the grim reality that the police already knew what he had done. He feared saying another word. He and the inspector looked into each other's eyes. The inspector knew there was a dead body. All he needed was the truth from those who committed the crime.

"Constable, please have him handcuffed and taken into custody."

For the first time in his life, Gibao felt the humiliation of being handcuffed and observed by people giving him accusatory looks as if he were a criminal.

Gibao slept in a prison cell that night. It began to dawn on him that he had brought shame on his name, his mother and grandmother, his wives and children, and his house. At five o'clock in the morning he was woken up and driven to the Alpha-man's house, in the company of the same police inspector who had arrested him, together with two of his assistants. The three policemen left Gibao in the van and went inside to talk to the Alpha-man.

The Alpha-man was saying his morning prayers inside his round hut. The officers waited outside until he had finished. Because they were in plainclothes, the Alpha-man thought they were clients, so he hastened to finish his prayers and invite them into his hut.

"Alpha, we want to talk to you, but not here," one inspector said.

What does the man mean by saying we want to talk to you but not here? He must be out of his mind talking to an elderly man like that, Alpha Finoh thought to himself. "Come into my room," Alpha Finoh ordered.

"Alpha, we want to see you at the police station. The van is outside your house. Please come with us," another inspector said firmly.

Alpha Finoh realized they were not customers. He closed his hut and came out to see the police van waiting. He was not unduly worried. He told the policeman that he would drive behind them in his Mercedes-Benz. The inspector did not agree to this. Finoh thought it strange that he was not allowed to drive himself. He walked to the van and tried to get into the front seat next to the driver. The inspector told him he had to ride in the back of the van instead. Alpha Finoh stood silent and stiff, with his prayer beads in his hands.

"You don't respect old age. You are telling me to sit at the back while you sit in the front. Ah! The children of today," Alpha Finoh complained as he took small steps towards the back of the van.

There were a few in Finoh's household who were awake to see him being taken away in the police van. He had never been in a police van before and they gave puzzled looks to each other about why the police should take him away before he had had his breakfast.

The driver started the engine. The door was opened and the inspectors helped Finoh up and in. He had on a long robe and a round white hat. He was fumbling with his spectacles, when he saw Gibao seated in the darkness in the back of the van and in handcuffs. The old man almost collapsed on the floor of the vehicle. He suspected immediately that the police must have learnt about the *sacrifice*. The inspectors monitored the old man's reactions. Gibao and Alpha Finoh barely looked at each other, and remained silent. The policeman knew something was wrong when these two "friends" had nothing to say to each other. Gibao's silence conveyed the same message as if he was saying, "We have had it."

By the time they reached the police station, the Alpha-man had realized that their "sacrifice" was no longer a secret. The Alpha-man was thinking he would be given a rough time until he confessed. He decided it was time to save himself. He had spent his life purporting to help others, now he should help himself out of this mess.

The inspectors took Alpha Finoh into the same room where

# THE DIAMONDS 229

Gibao had been interviewed. Finoh knew it was time to answer a lot of questions.

"Alpha, do you know Mr. Gibao?"

Alpha Finoh felt nervous. He trembled with anxiety.

"Yes."

"How long have you lived in Njama?"

"I was born here. This is my town."

"Alpha, where were you yesterday at about four o'clock in the morning when the first cock was crowing?"

There was a long silence. Alpha Finoh was looking in the policeman's face.

"Bo big man lek me na in una de ask den kayn question de? ("You ask a big man like myself such questions?")"

"Pa, dis not big man bizness, dis na di law."

"I was in bed," Finoh said, simply.

"You, Gibao, Mustapha, Kaanja and three others were in bed?" one inspector asked incredulously.

There was dead silence as the inspector waited patiently for the Alpha-man's answer.

"Ah, my son, the world has changed. I can't understand how you can ask an elderly man like myself where I was at that hour. I should be in my house and in bed, an old man like myself."

The inspectors decided not to ask any more questions. Mustapha had already provided information about the location of the crime to the police, so they drove Gibao and Alpha Finoh to the scene and gave them two shovels for the task of exhuming the corpse. After their digging was completed, Gibao and Alpha Finoh were taken back to the police station where they were both questioned again in separate rooms.

"Mi pikin den, du ya una help wi. Le big man den no disgrace ("My children, please help us. Don't let a big man be humiliated.")," Alpha Finoh said to the police inspectors.

"Wi go arenj una, una du ya ("We shall give you something in return.")," he pleaded more.

Three inspectors led Alpha Finoh into the room where Gibao waited.

"Alpha-man," the inspector said firmly. "You are said to be able to perform miracles. This is the time for you to save yourself."

"Pa, if you can save others, why can't you save yourself?" the other inspector taunted.

"Pa, if it was your daughter that was killed, how would you feel?" the third inspector asking, trying to make the old man talk.

Alpha Finoh sat stock still and silent.

"Who is your head man in this office?" Alpha Finoh asked.

"Pa, from all we know, the only person who can help you in this case has left. He has been transferred. Now, there is a very strict and upright man, Justice Wyse. He would never sell justice. I can assure you of that," one inspector told the Alpha-man.

Alpha Finoh was silent. He started thinking. He wondered if he knew this Justice Wyse. Did Justice Wyse know him? Would he be allowed to go back to his house until the day of the trial? He wondered how he could get back home. If he could only gain access to his house, he was convinced he could use his esoteric powers to kill the case. Perhaps, by the time the day of judgment came, Justice Wyse would be dead and this would drive fear into other judges who might want to try him and his accomplices. That was the only window of opportunity left now, the exercise of his powers. He had assured Gibao about this last possibility for their survival. It had become a matter of life and death now, for them and their accomplices.

# Chapter 24

■ ■ ■ ■ ■ ■ ■ ■ ■

Nature had taken offense at Tewoh's death. That was why the sun disappeared that day behind huge clouds that threatened a massive downpour.

By midday, Njama was saturated with the news that Gibao, Alpha Finoh and five others were charged with the murder of a fifteen year old girl. Mustapha and Kaanja had also been arrested.

Gibao was told that morning by an inspector that the murdered girl was his in-law, the sister of N'tuma, his wife. The letter, which the girl had brought to say that their mother was ill, was found in her pocket. The inspector read it to him. Gibao could say nothing. He only wept as he realized how much his crime had affected his household.

N'tuma was driven by the police to the station to identify the body. The sight of her sister's body sent her into a faint. For three days, N'tuma remained dazed and in a stupor.

Gibao and Alpha Finoh remained in custody. It was very late at night when Gibao woke up. The room was bare, except for a bucket as his toilet. He lived in that room with the smell of his own urine and feces. He was forced to accept these conditions, no matter how rich he was. He was now a confessed murderer and he had to share the prison conditions of every murderer.

Gibao sat on the bare floor trying to focus his thoughts amidst the stench and dirt of his cell. There was only one small crack in the wall that allowed in some breathable air. He got up and looked through the crack. He would have given up his riches to pass through it and start life over again in Semabu.

He thought about telling the judge he would give the court all his wealth, just to be free to go back to his home village.

He could see only darkness outside. There was no way to tell what time it was. The police had taken everything from him that could be dangerous in the event he wanted to commit suicide. He got up and paced back and forth from one wall to the other. He was thinking of Ndawa, the diviner of Kpetewoma. Why had this old man not told him about this aspect of his life in the diamond fields? Ndawa must have foreseen these events, Gibao thought. Why did he say nothing?

Gibao started wishing he had listened to Kinawova's objections. Kinawova must have had a premonition about his fate in Sewa. He remembered now how vehement the old man had been. His mother had even spoken about it to him. Now, look what has happened, he thought. Gibao was experiencing what others have often learned in jail: regretting the failure to heed the advice which he had so unconcernedly refused. Gibao suddenly remembered what his late father had told him, "Never rush with life." Gibao's rush to become wealthy had led him straight to this cell.

He reflected on having lost his opportunity to go home with the money he had made. His heart filled with regret, thinking about all the things he should have done. He thought about how Buya, Alie and others knew when to leave Sewa and return home safely. Yes, people always warned about the diamonds, Gibao thought. He remembered when his friend Ndoinjeh had died and how sad that death had been for everyone. Now, he wondered what his chances were of surviving his trial. He could not stop thinking and ruminating. He thought about his wives. N'tuma must be going through hell now at the hands of her co-mates. Were the other three wives sorry about what had happened to him? He thought Manu and Teneh might be sympathetic, but not Yebu. His mother, he thought, might not be able to live through this scandal. He could see his whole household collapsing under the weight of his guilt and shame.

# THE DIAMONDS

He began to lose his connection to the outside world. He bowed his head and prayed to God for forgiveness. He told God he had sinned. He had spilled innocent blood. He had violated one of the most sacred of God's Commandments, the commandment not to kill. A voice seemed to echo it loudly in his ears. His conscience stirred. Could N'tuma ever understand the circumstances? Would she forgive him? Would she understand that the *sacrifice* was not his idea? And that he especially regretted killing Tewoh? Would she ever see that the *sacrifice* had been a desperate but poorly chosen act to improve his own life and that of his household?

Gibao wondered what the possibilities were that the case might be dismissed. From what the policemen were saying, it was not possible to buy over the judge and free himself that way. Justice Wyse, the story went, was incorruptible. Gibao could see no immediate way out and he went back praying to God for forgiveness.

The Alpha-man, like Gibao, was stripped of all materials that would be potentially harmful to him, even his prayer beads were taken away. Why was I caught this time? Finoh asked himself. He wondered who could have revealed the secret. One could not trust people so readily any more.

Like Gibao, he prayed constantly in the hope that God would forgive him. What would happen to his numerous children if he did not survive this case? What would happen to his family? Such thoughts bedeviled his brain. He did not weep in sympathy for the dead girl or for his own guilt. He believed that in the end he would be spared. But even as he sat on the dirty floor of his cell, he vowed that he would cease to practice his profession.

Gibao and Alpha Finoh had to wait in their cells while the police pursued the three hired killers throughout Sewa.

In the evening, a stranger arrived from Semabu. Unfortunately, he was unable to see Gibao. He left a message that the old man Maada had died. There was a message for Yatta also. She was to persuade her son to return to Semabu. If not, Maada had warned that their family tree would disappear in Semabu. The stranger managed to deliver that message as well.

Mama Yatta wept bitterly. She knew she had left Maada ill, but she had hoped she would return and find him well. Now, Maada was dead. She had no chance of seeing him again. Maada's prayers were no longer available to help her or to help Gibao.

The young man went back to Semabu with the terrible news about the case of Gibao's human sacrifice.

■ ■ ■

One day Gibao's mother, grandmother, Miatta and N'tuma went to the police station. They wanted permission to talk to Gibao. They had gone many times previously, but were always told to come back. On this day, they found the police station as crowded as always. There was gossip circulating in the station about another murder case, not too different from Gibao's. The four women sat down and decided they had to wait.

Back at the house, Yebu was saying to Teneh, "we are not going to suffer for nothing, who knows whether he will be free in a case like this?" Yebu and Teneh took complete command of the house. "We will share his money so that our children won't suffer," Yebu firmly suggested.

The three of them managed to enter the room where Gibao kept every penny and they pried open his money box. They removed all the money they found and took it to Manu's room where they divided it among themselves. Each one of the notes was worth hundreds of pounds sterling. Teneh and Manu thanked Yebu for what they called her wise suggestion of going after the money box.

The news about Gibao's crime continued to be the topic around Njama. His name became a household word. Kemoh and Alhaji discussed his situation at length. Alhaji boasted to Kemoh that it was his curse on Gibao for stealing his wife that had got Gibao into trouble. Other people had committed such

# THE DIAMONDS

crimes but were not caught, Alhaji boasted not only to Kemoh but also to his friends.

Ya Digba was shaken by the incident, that her favourite customer was involved in the terrible crime. "What has become of the world?" she asked her other customers, who gossiped about the news every day. "Why do this evil? Is murder the only way to secure a fortune? Look at me. I have been selling cooked food for a long time. I am not a rich tycoon, but I practice an honorable trade. Yes, people have accused me of foul practices, but in the end they always find out the accusations are false." Ya Digba's conscience was clear of any deliberate wrongdoing. At her place, Gibao's participation in the *sacrifice* was talked about as the lowest form of crime.

When Gibao finally got to see his mother, grandmother, Miatta and N'tuma, he explained to them of his involvement in the death of Tewoh. He told them the whole story, nothing but the truth. His soul and his mind had to be cleansed of any lies.

The truth did not help N'tuma. From that day on, her relationship with Mama Yatta and Miatta soured. She no longer felt part of the family and wanted nothing to do with the blood on their son's hands.

The following day N'tuma left to attend to her sick mother. She took along all her belongings, as well as Gibao's money box, which she gathered up in haste without inspecting it. She loaded it into the lorry with her other belongings. No one went with N'tuma to see her off. Mama Yatta and Miatta were the only two who wept as N'tuma's lorry left. They cried, thinking she had left with a bitter heart against Gibao and themselves.

■ ■ ■

"Good morning, saa," Miatta said to Gibao's Lebanese friend. Miatta and Mama Yatta had gone to take a message to him from Gibao. Of course he had heard about the case on the very day the news was released.

"Una monin o, una osh fo wahala, good morning, and my sympathy for your trouble," the Lebanese replied.

The women appreciated the condolence. They were emboldened to speak. "My brother has sent us to you, master," Miatta said. "He wants you to help him in this case, since you know so many important people." Miatta's voice was humble and soft.

The man was alarmed. "Listen, Mrs. I can't interfere in this case. I am a foreigner and this is an internal affair. Please, I am sorry I can't do anything." The Lebanese was afraid that his own involvement in diamond smuggling could be uncovered in the process of Gibao's trial. "You see, I also am a father. I cannot condone such things. Believe me, if he had consulted me, I would have told him not to do it. It is against God and my religion Islam to take innocent life," the Lebanese ended.

Miatta and Mama Yatta realized they could never get his help, and they left him.

In Semabu, the news about the death of Tewoh and the arrest of Gibao and the soothsayer traveled fast. The people of Gibao's village realized the terrible effects of the diamond boom, how traditions and morals were wantonly subverted by greed. Human beings, the people said, became prisoners of the diamonds and innocent lives were lost through human sacrifice because of overwhelming greed.

"I feel sick," Kemoh, an elder in Semabu, told Sahr, another elder, as they discussed what had happened to Gibao. "It is hard to believe. That Gibao can come to this!"

"I understand, Kemoh. I feel the same way. I do not know how to react to the news. It is too horrible for words," Sahr replied.

"Sahr, diamonds are beautiful. God gave them to us in abundance in our land to enjoy them, to be happy with them, but see what evil one brother has done against another and against a sister. See the problems they have brought to our people. The diamonds are destroying us, enslaving us to evil. I

# THE DIAMONDS

don't know why we have fallen so low. I am thinking of my children and grandchildren. This diamond virus is going to finish us if we do not do something to stop it," Kemoh remarked.

"Kemoh, my brother, sometimes I say to myself that it would have been better if there were no diamonds in our country. You are right, we are now slaves to these stones. Believe me, these are diamonds of bondage. Instead of being a blessing, they are killing our people and we are killing each other for more of the stones."

"Yes, we are losing all our beliefs," Kemoh added. "Children no longer have respect for their elders. Adultery and drunkenness are rampant. People do not worship as much as they used to do. The mosques now are only half full on Fridays."

Kemoh and Sahr started walking towards the middle of Semabu. They saw people standing in small groups, all lamenting the sacrificial death of Tewoh. People were saying that the tranquil social order that Semabu knew was quickly descending into the lowest depths of hell when one of its most notable citizens like Gibao would take part in such a *sacrifice.*

The very day Gibao was to make his first appearance in court, his only other sister, Njabu, arrived at his house to visit, and with her two children. She had had no previous knowledge of what had happened and so, when she went to the prison after hearing the gossip, she was allowed to see Gibao.

On the day of the trial, many people refused to go to work. They wanted to see Gibao and hear his version of the story.

Gibao's first court appearance was brief. The magistrate wanted only to establish a *prima facie* case so as to commit the case for trial by jury. Gibao, his Alpha-man and the three actual murderers were brought into the court in handcuffs. All their relatives were crying, all except Gibao's wives.

The Alpha-man was a well-known personality. His feeling of shame kept him from lifting his head up and facing the many people he knew in the courtroom. All five men openly admitted their involvement in the death of Tewoh. The court was adjourned.

The trial before the judge was to take place in about eight days. People started counting the days till the trial could begin. They were determined to see if the trial would be a just one or whether Gibao would be set free, there was so much perversion of justice in Sewa. Gibao had money, and diamond money could buy his freedom. Diamond money could buy anything in Sewa. Perhaps Gibao would eventually be as free as the air.

"Whenever have you seen money men go to jail?" the cynics asked openly.

"Jail be for poor man," a worker would reply.

When Gibao's grandmother died suddenly, the rumor was that she died of a heart attack. She had not been ill, so her death was a surprise. Mama Yatta said that the old lady died peacefully in her sleep. Those who knew them said she died from the weight of too much shame on her chest that night.

Gibao, sitting in his dark cell, was informed of his grandmother's death by the prison guard. He was stunned by the news. He had just seen her in court the other day. She had looked well. How could she have died all of a sudden like that? he wondered. Or was the news simply fabricated by the police so as to torture him? Late in the afternoon however, a policeman told him that he would be allowed to go out accompanied to attend his grandmother's funeral.

Two days later, Gibao went in handcuffs to his grandmother's funeral. It was there that he learned that N'tuma was gone and that Manu had sent her children to her brother in Freetown. Gibao saw Njabu his sister, but he was not allowed to talk to her. Everybody was weeping. As the grave diggers were shoveling dirt into the grave, Gibao bowed down, strained to collect a handful of the dirt and tossed it into the grave. Gibao became the focus of everyone's attention, but it was only in wonder as to how this hardworking man could have fallen into such evil.

# THE DIAMONDS 239

Mama Yatta wailed. She had lost so much in just a few days: her son, her own reputation as a mother, her own mother and N'tuma. Yatta had untied her hair. She belted her lappa. Her breasts were bare and sagging. She wept unrestrained. "Why is God punishing me like this?!" she cried out. She was saying that many things had happened to her in her lifetime, but these incidents in Njama were too much. "What have I done against you, oh God, to deserve such punishment?" she wailed over and over. She begged God to spare Gibao's life, or, alas, she cried, "Take my life instead of Gibao's! Without him I cannot survive!"

The police took Gibao away from the grave. He was returned to his cell to await trial. Gibao's home had already disintegrated. Gibao thought N'tuma had abandoned him in his time of need. Gibao did not see that she might be thinking about helping her sick mother or that she might be very angry with him. He wept in his cell over the thought that N'tuma had already left. She had come to be his favorite wife, and now he had lost her perhaps forever. He grieved that N'tuma was now left to solve her own conflicts and problems without him.

# Chapter 25

Many people confessed they had never seen the court at Njama so crowded as it was during Gibao's and the Alpha-man's trial. The trial was to start at ten o'clock in the morning, but by eight o'clock the courtroom was already overcrowded. There was no standing room left. Fudia and Nande were there. Bintu, Brima and N'dora were across the room. Ya Digba had closed her restaurant to be there also. Gibao's mother, sisters, children, nieces and nephews sat near the front. Many people had taken time off work to see if justice could be done in Njama.

When Justice Wyse entered, the people in the court got up. When he sat down, everyone else sat down. Justice Wyse looked calm and comfortable. He was bald and had on spectacles with thick lenses. There was dead silence in the court as he took his time to assemble his documents. Gibao, the Alpha-man, the three other men, Mustapha and Kaanja were brought in to stand in front of him. Two policeman stood by them. There was an interpreter to translate the local languages into English.

Mustapha was asked to recall what happened that fateful morning. With meticulous thoroughness, he told the court all he knew. It was then that Gibao and the Alpha-man knew that it was Mustapha who had divulged their secret. The guilty ones lowered their heads and they listened as Mustapha related what had happened. They did not look at the judge.

When Mustapha finished, Justice Wyse spoke.

"I have heard about such atrocities, but this is the first one that has come before me. Never before in my entire career on the bench, have I had to deal with such diabolic and cannibal-

THE DIAMONDS                                                    241

istic practices. It is nauseating. I wish to state that, whatever the
objectives of this ghastly crime, you would not live to enjoy
the fruits of your ungodly misdeeds."

Justice Wyse's remarks were translated.

"You, Mr. Finoh," the judge went on, "you misuse religion
for evil purposes. You deliberately mislead innocent people. You
are an enemy of Islam. People like you should be destroyed.
You are a living embodiment of the devil. How can you reconcile the fact that you, as a father, can commit such a barbarous
crime on someone else's child?"

The crowd in the courtroom tilted their heads to hear every
word and watched the judge alertly. Men and women put their
hands to their mouths in astonishment. Some clasped their
bosoms as the judge condemned the old Alpha-man. Some
exclaimed in hushed voices, "Lord have mercy." They could
hardly believe what they were witnessing. But there were many
cynics in the audience who still believed that the culprits might
be acquitted on a point of legal technicality, such a thing had
happened in other cases in the past. Such an acquittal could
only leave people feeling utter dismay and sorrow. But Alpha
Finoh and Gibao were men of wealth and could bribe their
way to freedom.

The three men who had been hired to take Tewoh's life
were very young men who had also made the journey to Sewa
in search of wealth. They were well known in the Sewa area,
but very few knew exactly what their trade was, not until they
were apprehended now.

One of the three was named Joe Mbeke, but many called him
by the name he preferred; which was "HELL FIRE". He would
get mad at somebody and say, "Who born you?" ("Who gave
birth to you?") He liked to agitate people and to incite them to
a fight. In front of the judge he stood with his head bowed
down, knowing he now had to pay the penalty for his crime.

Another of the three was Alpha Kanu, alias "DANGER BOY"
or "MASUBA". He was known to yell out at people, "Gi mi rod,

Masuba de kam!" ("Make way for me! Masuba comes!") But his boasting stopped the day the police put him in jail.

The last of the them was Oporto Sesay, alias "BORN TROUBLE." His favorite saying was "Nor fred natin." ("I fear nothing.")

The three young men presented their versions of what happened to the judge. Gibao came next. Alpha Finoh was the last to give his version of the story of Tewoh's death.

Kaanja and Mustapha stood near each other. They were confident that they would be let go because they had only been forced at the last minute to participate in disposing of the body, and it was they who had brought the crime to the attention of the police.

Having heard the defendants' stories, the judge announced he would review the facts and give sentence tomorrow. The judge stood up and there was a commotion as everyone else also stood up. The seven defendants were led back to their prison cells, and people left to go back to their homes or to work in the diamond fields.

The next day the people gathered once again to hear the verdict. There was complete silence in the courtroom, except for the sounds of nervous coughing among the audience. The seven defendants glanced occasionally at the crowd to look for relatives and friends. The judge entered and everyone stood up. When the judge sat down, there was a loud rustling noise of other people sitting down, and after that a great silence.

Mr. Baker, the Greek diamond dealer whose real name was Mr. Kazantas, stood next to Gibao's mother. Of all the diamond smugglers, Mr. Baker was the only one brave enough to say that he missed his friend, Gibao. Gibao spotted him standing next to his mother, but he turned away in shame.

Justice Wyse put on his spectacles and surveyed the seven men in front of him. He was ready to pronounce their sentences.

"I hereby sentence you, Gibao Semabu, Alpha Finoh, Mbeke, Kanu and Sesay to death, by hanging. Mustapha and Kaanja, I

# THE DIAMONDS 243

find you not guilty of murder. You are both acquitted and discharged." The judge put aside his eyeglasses.

"Born Trouble!" a cynical voice shouted in the courtroom. There was subdued laughter, then, silence again.

The interpreter told the five guilty defendants what Judge Wyse said: that they were guilty and would be hanged. The judge pounded the gavel and the trial was over.

There were gasps throughout the courtroom. There was loud whispering. Some of the people were amazed that not one of the five had been able to buy freedom. The relatives of Gibao and Fino started weeping. The girlfriends of Joe Mbeke, Alpha Kanu and Oporto Sesay started weeping also. For their part, they wept more out of frustration for not having ever known what type of business their boyfriends were engaged in. They, too, felt a sense of great shame.

Gibao's mother shuddered. In those last moments of that humid morning, when all the audience in the courtroom was as still as death itself, Gibao's imminent end seemed real to his mother for the first time. It was the worst moment of her life, that moment when she heard that her son was to be executed. She could only remember the good son she had always known. She swayed and moaned in agony, and Mr. Baker and Miatta had to support her to keep her from falling.

The crowd in the courtroom was leaving. People walked out slowly, as if leaving a funeral. Relatives cried out the names of the condemned, there was nothing else that they could do. The guards led the five guilty ones back to their cells, perhaps never to be seen again.

Outside the courtroom, people congregated in groups. Fudia the prostitute, and Nande her friend, stood together and looked around in confusion like the rest of the people. Five men altogether had been condemned to be hanged, and two of them were important and wealthy men in Njama!

"Fudia," Nande said, interrupting her friend's thoughts, "You could have been in N'tuma's place."

"I am lucky," Fudia replied. They took hold of each other's hand, they walked slowly, and thus they melted into the crowd.

The people were convinced that Gibao had tried to force his fate and play God. They talked about how one cannot rise to wealth by standing on the murdered corpses of others. Diamonds that come from blood have the eternal curse of the devil. The profits from them would finally end up with the devil.

■ ■ ■

Gibao was ushered into a tiny prison cell by a prison officer. This cell was one that was used for prisoners on death row. He immediately smelled the foul, acrid stench of stale urine and feces in the old corroded pail. Its contents had been left there by the last inmate, who was executed for the murder of a petty trader.

Gibao squatted delicately on the pail with his emaciated body. His head bowed. His entire body absorbed the concentrated heat in the cell, and he sweated profusely. Gibao tried to secure a more comfortable posture. His heartbeat increased as he strained over the foul pail.

He squatted alone in the solitude of his cell. He remembered the day he found himself sitting on the mortar and dreaming about diamonds. Now, time had become eternally empty in his reckoning because, within this dark holding cell, he could not tell the difference between day and night. His only communications were mostly the phantoms of people who floated through his mind, or an occasional twice-daily visit from a guard. Sleep escaped him. The reality of his situation haunted him. His eyes had become bigger in the darkness, only to flood with tears of regret.

Tonight Gibao was to have light for thirty minutes. Many a time the light, a small overhead 60 watt bulb, would not be provided for days, especially for inmates awaiting execution. They would not complain. This night Gibao was not expecting

## THE DIAMONDS 245

the light. However the light came on, to his pleasant surprise. His only cell mate turned out to be a fat-bellied gecko glued onto the wall. She was fat with advanced pregnancy. Life was in her belly, pulsating with unborn geckos.

Gibao fixed his eye on the gecko. His first thought was to kill the gecko, but this thought vanished very fast from his tormented mind. Instead, he felt grateful for the delicate creature. The gecko ate up the flies and treacherous mosquitoes which were fattening themselves on his blood. He watched with delight as the creature successfully hunted the flies and mosquitoes that flew by. The exercise quite fascinated him, for as long as it lasted.

A rude knock on the door jolted him. He wondered what was the matter. He had lost all sense of time. For him, it was already living eternity in the cell's darkness. A small opening in the door appeared and he saw the guard's eyes looking in at him.

"We're making arrangements for your eldest daughter to come and see you before your execution, as you requested. The request has been approved," the officer said. "I cannot remember the last time such a thing happened. Most inmates here do not care about talking with their loved ones in their final moments. I guess it is very painful to say goodbye." The officer closed the door again.

Gibao could hear the echo of his footsteps walking away. He began to watch the gecko again. How many little geckos was the mother carrying inside her belly? He kept thinking about the gecko. If it gave birth to many little ones, they would grow fat fast as they feasted on the hordes of flies and mosquitoes that constantly tormented him. He looked forward to the day the gecko would deliver the little ones from its bloated belly.

The cell remained silent. The light went off. Gibao closed his eyes.

*I shall tell my daughter everything I have been thinking*, Gibao told himself. *I shall empty out my mind. I shall tell her that I never meant to kill my sister-in-law. I never planned it, I never did. How can anyone kill his sister-in-law? My wife, N'tuma, I want Jeneba to tell her I am sorry. N'tuma must know how things are in this town. It is a dog eats dog world. I shall tell Jeneba how remorseful, how repentant I am and how I pray for God's forgiveness. I shall ask her to take a message to her brothers and sisters, her mother and her step-mothers. I beg all of them to pray for me, that God may forgive me.*

Gibao's confession flooded out of him before the imaginary image of Jeneba. *I will tell my daughter that I was wrong to have involved myself with Alhaji's wife. I was wrong to have continued to stay on in this land even after I had secured my first good fortune, which was more than that of Pesima. I shall tell my daughter that it is good discipline and virtue to have a contented mind. I shall ask for forgiveness from all those I have wronged. I know that God forgives sinners. As I sit here, in my time of torment, I still hope that fate would intervene and my life would be saved. That I shall be given life imprisonment and not face execution. Fate has mysterious ways of helping someone in need. Something deep inside keeps telling me not to give up. But if fate decides otherwise, I know that God has heard my prayers and shall forgive me. Ngewo, the Divine, may His will be done.*

■ ■ ■

The only way Gibao could get away from the horrific stench in the cell was to transport his thoughts back to a time of innocence. The rainy season cleansed the earth. That was what he needed, the rain, because it cleansed not only the body but also the soul. He remembered the rains that brought the whole of nature into luxuriant bloom, with beauty and in full growth. Flowers grew all around and without human support, unfolding their petals and inviting butterflies to feast on their nectar. The flowers pervaded the wet air with their delicate aroma. He laughed as he remembered how the rainy season

## THE DIAMONDS 247

interrupted the currents of life. People would be enclosed and held captive in their houses. Chickens, dogs, pigs and goats, all of the domestic family that lives in the village would also restrict their movements because of the rain. The birds would not venture out and would not disturb the worms. The insects would hide. Monkeys would be in the treetops overlooking the swollen rivers.

When the pangs of hunger moved their stomachs, men and women would grab their implements and challenge the rain in pursuit of food. They would go into the bush in search of bush yam, cocoyam, cassava and snails to fill their hungry stomachs. The rainy season was the hungry season, everything was maturing and would not be ready to eat until it ended. He remembered how the produce of the dry season would be exhausted, when the rice barns would stand empty, creaking with age and the ravages of bugs. In the rainy season, men and women would search wet forests and bushes to demand their share of whatever nature provided then. They would return home in tattered clothes, wet and shivering, but confident they would not go hungry. He remembered that after supper, the adults would spend the evening hours around a fire telling animated stories about the old times to themselves and their children.

Gibao was still thinking about the rain some days later, when the prison officer came with two other officers to his cell. His mind was brought back to reality. The officers had come to accompany Gibao to the death chamber. Jeneba had still not come.

Word had gone round that the prisoners were to be taken away and a crowd had gathered outside the prison for one last look. The van was standing there in which Gibao and the others were to be transported. As the doors of the van were opened for them to enter, Gibao turned and gave his weeping mother a last glance. He was the last to enter before the door was slammed shut. Gibao sat down next to "BORN TROUBLE". Gibao's mother's began wailing, first softly, then with increasing loudness, and then ascending into a high pitch that pierced the crowd. The continuous, sharp wailing echoed in the van. The van started moving slowly as it progressed through the crowd. Once past the people, the van sped away into the distance. Mama Yatta pleaded in her tears for mercy for her son. But others in the crowd were only filled with a sense of justice, as they considered it, for the death of the young girl Tewoh.

Gibao was never told what happened to his wealth or his family. It was God's judgment, people said, that his family was dispersed because of his murderous crime and greed.

Gibao was the last to be hanged that rainy day, on a wood frame made from the kola nut tree. Before the trap door was released, Gibao smiled to see the heavy rain clouds above, and to know that his beloved earth would be cleansed once again.

■ ■ ■

Events characterize historical moments. The discovery of diamonds in Sierra Leone in 1929 will be remembered as a significant historical moment that has had an indelible socio-economic impact on the country. The economic benefits of diamonds were to dramatically change the well-being of Sierra Leoneans. However, as time progressed, what was to be a diamond boom became a curse on the nation. Herein lies the irony. The economic benefits of diamonds, which were meant to free people from their shackles of poverty, instead enslaved them in the clutches of greed.

## ABOUT THE AUTHOR

J. Sorie Conteh was born in Sierra Leone. He went on to the United States to pursue higher education and received a B.A. from the University of Rochester, NY, and Ph.D. in Anthropology and African Studies from Indiana. He is a former Research Fellow of the Department of African Studies of Fourah Bay College, the University of Sierra Leone and of the Afrika-Studiecentrum in Leiden, the Netherlands, as well as Political Affairs Officer at the Permanent Observer Mission of the Organization of African Unity to the United Nations in New York. Dr. Conteh has published several short stories, articles, monographs, booklets and conference papers. His writings cover a wide variety of African topics and concerns: the effects of diamond mining in his home country, female circumcision, secret societies, African culture, and democracy in Africa. He is currently with the United Nations IRAQ–Kuwait (UNIKOM) Observer Mission in Kuwait.

Printed in the United States
47044LVS00002B/119